A CLASSIC ENGLISH CRIME

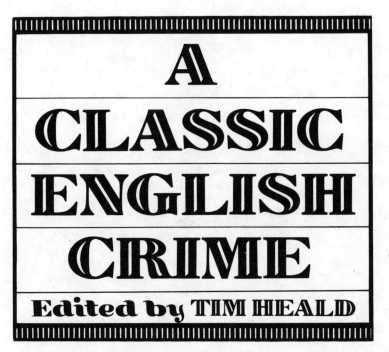

A CLASSIC ENGLISH CRIME

Edited by TIM HEALD

13 Stories for the Christie Centenary
from the Crime Writers' Association

THE MYSTERIOUS PRESS
New York · Tokyo · Sweden · Milan
Published by Warner Books

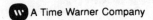 A Time Warner Company

First published in Great Britain in 1990 by
PAVILION BOOKS LIMITED
196 Shaftesbury Avenue, London WC2H 8JL

Means to Murder © Margaret Yorke 1990
Smoke Gets In . . . © David Williams 1990
Holocaust at Mayhem Parva © Julian Symons 1990
All's Fair in Love © Susan Moody 1990
The Lady in the Trunk © Peter Lovesey 1990
Jack Fell Down © HRF Keating 1990
Experts for the Prosecution © Tim Heald 1990
A Fête Worse than Death © Paula Gosling 1990
Wednesday Matinée © Celia Dale 1990
Spasmo © Liza Cody 1990
A Little Learning © Simon Brett 1990
Good Time Had By All © Robert Barnard 1990
Cause and Effects © Catherine Aird 1990

Mysterious Press books are published by
Warner Books, Inc., 666 Fifth Avenue, New York, NY 10103.

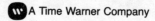A Time Warner Company

The Mysterious Press name and logo are trademarks of Warner Books, Inc.

Printed in the United States of America
First U.S. printing: June 1991

10 9 8 7 6 5 4 3 2 1

Library of Congress Cataloging-in-Publication Data

A Classic English crime / edited by Tim Heald.
    p.   cm.
  ISBN 0-89296-456-1
  1. Detective and mystery stories, English.   I. Heald, Tim.
PR1309.D4C56   1991
823'.087208—dc20
                                              90-84897
                                                  CIP

CONTENTS

INTRODUCTION
TIM HEALD

The legacy of Agatha Christie hangs heavy on Britain's crime writers. In her lifetime she was already a legend, but in her centenary year her posthumous presence looms impossibly large. She has become an industry: the most widely read novelist in the English language. Films, television adaptations, re-issues of books, even spoof biographies of her best-known characters, and now this. The tide of Christiana makes Canutes of all of us.

The Crime Writers' Association is essentially a social organization but it is also the nearest we have to a trade union of would-be Christie heirs and heiresses. This is their – our – little act of homage, a sort of corporate genuflection.

When I was asked to edit it, various ideas suggested themselves. At one extreme we could have attempted a complete crime novel in the classic style with a number of modern crime writers contributing a chapter; at the other we could have simply asked a representative sample to do a short story in their own style without any constraints or disciplines at all. In the end I went for a good old English compromise. 'The only guidelines,' I said, 'are that each story will be set in "The Golden Age" between the two world wars and will contain what the authors perceive to be the essential ingredients of a classic English murder. These ingredients must include a corpse but otherwise such items as butlers, libraries and small Belgian detectives will be left to the discretion of the writers.' In other words this is a collection of individual original short stories, unified by the notion of paying tribute to Agatha Christie and therefore all set in the period at which she was in her prime.

Not everyone accepted the challenge. One or two of our brightest and best flinched, but the baker's dozen who did accept are, I believe, a fine representative of the best of contemporary crime writing – a genre in which we still lead the world. They are, as you can imagine, a difficult crew to discipline, so not everyone has even included a corpse and some have scarcely even told a story. Simon Brett, for example, may well be a genius but he is also uncontrollably wayward.

I was keen too to have a go myself. When I first embarked on a writing career I was told that 'An editor who writes has a fool for a contributor'. The maxim has the resonance of authority but like all such rules there are exceptions which prove it. In this case I take refuge behind the publisher's editor, Steve Dobell. Although he gets no credit on the jacket he has been the final umpire, the man who spots the minimal inconsistencies and errors to which we are all prone. I placed myself in his hands as far as my own entry is concerned and would have removed it if he had thought fit. He didn't and I hope this is a tribute to his judgement and not his tact.

The contributors all, I think, enjoyed attempting the challenge. At the same time the attempt itself reminded us that the Dame, whatever her faults, had inimitable gifts and talents. I hope that you enjoy reading this as much as we enjoyed writing it. Modern crime writing has advanced in a number of ways, and its protagonists would argue that it has attained a sophistication undreamt of in the so-called golden age. At the same time it is no denigration of this collection or of the modern generation to say that in this her centenary year Dame Agatha Christie remains a law unto herself and an incredibly difficult act to follow.

This, dear Agatha, is the best we can do and it is done in homage, however disrespectful it may seem. I hope it may find favour in the great library in the sky where you sit in judgement on us all.

A CLASSIC ENGLISH CRIME

MEANS TO MURDER

MARGARET YORKE

In my brown Jaeger dressing-gown and striped viyella pyjamas, I knelt on the landing, watching between the banisters as, below, the guests arrived. I recognized Dr Pitt, who often came to see Mother. The small plump lady with him must be Mrs Pitt. She took off her fur coat and handed it to Trotter, the parlourmaid, who was helping Fitch admit them. Outside, John was in charge of parking the cars, directing them into position with the aid of a torch. Each lady was dropped at the door before the car drove on to its space.

Lady White had a chauffeur and her car was a Daimler. I knew this because I had discussed the arrangements with John earlier in the day while he was polishing my father's Invicta. Among his duties was that of maintaining the car and even, sometimes, driving it, if Mother, who did not drive, had to be fetched from the station after a day in town, or wanted to pay a call on a neighbour.

It was New Year's Eve.

An enormous Christmas tree stood in the hall, its topmost branches level with the banister rail, and opposite me was one of the bright painted birds with feathery tails clipped to its boughs. Dozens of brilliant baubles hung on the tree, and fairy lights, but I liked the birds best; there were three of them, one blue, one red and one green. The red one was on a low branch and I had been allowed to put it there when Mother, helped by Fitch, who stood on a ladder, was dressing the tree.

Fitch was the butler. He was bald, and very thin, with creases all over his face, and he was good at card tricks. If he wasn't too busy, he would entertain me with them when I visited him in his pantry. Sometimes I helped him clean the silver, and he said if I kept on with it I'd get a butler's thumb, which would be a great help with the spoons. His own right thumb was smooth and flat, much broader than the one on his left hand.

Fitch had been at the Manor for ever, even when Mother was young, for this had been her home until she and Father married. They met when he was on leave from the Indian Army, and they returned there together after the wedding. I was born in India, and I had a good life there with a kind ayah and other children to play with, but the climate didn't suit Mother, who often felt faint and ill. When I was seven my grandfather, who owned the Manor, died of pneumonia, and Mother and I came home to be with my grandmother for a time, but we never went back because my grandmother, pining, soon died too, and after that Father sent in his papers and left the Army.

It seemed rather strange. Was it copies of *The Times* he had sent to Colonel Swethington, or a series of notebooks or letters? I hadn't understood what papers they were, but it meant we could all be together and I wouldn't be sent home alone to boarding-school, like the other children older than me.

At my post on the landing, I sighed with happiness. On Christmas morning a gleaming new bicycle was waiting for me at the foot of the tree. I had ridden it round and round on the frozen lawn, and I'd soon learn to balance without hands and do tricks, like Peter, the garden boy, whom I'd seen riding along with his hands in his pockets, swaying from side to side and whistling. His mother had been my mother's nanny and they lived in a cottage in the village.

Now the Manor belonged to Mother and Father, and we should live there always, and though I was sad about my grand-parents, after all, they were old.

Mother was looking beautiful tonight in a shimmering dress of gold, which matched her hair. For a year she'd worn black or grey, in mourning, but now that was over. In India, she had always been pale and tired; here, she was different, and though she was still sometimes unwell, she wasn't so thin and her cheeks were often quite pink. I watched as she led the way in to dinner, crossing the hall on the arm of a tall man with white hair whose name I didn't know. How wonderful they all looked, the men in dinner jackets with gleaming white shirts and the women in long dresses of every hue.

One woman wore black. That was Mrs Fox, from Summer Cottage. We had known her in India, where her husband, Captain Fox, had been killed during some riots, or so I was told. I wasn't sure what had happened, exactly, but, as a result, Maxwell Fox was an orphan.

Tom Swethington said he couldn't be an orphan as his mother was still alive; you were only an orphan if both your parents died; but whether he was right or not, it was sad. Max had stayed with us for a time while his father, who did not die at once, was in hospital. I heard one of the servants telling Ayah that the Captain's horse had fallen, throwing Captain Fox to the ground, and he had been trampled on. This didn't sound quite the glorious death in battle that Max had seemed to believe was his father's fate, and Tom Swethington muttered that there was some talk of the girth having broken, causing the saddle to swing, but I didn't really understand what that meant.

Tom said that we mustn't talk about it to Max. He believed his father had died a hero's death, and that was how it should be.

'He'll probably get a medal,' said Tom, confident of his own father's ability to arrange such rewards.

Mrs Fox and Max remained in India for some months after we left, and then they returned to stay with relations in Kent while looking for somewhere permanent. Three weeks before Christmas they had come to Summer Cottage, when its lease was up.

'It's cheap and convenient, and it will be a kindness to tell her about it,' Father had said one day at breakfast, and Mother had agreed.

'It will be nice for the boys,' she said.

I wasn't so pleased. I didn't like Max, though I knew I must be sorry for him and allow him to play with my toys. He was a year older than me, tall and thin, with straight dark hair like his mother's, and he would bend my arm behind my back to make me do as he wished, if I didn't agree at once. He'd do Chinese burns, too, twisting his hands round my wrist till it hurt and I yelled, and then he'd call me a crybaby.

I hadn't seen much of him since they arrived, to my relief, as he had been sent to boarding-school, but he'd come with his mother that morning when she called to ask if she could help prepare for the party. She'd brought an apron in a holdall and offered to arrange flowers, but Mother had done them the day before, so Mrs Fox didn't stay long and I didn't have to let Maxwell try my bike.

I didn't go to school. I had lessons at the Vicarage from Mr Hastings, the vicar, and his daughter Jane, who looked after him. His wife was dead. This worried me a little; neither she nor Captain Fox had reached three score years and ten, which was man's allotted span, I knew.

When the dining-room door closed behind the last guest, Daisy, the housemaid who looked after me when Mother was busy – thank goodness it had been decided that I was too old to have Ayah replaced by a nanny or governess – came bustling along to put me to bed. I had seen Father take in Lady White, and Mrs Fox had entered the dining-room on the arm of the curate from Little Marpleton, a pale young man, a bachelor. She, too, was pale, in her long black velvet dress with sleeves to her wrist and a single strand pearl necklace.

I had been asleep for some time when the music woke me. It was faint, a reedy sound, not the same as when Mother played the piano. Sometimes we sang rousing ditties like *Clementine*, and sentimental ballads, and in the weeks before Christmas it had been carols, even Father joining in with his deep voice for *Good King Wenceslas* while Mother and I were the page.

Gradually, the music grew louder, the strain taken up by some harsher instrument than the first. I lay for a while and listened, until a jiggy little tune made my feet twitch and want to dance. Who was playing?

I got out of bed, found dressing-gown and slippers, put them on and slipped out on to the landing again. As I did so, Trotter opened the drawing-room door to let Fitch go in with a tray of drinks and the music swelled up more strongly. Trotter went off through the green baize door that led to the kitchen regions, and I ran down the stairs and crouched behind the big Christmas tree in a position that would let me peep round the branches and look through the door when Fitch emerged, as he must in time. If he saw me, he wouldn't be cross, though he might send me back to bed. He wouldn't tell Father; I could trust Fitch.

It was a little while before the door opened and I caught a glimpse of some men in fancy dress, with coloured frock coats and knee breeches, like George III in my history books. They sat before music stands, and the gleam of brass caught my eye. I knew it came from a French horn; I'd heard the military band often enough to recognize some instruments.

I must have dozed off, tucked there behind the tree, waking at intervals when the drawing-room door opened to let someone in or out, usually a man on his way to the cloakroom. I saw Dr Pitt, and the curate, and I saw Mrs Fox come out and go into the study.

I drowsed and woke, drowsed and woke. Then I saw the ghost. A figure in a green frock coat, ruffles at throat and wrists, and wearing pale breeches and black shoes, came down the stairs and disappeared into the study. That frightened me, and as soon as the door had closed I hurried upstairs and jumped back into bed, only then realizing that it must have been one of the musicians. After that night, I never saw my mother again.

The day after the party, Daisy's face was all blotched, as if she'd been crying, but she told me it was only a cold. She set me to tidy my toys in the morning, and in the afternoon she took me for a walk in the village. We went to the smithy, where Bob Pearce was shoeing a carthorse, and I was allowed to pump the bellows to fan the coals as the huge shoes were heated and shaped. There was a strong smell as the hot iron was placed on the horse's hooves and hammered into place. Surely it must hurt the horse, having nails driven into its feet like that? The smith assured me that the hoof felt no more than a human fingernail, and I was mollified.

Mr Giles, the farmer, asked Daisy and me back to tea at the farm, and let me ride on the back of the big gentle animal. Clip, clop, went the new shoes on the big hooves with the long feathers of silky hair hanging over them. I clutched a hank of the horse's mane to keep my balance.

'I'm surprised you haven't got a pony to ride, young fellow,' said Mr Giles.

I'd ridden in India, and Father had talked about getting me a pony soon, but I wasn't keen.

'A bike's more in my line, Mr Giles,' I replied.

We stabled the horse, shutting him into a stall with a bale of sweet-smelling hay hooked in the corner, and Mr Giles left Daisy and me to find our own way into the house while he went to help his son, Fred, with the milking. I could hear the spurt of the milk hitting the pail as we passed the long shed, and a cow uttered a low, soft moo. Daisy said she wouldn't mind working on a farm, among beasts.

Soon we were in the warm kitchen and Mrs Giles was giving me home-made scones with butter and strawberry jam, and milk fresh from the cow, still warm.

'Poor lamb, what a start to the New Year,' she said, and then, 'When's the . . . . ?' but Daisy cut in before she could finish, and I wondered what had happened to the lamb to render it pitiful. I'd seen no lambs on the farm.

It was dark when we reached home, and I wanted to know where Mother was, but when I asked Daisy, she didn't answer. There was no sign of Father. I had my bath, then milk and biscuits and a game of Racing Demon with Daisy. I was tired after so much fresh air, and fell asleep as soon as I was tucked into bed.

Next morning Father was at breakfast, but he showed no interest when I told him about my visit to the forge. He ate quickly, glancing at *The Times* as he drank his coffee, and he left the table before I had finished. Mother would be having her breakfast in bed, as she often did. I decided to go and see her.

She and Father had separate bedrooms. She sometimes spent a day in bed, but she was never too ill to welcome a visit, and we would play Battleships, or Hangman, or she would read to me, so I set off confidently and tapped on her door. When there was no answer, I opened it and went in. The room was very tidy, the bed made, and all her things were gone: there were no brushes, pots, or books to be seen, not even the photograph of me with Ayah which she kept on her dressing-table. Everything had vanished, and so had she.

Father found me standing there, bewildered.

'What are you doing here, Dick?' he demanded, and I said I was looking for Mother.

'She's gone away,' he told me. 'And she won't be coming back. You'd better forget her as soon as you can. I don't want to hear you mention her ever again. Out, now,' and he chivvied me from the room, locking the door after me.

I cried, of course, running along the passage to my own room and flinging myself on the bed in misery, but soon Daisy came and cuddled me against her soft apron, crying too.

'But where is she?' I wailed. 'And why didn't she say goodbye?'

'She couldn't,' said Daisy. 'Of course you're sad, Master Dick. So am I – so's cook, and Fitch and Trotter and John – we all are – but the master has said no one's to talk about it, and that's that. You'll get over it in time, my lovey, and you're to go off to school, so that'll be exciting, won't it? You're going to Pitcairn House with young Maxwell Fox, and there's all your clothes and things to get.'

I'd expected to go to school next year, when I'd be nine, but not as soon as this, and at first I didn't like the idea much, but without Mother things weren't the same. Father was out a lot – something to do with business, he said – and I had no one to play with, though Daisy spent a lot of time with me and there was still my bike to enjoy. We went to the farm again, and Mr Giles gave me a calf to look after and said that it could be mine. Before term began, the flooded water meadows froze and I slid on the ice, a novelty after India.

Then came a trip to London with Father to buy my uniform.

We went to Harrods, where we met Mrs Fox and Maxwell in the boys' outfitting department. It seemed he needed things too, and we bought shirts, shorts, socks and football boots. I quite enjoyed the day, especially the large lunch we had at the Hyde Park Hotel, where I drank ginger beer and Maxwell had cider. Father and Mrs Fox shared a bottle of champagne and were in a very cheerful mood, which I thought strange after Mother had only just gone away, but it was true that for a while I had forgotten about her, bearing out Daisy's prophecy. I felt bad about it, and cried in bed, later.

Mrs Fox and Maxwell had travelled up by train, but we all came home in the Invicta, and when Father jumped out of the car to open the door for her I heard him say, 'The time will soon pass, Lois. June, I think.'

What could he mean? What would happen in June?

When it arrived, I understood, for in June Father and Mrs Fox were married, and she and Maxwell came to live at the Manor, which seemed to belong entirely to Father, now that Mother had gone.

Things changed again. During the summer holidays Father and Mrs Fox, as I still thought of her though I had been told to call her Aunt Lois, went touring in Europe, and Maxwell stayed with his grandparents in Cornwall. I remained at the Manor, for I had neither grandparents nor uncles and aunts, but there were plenty of people to look after me. I spent a lot of time at the farm, where my calf was growing, and I began riding Mr Giles's old cob, a quiet creature. She was too big for me, but I grew bold and imagined myself to be a cowboy taming a bronco. I went to the forge, too, and Bob Pearce helped me make a trivet for Mrs Giles to rest her kettle on.

Maxwell came back after a month, and he wanted to come to the farm. He rode the cob, galloping her about the fields, whipping her with a stick cut from the hedge until Mr Giles told him he would not be allowed to ride again.

'Let your mother pay for you to have lessons at the stables,' he said. 'She can afford it now,' and he stormed off while Maxwell shouted after him that he was not to be spoken to in that tone.

Daisy became silent and grim, and the atmosphere in the house altered as Maxwell demanded special dishes from cook, and complained, unjustly, that John had not cleaned his shoes properly. I remonstrated with Maxwell, but timidly, because at school he was a hero, admired because he was good at games and cared nothing for discipline, daring other boys to carry out deeds requiring courage. I noticed that he never did them himself. He called me a little squit, and his friends commiserated with him for having such a poor object as myself as his stepbrother, while my own contemporaries envied what they saw as my good fortune.

Father and Mrs Fox – Aunt Lois – returned, and she slept in what had been my mother's room. While I was away at school it had been repapered and painted, equipped with new curtains and different furniture, but to me it was still Mother's room, and Father was in there, too. His own room was now called the dressing-room.

Then Daisy said she was leaving; she wouldn't be there when

I came home for the Christmas holidays.

I clung to her, sobbing that I'd never see her again and she laughed and hugged me, telling me not to be a silly boy, that she was only marrying Bob Pearce, the smith, and would be in the village where I could come and see her as much as I liked. 'I shan't be dead, like your poor mother,' she said.

'Dead? Is she dead?' I stared at Daisy.

'Why, didn't you know?' Daisy exclaimed. 'Didn't anyone ever tell you?' she cried, then reminded herself, aloud, that Father had forbidden everyone to discuss what had happened, thinking least said, soonest mended. 'But I thought he'd told you something,' she said, and she took me to the churchyard, where beside my grandparents' grave was another, with a simple headstone bearing my mother's name and the dates of her birth and death.

'We'll pick her some flowers,' said Daisy. 'You'll feel better then,' and she explained that the old illness my mother had suffered from so badly in India had returned, to prove fatal, the night of the New Year's Eve party. The funeral had been on the day we spent at the farm, when Mr Giles gave me the calf.

In the years that followed I often went to the churchyard with roses or sweet peas, or sometimes just flowers from the hedgerows, primroses, or poppies, and wild scabious, and Daisy was right: to do so made me feel better. Even now, more than fifty years later, I can still recall the sweet smell of newly-mown grass and the scent of the flowers I had brought.

Today, I took daffodils and iris, bought on my way from the airport, and after my visit to the grave I called to see Daisy, who is still alive. Indeed, it is because of her that I have returned after all this time.

I did well at school, and was separated from Maxwell when we left Pitcairn House, for he went to Harrow while I was sent to a lesser establishment. After my war service, as there was nothing to keep me in England I emigrated to Australia, where I did well from sheep and bought into mines. Now I am a rich man. My father died in 1972, leaving the Manor and everything else to his widow, and some time after that Maxwell joined her there, with his painter friend, Trevor. Trevor, eventually, had died, but the other two were still living in what had originally been my mother's house. Lois must be nearly ninety by now.

It seemed that they had run out of money. Daisy had written to me through the years, and I knew that Maxwell had tried several methods of raising funds, investing in various ventures and speculating on the stock exchange, but the upkeep of the place had drained the available cash, and his attempt at marriage had ended in an expensive divorce on account of Trevor. Now he intended to sell the estate to a development company which planned to build an entire town with schools, shops and even light industry in a beautiful piece of country, destroying for ever the water meadows, which would be filled in and the flood water presumably diverted elsewhere, into, perhaps, the village. How could an ageing, childless man be so greedy?

Daisy, a widow now with three children of her own and seven grandchildren, lived with her elder son and his wife in the old forge, which had been renovated, extended and modernized. Her son was a smith, like his father, but he made wrought iron-work, gates, weathervanes and the like. The other son was an accountant, and the daughter was a doctor. They had moved up the social scale. Daisy herself had white curls and the same deep blue eyes in a face that still smiled though it was wrinkled. She gave me a hug as warm and as welcome as when I was a lad.

I had offered to buy the estate from Maxwell, but he would not accept my bid. He would make millions from the developer if it went through. Now I was going to see him, to make a final appeal.

Sitting by Daisy's fireside, I asked her to tell me all that she knew or could remember about my mother's death.

Daisy screwed up her face and touched her eyes with a hand-kerchief, moved, still, by that experience when, on New Year's morning, she had taken in my mother's breakfast tray and found her still asleep, as she thought. But the sleep was the sleep of death.

'It was diabetes she had, poor lady,' said Daisy. 'She'd been ill in India, but when she came home Dr Pitt found out what was wrong and she gave herself injections every day. She must have forgotten her dose, that night, or perhaps something went wrong because she had eaten things she shouldn't have had. Dr Pitt said anything like that could have happened. There'd been a big party that night. You'd been watching the guests arrive. Then I put you to bed.'

'I got up again,' I told her. 'I heard the music and crept down to the hall to see the musicians when Fitch opened the drawing-room door. I fell asleep down there, hidden behind the Christmas tree. But I saw them, in their silk coats and their breeches and their white wigs. Regency minstrels.' I could conjure them up, even now. 'One of them went through the hall alone – he went into the study – to have a quick nip of my father's brandy, I suppose. He had come down the stairs.'

'Funny you should have remembered that,' Daisy said. 'There was a whole suit of those fancy clothes, and a wig, pushed under the big leather chair in there when I went in to clean in the morning. I took them upstairs and put them away, meaning to mention them to my poor lady.'

'What happened to them?' I asked. 'Were they reclaimed?'

'No, they weren't. I think they may have been all packed up with your mother's things,' said Daisy. 'It was odd, though, I thought at the time, because the musicians all got dressed in one of the bedrooms, and changed there again before leaving. Why should one of them leave his clothes in the study?'

'Was it a green coat?' I asked.

'Yes,' said Daisy, surprised.

I'd seen Mrs Fox go into the study, too, but I must have been asleep when she and the musician came out, for surely, I thought now with hindsight, they must have had a rendezvous there? But why was the suit left behind?

'What happened to all my mother's things?' I asked.

'They're here, in the attic,' said Daisy. 'Your father gave orders that they were to be got rid of, but somehow it didn't seem right to throw them away. They were all that was left of your poor mother, and rightly the whole place should have gone to you, not that Maxwell and his mother. Trotter and I decided to keep everything safely so that you could look through them when you grew up. But the war came, and then you went to Australia. There were papers, photos, diaries. Mrs Giles at the farm kept them first – all packed in trunks, they were – and later we brought them here.'

She paused. 'Trotter and I took a few woollies for ourselves, they'd only have got the moths, otherwise, but nothing's been touched, since. Funny how moths don't seem a problem now, isn't it?'

'I'd like to look at them before I go up to the Manor,' I said. I hadn't announced my visit: I wasn't expected.

First, I telephoned Daisy's daughter, the doctor, and asked her some questions. Her replies made me very thoughtful. Then Daisy's son helped me bring down the trunks and we unpacked them in a bedroom, laying the things we removed carefully on the bed. We found the frock coat, packed in tissue paper, and the breeches and silver buckled shoes, and the wig. We laid them aside, careful not to disturb them.

'If a murder was done,' I said quietly, 'there might be evidence, even after all this time. The old woman is still alive, after all. Her blood can be tested. I think she wore the suit so that she could move round the house without being recognized. People seeing her would take her for one of the minstrels.'

Daisy's daughter had said that it was possible, if my mother's insulin had been replaced with water, for her to have injected herself and then gone into a coma and died. She might have felt dizzy and thirsty, but as she was alone in her bedroom, no help would be at hand. Without knowing what dosage she was on, and more details, it was impossible to say what the effect might be, perhaps not fatal at once; that would depend on all sorts of things. Such a death might raise no suspicions in a doctor regularly attending; he would assume she had forgotten her medication and if there had been an inquest, accidental death was the likely verdict. These days, stringent rules might make such a means of murder easier to detect, and today there were tests which could prove whether Mrs Fox – Lois – had handled or worn the garments, for she would have left traces – a hair in the wig, perhaps – of herself on them. She could have hidden the suit in the house earlier: suddenly I remembered her call that morning, and how Maxwell had wanted to ride my bike but there wasn't time. She knew her way round; she could have made the opportunity while we boys were having milk and biscuits in the schoolroom.

The law could not permit gain from the result of murder, if it were detected. My mother's will, leaving everything to my father, had been made in London after her marriage, a year before my birth, and she was her parents' outright heir. If Mrs Fox had killed my mother in order to marry my father, her right to his estate must surely be invalidated.

I am waiting at Daisy's for a senior police officer to arrive and accompany me to the Manor. An experienced forensic scientist has already taken away the wig and the garments. He saw a small bloodstain on the breeches, and muttered something about it possibly being menstrual blood.

'It will be interesting to test it, after so long,' he said with enthusiasm. 'Genetic fingerprinting is making positive proof much easier to obtain.'

Had my father known the truth? Had he been party to the crime? He and Lois had known each other in India. I remembered the story about Captain Fox's broken girth and wondered if that had really been an accident. In those days divorce meant social disaster and would ruin an army officer's career; she and my father could not have got married without being ostracized and rendered penniless, since neither had private means. As it was, they enjoyed prosperity for many years. During the war they had stayed at the Manor, which had become a convalescent home, with Lois in Red Cross uniform carrying out some administrative function. My father, re-commissioned, had had a desk job at a supply depot nearby. I didn't want to believe that he was her accomplice; only one of her victims. If he'd been involved, he would have made certain that all proof was obliterated – the disguise, for instance, and the bottles of insulin. Three had been found among my mother's things; perhaps all had been tampered with, in case one negative dose was not enough. Lois, however, would not have wanted to draw attention to herself by searching for the clothes or the drug; she must have assumed they were destroyed, perhaps had suggested to my father the very action he had ordered.

Unlike Maxwell, I have children, and one of my sons, daughters, or grandchildren might like to run the Manor estate once the law has returned it to me. For certain, it will not be sold to a speculator, and as there's a nearby motorway already, it shouldn't be subject to compulsory purchase.

I can see a car drawing up outside, a Jaguar with three men in dark suits inside. There's another car, too, with uniformed officers, two of them women.

They may need a doctor. The old lady may die of shock. Still, that won't prevent tests being carried out.

It's too late for vengeance, but it isn't too late for justice.

Margaret Yorke says she first began reading detective stories when she was ill at the age of twelve. The first of her classic whodunnits, featuring amateur detective Patrick Grant, appeared in 1970. Since then she has published fifteen psychological suspense novels.

SMOKE
GETS IN...

DAVID WILLIAMS

'Morning Mummy. Morning Daddy. What a peachy, heavenly day. Aren't we just lucky to be alive?' Diana, dressed in a white blouse and jodhpurs, was petite, pretty, nineteen, engaged to be married, and glowing from her early ride. She circled the breakfast table, kissing her father and mother in turn, then helped herself to kedgeree from one of the serving dishes on the sideboard before joining them both at the table.

'Good mornin', m'dear. Suppose all this bonhomie's because Ber. . . Berty's arriving this morning,' said Sir Percival Balderneck, Baronet, owner of Codlum Hall, the several thousand surrounding acres, and a cultivated sort of stammer – all inherited from a long line of Baldernecks. Grey hair, a florid face, arthritis, and over-indulgence in vintage port made him feel as well as look older than his fifty-five years. From what he had just read in the stock-market report, the suggestion that he was lucky merely to be alive he considered more than a touch extravagant.

A solid conservative, given more to intuition than to heavy reasoning, Balderneck regarded his fourth and only unmarried daughter with guarded tolerance over the top of *The Times* and his gold half spectacles.

'And to think I'd nearly forgotten Berty was coming,' said Diana with affecting innocence. 'Can he stay till the twenty-fifth, Mummy? Please, Mummy? Till after the Fitzherbert dance?' The appealing look she beamed at her mother showed Diana at her very best: she practised it from time to time in her looking glass – it was one of her very few unbecoming habits.

'I should think so, dear. If he wants to.' Lady Monica Balderneck looked up while responding absently. Known to her friends as Bubbles, she was some years younger than her husband. As a debutante she had been considered ethereal but, although she had kept her looks and figure, vaporous was now a more apposite description. Picking up the small silver handbell near her plate, she gave it a prolonged tinkle. 'There's no one else staying before August, is there?' she questioned, in the same vague and preoccupied tone as before, and – ahead of anyone providing an answer – returned her attention to the unexpectedly riveting, Codlum edition of the *Worchester & District News.*

'Can we have more coffee please, Ethel?' Diana asked the maid who had just appeared in response to the bell.

Lady Balderneck lifted her gaze again. 'And Ethel, remind cook that Miss Diana's guest will be here in time for lunch.'

'Yeth, m'lady.' With a penetrating sniff, the large and adenoidal girl removed the empty coffee-pot and stomped back through the green baize door, providing a reprise sniff from the other side.

Lady Balderneck gave a painful wince, exhaled something between a snort and a sigh, then announced in a fairly despairing tone: 'The second case of arson is on the front page. It doesn't say who the police suspect.'

'Well it's not li. . . ikely they would, is it?' responded her husband with a frown and a twitch of his bristling moustache. 'They're far from sure it's arson yet. Might well be coincidence.'

'Nonsense. They know perfectly well who's doing it.'

'Knowing is one thing. Pu. . . proving's quite another.' Balderneck was given to the odd profundity.

Diana wrinkled her retroussé nose – an organ frequently described by suitors as adorable. 'Are we absolutely sure it's Ted Grunnow?' she asked.

'Yes we are. Plain as a pikestaff,' insisted Lady Balderneck, who had never set eyes on a pikestaff. She knew Grunnow well enough. He was a smallholder in Upper Codlum whom her husband, as chairman of the local bench of magistrates, had sent to prison for a well deserved four weeks, without the option. This was after Grunnow had been caught, for the umpteenth time, stealing chickens with his handcart and on a fairly substantial scale.

'We can't be certain it's Grunnow,' replied Balderneck. 'And for heaven's sake, Bubbles, don't let anyone hear you say we can. Especially the servants.'

'Well Ogden had better catch him at it soon. Before he sets fire to us all in our beds.' Ogden was the village bobby. 'Why can't you just . . . ' Lady Balderneck shrugged her delicate shoulders while circling the air with a well manicured hand, '. . . just order Ogden to arrest him, or something?'

'Ogden's doing his best. The police generally are keeping a cu. . . careful eye on the fella,' her husband replied, but without too much conviction.

'They were supposed to be doing that from the day he was let out two weeks ago. Hasn't stopped him firing poor Benson's barn.' Benson was a local farmer who had borne witness, with others, to Grunnow's chicken rustling. 'And they should have been watching him like stoats when he set fire to Algy Wrightson's greenhouse,' Lady Balderneck persisted, patting her permanently waved hair. Wrighton was another of the Worchester Justices of the Peace who had sat in judgement on Grunnow. His house was under a mile from Codlum Manor.

'But there's no proof he started either fire. In any case, there's no reason why he should pu. . . pick on us.'

'Daddy, I'd say there was every reason,' Diana intervened. 'He threatened revenge on everyone involved with his conviction. What he called his wrongful conviction and cruel sentence.'

'Tosh. He was caught red-handed,' boomed her father, the volume failing to disguise the doubt.

'But it was you who did the sentencing all the same,' Lady

Balderneck concluded darkly.

'Jolly hard luck on your Pater, what? I mean, if every joker he sends to jug tries to burn down the family seat when he gets out. Dash it, what's the world coming to?' questioned Berty, Diana's fiancé, a few hours later, as the two strolled back from the tennis court arm in arm, carrying their racquets. They made a handsome couple, she in a calf length Lillywhite's tennis dress with a flimsy sash at the hips and a soft white band of the same material knotted around her bobbed, raven-coloured hair.

Berty, a knife-edged crease in his white flannels, was a short, spare, muscular young man with a limited cerebral range but an Oxford half-Blue for boxing, a warm disposition, and undeniable career prospects in the City. His family owned a merchant bank: all of it. He was head over heels in love with Diana, and the feeling was reciprocated. Sir Percival Balderneck had warmly sanctioned an engagement based on such commendable, not to say, sterling foundations: Berty was also heir to a Viscountcy.

'I think your Mater's absolutely right too. This cove Grunnow ought to be put down, once and for all, what?' Berty offered a metaphor familiar to those who managed livestock and agricultural labourers. He cleaved the air with a fierce backhand stroke, emulating Fred Perry, the new 1933 Wimbledon champion – while inadvertently propelling a surprised wasp for several hundred yards. 'Hello, there's been a visitation from the local constabulary.' He pointed his racquet at the blue uniformed figure just leaving the house on a heavy bicycle and heading in their direction. 'A harbinger of good news perhaps? What?'

They paused at the edge of the gravelled drive as PC George Ogden drew up beside them and dismounted. He was a large and ponderous countryman in his middle thirties, with a sorrowful face, hairy brows over bovine eyes and skin the colour of a lightly smoked kipper, glistening in patches.

'Hello Ogden,' said Diana. 'Been to see Daddy, have you?'

'Morning, Miss Diana. Morning, sir.' The constable saluted deferentially. 'Been another fire like, I'm afeared. Middle of last night. Arr. This time it were Mrs Cranleigh-Boys's 'ouse, this side of Worchester.'

'Golly, wasn't she the third magistrate on the bench? The day Grunnow was tried?'

'That be the long and short of it, miss. Arr.'

'Much damage?' asked Berty.

'No that much, sir. They caught it in time, see? 'Twere the back wall of the kitchen, like. Part of the main 'ouse this time, though.' There was an extra long pause before Ogden's punctuating and, this time, deeply ominous 'Arr.'

'You mean the other fires were both in outhouses?'

'That's right, sir. Empty barn the first time. Major Wrightson's greenhouse after that.'

'Have you arrested Grunnow?' Diana demanded.

The constable shook his head. 'Still no evidence, see miss? His cottage was being watched at the time.'

'By whom?'

'By me. Arr. Haven't had no sleep to speak of these ten nights past, what with watching out for that beggar.' The policeman opened and closed his mouth several times, making a noise each time like the droppings from a leaking tap. 'It's Codlum 'all as I'm watching out for.' He nodded over his shoulder at the pink stone, Georgian house behind him. 'Can't risk nothing 'appening to that. Or the folk in it.' His gaze dropped in a seemly but purposeful manner.

'Quite right. So where was Grunnow at the time the fire started?' asked Berty.

Ogden glowered. 'In 'is cottage, sir. Supposed to be. And I never did see 'im leave it, or come back.' He removed his helmet and wiped the inside with the elbow of his sleeve as he continued. 'And he was there all right when they got news of the fire to me. Sergeant come over by car from Worchester. Fred Grunnow answered the door to us. Mark you, 'e took 'is time. Livid 'e was too, when 'e did come down. Arguing 'e's being persecuted. Since 'e's been in prison, like. See, 'e still says 'e was innocent over that. Codswallop, of course. Arr.'

'Was there time for him to have got back since the fire start-ed?' Berty enquired. His eyes narrowed, indicating careful thought.

'Just about, sir. At the time they *reckon* it started, that is. It's a mile and a 'alf through the woods to Mrs Cranleigh-Boys's. But 'e could have done it.'

'On foot?'

'Depends.' Ogden thought for a moment. ''E could 'ave used a bike, I suppose. And left it in the wood at the back of 'is place. Otherwise I'd have 'eard 'im coming or going.' He paused again, while the jaws opened and closed twice. 'Except, of course, 'e 'asn't got a bike.'

'What about the other fires? Was he at home for those too?'

'For the first one 'e swears 'e was. But then, we wasn't watch-ing him at the time, like. In the case of Major Wrightson's place, it's less than a mile from Grunnow's cottage.' Ogden frowned. 'Like it is from here too.' He glanced meaningfully at Diana. 'Across the fields. Grunnow could have done it both ways in twenty minutes easy. Under cover along the 'edges like.'

'But you were watching him that night,' Berty insisted.

'Right enough, sir. And the way 'e got in and out must have been by magic.'

'Does he keep petrol or paraffin on the premises?'

'Paraffin, sir. For lamps, like everyone else in the village that 'asn't got gas. And 'e smelled strong of it when we got there last night. Me and the sergeant noticed particular. Except Grunnow said 'e'd been filling lamps. Mark you, the fire brigade say them other fires was started normal like. That's why my 'eadquarters won't believe it's arson. Not yet they won't.'

'So what's a normal fire?'

Ogden considered for a moment. 'One that's not started on purpose, sir. Like because a cigarette end's left burning. Or a matchstick's dropped careless. Everything being tinder dry since this drought's been on. Arr.'

'Grunnow's house is at a T-junction,' put in Diana. 'One person watching can't cover all possible approaches, surely?'

The policeman nodded. 'Exactly what I've just been explaining to her Ladyship, miss. Rank impossible 'tis, the way things are. They ought to draft in more constables for the work. But the County be short of everything at the moment. Money's the root of it, of course. Like everything else since that there crash in America. And there being no proof against Grunnow, you can't 'ave a round the clock watch, like. Not that round the clock's needed. We mostly knows where 'e is in the daytime. Like today 'e's running 'is market stall in Worchester. Won't be back till after eight. He walks it both ways. With his cart.'

'You couldn't get more people to watch him, even if my father insists with the Chief Constable?'

There was an awkward pause while the girl and the policemen simultaneously recalled that Sir Percival Balderneck and Colonel Winstable, the Chief Constable of the County, hadn't been on speaking terms for six months, following an altercation on the hunting field.

'Nothing's easy, at the moment, miss,' said Ogden half apologetically. 'Well, I better be on my way.' He prepared to mount his bike. 'Another sleepless night ahead, no doubt. Good-day to you both, then.'

'Salt of the earth, what?' said Berty, when the big policeman was out of earshot. 'Your Pater said he was gassed in the war.'

'Not badly,' Diana replied as they resumed their stroll toward the Hall. 'Otherwise he couldn't be a policeman, could he? His father used to be one of the outside staff here. I believe Ogden himself started working for us as a garden boy in 1912. It was after the war he joined the police, but he's still jolly loyal to Daddy.'

'Is he married?'

'No. Sort of permanently, unofficially engaged to Audrey Ruckle, the barmaid at the Spreadeagle. They can't afford to marry. Not until he gets promotion, I think. His parents are both dead. He lives with a widowed aunt, Mrs Hagler.'

'In a police house?'

'No, in her cottage. There isn't a police house in Upper Codlum yet, though one's been promised for ages. Mrs Hagler had no children of her own. Her husband was killed in France, but he left her well provided for. Anyway, she dotes on Ogden. She owned the village shop till she retired. Used to give me free sweets when I was little. She doesn't care for Audrey Ruckle though.'

'Who's a blousey barmaid?'

'She is a bit.'

'Hmm. Care for a gasper?' He offered her a Balkan Sobranie from his silver case.

'No thanks.'

Berty lit a cigarette himself. 'Well I think Ogden's doing his best in a bally lonely situation, *vis-à-vis* the arson, don't you know? He's obviously mad keen to protect your family and the Hall. I think we should help him.'

'How?'

'Well if he and your Mater are right, and this bounder Grunnow is setting fire to places right, left and centre, there's got to be a secret way he's getting in and out of his cottage. It's obvious Ogden's baffled, but I bet we could twig how Grunnow's doing it in no time, what?'

'But we'd have to get in to do that?'

'Abso-bally-lootly.' He expelled smoke through his nostrils. 'Does he live alone, d'you know?'

'Yes he does. But they say he hardly ever goes out. Except on market days.'

'Like today. So all we have to do is slip in now, while he's still in Worcester. Or I can at least, with you keeping *cave* in the car.'

Half an hour later, Berty had entered Grunnow's small cottage through the back door. Diana was in his open Lagonda parked at the junction of the main and side roads that enclosed the narrowish, two-acre holding on its southern and eastern sides. Woodland came nearly up to the northern boundary, with a continuous, four-foot wire fence set close to the rear of the cottage. Grunnow's own holding was spread out to the west, between the fence and the hedge that separated it from the high road.

The thatched dwelling was single storey with a dormer window in the attic. It was built of rubble and plaster, and whitewashed, but not recently. The roof thatch needed repair. There were several small outhouses – a privy with a broken door, a rickety woodshed, and a lean-to, its earthen floor rutted by the wheels of the absent handcart. There were some blacksmith's tools hung up over a bench on one side of the lean-to, and, on the other, piles of empty wooden vegetable boxes stacked to the roof. There was a hand pump outside the back door with a long dog chain attached to it, and a covered well in the dusty yard next to an empty, netted chicken run. The smallholding itself was better tended than the buildings – well weeded, with vegetables and fruit bushes in ordered ranks occupying almost all of it.

Berty, who had changed out of his tennis clothes, had scouted around the building on his arrival, looking for a covered way leading off the property, but not finding one. Getting inside the cottage had been easier than expected. A searching along the back door lintel had revealed a key. The dim interior was illkempt and sparsely furnished, and its bulging walls and flagstone floor yielded nothing by way of a secret exit or trap-door.

It was just after he had climbed the narrow stairs to take a quick look at the attic that Diana urgently sounded the horn of the car and started the engine. Although it was barely six o'clock, Grunnow had appeared from around the bend, two hundred yards away, pushing his empty handcart along the road from Worchester. He was a big man, about the size and shape of George Ogden, and although he walked with a limp, he was moving fast. Berty could see him through the dormer window – as well as the fierce-looking mongrel dog that was already lurching ahead of master and cart, hurrying for home.

Berty turned about sharply for the stairs, tripped on the top step, and went crashing down to the bottom. Picking himself up from the flagstones, he hopped to the door with a searing pain in his right ankle. He had locked the door, replaced the key, and was vaulting the rear fence when the snarling dog raced in from the road. The animal leaped at the receding intruder, in time to sink its teeth into still vulnerable nether regions, luckily closing on nothing more sensitive than grey flannel. There was a rending sound, but Berty kept going. He cleared the fence and beat aside the lower branches of conifers as he thrust diagonally through the wood toward the side lane where he could hear the Lagonda. Scratched, torn, dazed and with the pain worsening, he staggered through the hedge into the lane.

'Here, darling!' shouted Diana at the wheel of the car just behind him.

'Keep going,' he cried, waiting for her to draw alongside, then stepping on to the running board.

''Ere! What's going on?' protested an angry, rough voice from the upper road where the figure of Grunnow could be seen gesticulating wildly.

The mongrel, baulked from further pursuit by the height of the fence, was howling without cease.

'Grunnow must have finished early,' called Diana, shifting the powerful engine into second gear, and for some reason blushing furiously. 'Did you find anything?'

'Nothing. Except he's got enough paraffin to burn down the Houses of Parliament.' Grasping the top of the windscreen, Berty levered himself into the car over the passenger door. It was only when he sank on to the cool leather beside Diana that he realized why she was blushing. The seat of his trousers seemed to be entirely missing. 'I say, now you'll have to marry me, what?' he chortled, making her blush even more.

'He jolly well has to be getting out through the wood. It's the only way except . . . Well it's a mystery,' said Berty, returning to the subject of Grunnow late that evening. He and Diana were both in evening dress and leaning on the balustrade of the terrace, outside the drawing-room at Codlum Hall. Sir Percival and Lady Balderneck had already retired to bed.

It was a clear night with a warm breeze from the south. Berty was sipping the last of a brandy which, along with a good dinner, had almost banished the pain in his ankle. The couple were taking a breather after dancing to records of the Savoy Orpheans on the gramophone. The reprise of Jerome Kern's latest foxtrot was drifting through from the machine they had left playing in the drawing-room.

'Ogden's been watching from the Worchester road, of course,' said Diana, choosing another marron glacé from the box Berty had brought her from Prestat in South Molton Street.

'Only because he says he can't go into the wood.' Berty had called to see PC Ogden just before dinner.

'Because he'd be trespassing?'

'That's right. Pretty footling reason too. But he insists he has to abide by the law. He nearly had a fit when I said I'd broken into the cottage.' Frowning, Berty scanned the Dutch garden below them which was prettily illuminated in the moonlight. 'But I told Ogden he ought to position himself down the lane,' he went on. 'He can hear the bounder leave from there at least, even if he can't see him. And I think we should mount guard on some nights in the wood ourselves.'

'All night?' she linked an arm through his.

'No, for a couple of hours say, after one o'clock. That's when Ogden's been knocking off. I've told him we would. He sounded jolly grateful!'

'But they say all the fires so far have been started between midnight and one?'

'All the more reason why Grunnow should break the sequence, what? Because the police have worked out the pattern. But there's no point keeping watch on a night like this.'

'Because all the fires have been on cloudy nights?'

'Mm.' He looked at the time. It was just after midnight. 'He wouldn't dare attempt anything up here by moonlight. Not like me.' His voice had softened as he put his glass down and drew her close.

After they had kissed, Diana opened her eyes and gazed at him adoringly, his manly head boldly outlined in a coloured halo against the night sky. 'Oh darling,' she murmured. Then, her body suddenly stiffened. 'Darling,' she said again, this time more loudly and with decided urgency as she broke away from his embrace, 'just look over there.' She was pointing to the bright red reflection in the middle distance.

'By jove, it's a fire all right. And not far away.' Even as he spoke they both saw a great lick of naked flame leap high into the sky.

'It looks as if it's in Lower Codlum. Come on,' cried Diana already half-way across the terrace.

As the two disappeared, the recorded voice in the drawing-room was crooning: '. . . *all who love are blind. When your heart's on fire . . .*'

'Fire brigade came as fast as they could, but the cottage was burnt to the ground by the time they got there. Old Mrs Hagler couldn't have stood a chance. She was asleep upstairs,' Berty explained to Balderneck nearly an hour later, after he and Diana had returned to the Hall. Diana's father had been waiting for them dressed in pyjamas and an unseasonably heavy dress-ing-gown. The noise of the fire engine had woken him and his wife. Diana had gone up to tell her mother the bad news. The two men were standing in the hall.

'They got the body out, though?'

'What there was of it, sir. It wasn't a pleasant sight.' Berty swallowed at the memory. 'Diana was very cut up. She was fond of the old lady, don't you know?'

'It's a fu. . . fairly isolated cottage, of course. Not really in the village. Algy Wrightson's place isn't far away. You say he was first on the scene?'

'Yes. The smell of fire woke him.'

'Would have done, with tonight's breeze. Pretty sensitive to fire too, since his gu. . . greenhouse was burnt down.'

'It was he 'phoned in the alarm, then dashed over in his car, but he was too late to do anything. He said the place was already an inferno.'

'Those old thatched cottages go up like matchwood once fire takes a hold. All over in minutes, no doubt. Ga. . . ghastly thing. And Ogden wasn't home with his aunt,' the older man uttered dully, shaking his head.

'No. He was out watching Grunnow's cottage, of course. Since eleven.'

'How did he take it?'

'Like a soldier, what? But jolly well stunned all the same.'

'Angry too?' A firm finger and thumb went to smooth the moustache.

'I imagine he will be later.'

'It was Grunnow who did this all right. In revenge for Ogden arresting him over the chu. . . chickens. We all overlooked he'd have it in for Ogden too. And that includes Ogden, I expect. My wife was sure he'd go for this house if he could. But who'd have guessed he'd take it out on Ogden's aunt? Swine.'

'Naturally, Grunnow swears he's been home all night. And once again, Ogden never saw him leave or return.'

'But you said he could be getting out under cover?'

'Yes. If there's a tunnel or something I never found it. But if he's quiet, he could be going over the fence and through the wood at the back of his place. I didn't like to ask Ogden just now, but if he was watching Grunnow's cottage from where he's been doing it on other nights, he could easily have missed seeing him again.'

'Well at least the Worchester police seem convinced this time that Grunnow's our arsonist. I know I certainly am, whether or not they've fu. . . found witnesses yet. They've taken him in you say?'

'For questioning, and I think for his own protection, what? A lot of people at the scene were about ready to string him up there and then.'

'I'd guess Ogden'll feel the same in a bit. Best they keep Grunnow locked up till he comes before the bench. The charge'll be mu. . . murder this time. Case for the Assizes,' completed Balderneck – except he was wrong.

'They've let Grunnow go?' questioned Lady Balderneck in a shocked voice at the start of lunch three days later.

'Had to. Not a shred of firm evidence to connect him with any of the fires. No witnesses. Nothing. Except the revenge theory,' replied her husband who was standing to carve the large cold ham in front of him at the end of the table. Ethel the maid was taking round the plates after he filled them. 'Damned disgrace all the same.'

'And with only this house left on his list. Isn't it enough he's. . . ?'

'No, I'm sure we're safe. Fu. . . fella knows the authorities are on to him now,' Balderneck interrupted with more conviction than he felt.

'That's probably right,' said Berty in support. 'He's had his revenge. More than that if he never meant to kill Mrs Hagler. And I don't suppose he did, what? The fires were only intended to destroy property, don't you think?'

'Not necessarily the one at Mrs Cranleigh-Boys's,' put in Diana slowly. 'She could have been trapped in the house, like Mrs Hagler. If the fire from the kitchen had spread.'

'No, she'd have got out. It's a big place. There's less danger to life from fu. . . fire in a large house,' her father offered quickly and not altogether logically, but he was concerned that his wife shouldn't be unduly alarmed about Grunnow setting Codlum Hall alight. 'I imagine Grunnow would do well to keep clear of Ogden,' he concluded pointedly.

'We ran into Ogden this morning,' said Berty as Ethel brought him his plate of ham. 'He seemed pretty normal. Gone back to work, even before his aunt's funeral on Thursday.'

'Best thing,' Balderneck commented stoutly, sitting down after finishing the carving. 'Work keeps the mind occupied.' He had been working on the *Times* crossword for most of the morning. 'Where's he living?'

'He's taken a room at Mrs Jenkins's,' answered his daughter. 'She's just lost one of her regular lodgers, so it suits everyone.' Mrs Jenkins's house was on the fringe of Upper Codlum on the same side as the Hall.

'D'you suppose Ogden and that Ruckle girl will get married now?' Lady Balderneck questioned, while closely studying the contents of the chutney dish.

'He didn't mention it, Mummy.'

'He was sure Grunnow would still need careful watching,' said Berty.

'Why?' asked Balderneck.

'Because the blighter still has this secret way of getting in and out of his cottage at night.'

'That's why Ogden thinks he'll start another fire. Because if he can prove he's not left his cottage again, it'd make him innocent for ever,' said Diana.

'Nonsense,' expostulated her father with his mouth full.

'Of course it is,' Berty countered, 'but not to Grunnow. Nor to the Worchester police, who can't be convinced he's guilty, or they'd never have let him go. But all the more reason for us to mount an extra watch on Grunnow for a bit, what? I mean at the times when Ogden isn't doing it. We've agreed a time-table with him for the next few days.'

'Well I think it's all completely unnerving,' Lady Balderneck responded before turning to speak to the maid. 'Ethel, this isn't mango chutney is it?'

'No, m'lady.' Ethel uttered through a bunged up nose. 'Please m'lady, cook seth we've rund out of the mango and will thith do?'

'No it won't. Sir Percival never cares for anything but. . .'

'Oh, don't trouble, my dear,' put in her husband, glad they were on a new subject. 'Good idea to break a pu. . . pattern. Only way to know what you might have been missing all the time.'

Sir Percival Balderneck, busy with his victuals, missed the look of enlightenment on his daughter's face that his last words suddenly produced.

'I still think we're in the wrong place at the wrong time,' said Berty to Diana much later that day. It was shortly after midnight and they had been crouched together in the clump of trees for nearly an hour. 'I mean we said we'd watch from. . . '

'Ssh,' she whispered back. 'Look.'

The stooping figure of a man had appeared silhouetted against the skyline. He was only fifty yards from them and moving very fast. They watched while he crossed the short piece of open scrubland that separated the last village house from the dry ditch under the boundary wall to the Hall

'Don't move till he's over the wall,' Diana whispered again.

They watched until the familiar outline rose up again below a broken part of wall and scrambled over it.

'Did you see? He's carrying a can? We've got him,' hissed Berty. 'I'll follow. You telephone the alarm. Then bring the car when he's had time to reach the house.'

It was one of the action plans they'd agreed. The Lagonda was parked two hundred yards away in shadow next to the 'phone box in the centre of Upper Codlum.

Once over the wall himself, Berty, in dark clothes and tennis shoes, had no trouble in silently shadowing the figure ahead of him who seemed never to look back. Keeping his distance through the shrubbery, skirting the drive and the south lawn, then the orchard, Berty was sure his target was making for the rear of the main house when suddenly the figure swung away towards the stables on the right.

'Rotter,' muttered Berty to himself. 'Going for defenceless animals.'

He waited poised when the man stopped next to some hay bails stacked against the last of the row of loose boxes, but as soon as he saw the paraffin can being unscrewed he rose from hiding, sprinted across the stable yard, and with a roar grasped the criminal by the shoulder and swung him about.

With a gasp of surprise the man dropped the can and reached too late inside his jacket. Berty punched him hard with a perfectly timed right to the head, followed with a left to the solar plexus and, finally, threw another and even more devastating right to the jaw that sent the victim sprawling on the ground. Then he pounced on the man's chest, pinning him down as the sounds of a motor engine, running footsteps and excited voices filled the air nearby.

'Once too often, what?' said Berty breathlessly and still kneeling on his captive. 'I'd never have believed it. You've been clever, Ogden. But not clever enough.'

'It was all thanks to Diana,' said Berty next morning at breakfast. He gave his fiancée an adoring look. 'It was she who twigged the arsonist was Ogden not Grunnow, what?'

Diana smiled modestly. 'I got the feeling Grunnow might have been telling the truth all the time when Berty couldn't find that hidden exit. That we might just have got into the habit of suspecting him. Like always eating mango chutney, Daddy.' She shrugged. 'After that, Ogden was the obvious suspect. Of course, no-one had thought of him before, because every time there was a fire he said he was watching Grunnow's cottage. And we all believed him. It was the most marvellous alibi. Nobody would be watching Ogden.'

'That's the choice part,' put in Berty again.

'*Sed quis custodiet ipsos custodes?*' Balderneck solemnly pronounced a tag remembered from schooldays, and which, in response to a mutinous sigh from his wife, he proceeded to translate as: 'But who is to gu. . . guard the guards themselves? Or in this case, guard in the singular,' he completed defensively.

'Absolutely,' Berty agreed. 'We'd even agreed with Ogden about the times when Diana and I would be out watching. So he knew he was completely safe during his own stint.'

'You see,' continued Diana, 'all the fires except the one that killed Mrs Hagler were red herrings. Meant to have everyone think we had an arsonist in the village. Suspicion would fall on Grunnow because of what he threatened when he went to prison. Ogden encouraged that.'

'But the whole dirty business was because Ogden needed his aunt dead,' said her father, shaking his head at his scrambled eggs.

'Yes, Daddy. He knew Mrs Hagler was well off and was leaving him everything. She adored him, but loathed his girlfriend. The old lady could have survived for years, of course. But until she died, Ogden couldn't marry Audrey Ruckle.'

'He confessed as much last night,' said Berty.

'But surely. . . ?' began Lady Balderneck, inserting a black cigarette with a gold tip into a very long white holder.

'Oh, it wasn't just because he couldn't afford to marry her,' provided Berty, leaning forward quickly with a lighter. 'It was because he was sure his aunt would have left her money to someone else if he had.'

'But why did he need to start a fire here last night, when he'd already achieved his aim?' questioned Balderneck, coffee cup poised at his lips.

'That was the most important red herring of all, Daddy. He was afraid that otherwise when his aunt's will was read people might start putting two and two together. He needed another fire *after* he'd murdered Mrs Hagler for camouflage.'

'God bless my soul.' Her father put down his cup sharply, forgetting to drink from it at all.

'Appalling man,' said his mother.

'A rogue policeman is a most exceptional thing, of course,' mourned Sir Percival. 'In all my years on the bench, never come across one before. There are damned fu. . . few in England. Now in America. . . '

'Of course, we couldn't have caught Ogden if we'd been watching Grunnow's house,' Berty put in. 'Especially at the time we'd intended doing it. It was Diana insisted we should hide between Mrs Jenkins's house and the Hall, at the very time Ogden was supposed to be watching Grunnow's place. I was against it. Glad I took her advice. What?'

The last comment was one that Berty, the future Lord Greenwood, was to repeat constantly through a long and happily married life.

David Williams created his own successful advertising agency but suffered a stroke after which he turned to full-time writing. He has now written fourteen urbane whodunnits since *Murder for Treasure*, all of them using his suave merchant banker and amateur sleuth Mark Treasure.

HOLOCAUST AT MAYHEM PARVA

JULIAN SYMONS

A fine summer morning in Mayhem Parva. Through the leaded light windows of her cottage in the High Street Mrs White, who thought of herself as the merry widow, watched Professor Plum walking along erratically as always, taking care to dodge the cracks in the pavement. He looked deplorably untidy in that old pullover, but still she thought was a fine figure of a man, and one said to be susceptible to feminine charm. If she was at his table at the Vicarage tea party that afternoon, and sparkled – and she knew how to sparkle, who better? – anything might follow. A supper *tête-à-tête*, a little gentle dalliance, and then – well, she had really exhausted the pleasures of being a merry widow, and although the Professor had the reputation of being a permanent bachelor, interested only in the odd concoctions he brewed up in his laboratory, he had never seen the merry widow really sparkling. But of course it was necessary to arrange that she *should* sit at the same table. She picked up the telephone.

Outside Mr Bunn the baker's the Professor had to sidestep dexterously to miss a couple of tricky hairline cracks in the pavement. An ancient Morris pulled up behind him with a shriek of brakes, the window was wound down, and the Reverend Green's round shining countenance looked out at him.

'Is it not a beautiful day, Professor? All the live murmur of a summer's day, as the poet puts it. And where can the summer day murmur more seductively than here in Mayhem Parva?'

'Ha,' said the Professor.

'We look forward so much to seeing you this afternoon.' At that Professor Plum merely nodded. The Reverend Green put his head on one side and said coyly, 'A certain temptress has asked my dear Emerald if she may share your table.'

'Ha,' the Professor repeated.

'That makes you curious, I'm sure.' In fact the Professor had shown no sign of curiosity. 'I fear you must wait for curiosity to be satisfied. What I can promise is that Emerald has prepared a sumptuous spread. But I have duties, I must fly.' The ancient Morris moved off in a series of jerks.

The infernal Mrs White, I suppose, the Professor thought. Stupid simpering woman, not a patch on that fine little filly Mrs Peacock – what's her name, Paula. Now if it had been Paula Peacock who'd asked to sit at his table – but that wasn't likely, and it wasn't the problem, which was what to do about the Vicar. Should he go to the boy's parents, or confront the Vicar face to face and tell him he was a disgrace to the cloth? But suppose the man just laughed at him, and the boy's people sent him off with a flea in his ear? Difficult, difficult. Better have a word with the Wise Woman, he thought, which was his name for Miss Harple.

Back in his ugly little house near the station the Professor retired to his lab. He was working at the moment on a mixture made from spotted hemlock, which he believed to be good for asthma. Multiplex Chemicals had shown interest in taking it up on a commercial basis. But the problem of the Vicar was on his mind, he found it hard to concentrate and after half an hour gave up. He telephoned Miss Harple and asked if she could come over, as there was a confidential matter he couldn't discuss on the telephone.

'A garden is a lovesome thing, God wot,' the Reverend Green said as he leaned over the fence that separated the untidy Vicarage garden from Miss Harple's neat rose beds, primrose and polyanthus borders, and rock garden cleverly devised in stripes of red, white and blue. Miss Harple, who was weeding the rock garden, straightened up but did not reply. Even in gardening clothes she looked elegant, her beautiful white hair perfectly dressed, her china-blue eyes innocent, or as some said icy.

'What does the philosopher tell us? That God Almighty first planted a garden, and that it is the purest of human pleasures.'

'But it was entered by the serpent,' Miss Harple said.

'Ah, you are too clever for me.' She did not deny it. 'Dear lady, may I venture to remind you that Emerald and I look forward to seeing you this afternoon in our rambling wilderness.'

'I have a guest coming down from London.' She elaborated, 'A gentleman.'

'Of course he will be welcome, the more so because he comes as the escort of our dear Miss Harple, solver of all our mysteries, elucidator of every puzzle.'

The Reverend Green passed a handkerchief over his face, smiled, bowed, opened his garden gate. Miss Harple looked after him for a moment, finished her weeding, went into the kitchen. She had much to do before her guest arrived.

The letter plopped on to the mat. Mrs Peacock, eating her single slice of dry toast, drinking her sugarless tea – she knew the importance of preserving her figure – heard it, and shivered a little. When she saw the square envelope with its carefully printed capitals she had to force herself to open it.

She read:

I KNOW WHAT YOU WERE DOING WITH
PROFESSOR PLUM IN THE CONSERVATORY.
GET OUT OF MAYHEM PARVA YOU FILTHY WHORE

She put the letter beside the two others, deliberated during a long hot bath, and then went round to see Miss Harple. Mrs Peacock had come only recently to the village, and almost the first person she met was Miss Harple. They had met before, when Miss Harple solved the mystery of the missing Egyptian diplomat, at a time when Mrs Peacock was the Egyptian's mistress, and was known as TouTou the Peacock Fan dancer. Her maiden name, which in fact she had never changed, was Betty Sludge, but not unnaturally she preferred Paula Peacock and, as she told Miss Harple, wanted only to live quietly in Mayhem Parva, her days as TouTou forgotten.

Miss Harple read the letters, and then looked at Mrs Peacock with those blue eyes that, as TouTou had said when being questioned by her during the Egyptian diplomat affair, could see through a brick wall.

'Is there any truth in these stories?'

'None at all.' She giggled, then stopped as she saw Miss Harple's frown. 'Though Professor Plum is an attractive man.'

'But you were not with him in the conservatory – or the library as another letter says – or his study?' A shaken head. 'And you have met nobody else in the village who knew you in the past?' Head shaken again. The china blue eyes looked hard at her. 'Of course if you left Mayhem Parva and returned to London. . .'

A third head shake, and the most decisive. 'I've bought my house. And I love it here. It's so peaceful, so *English*.'

'Very well. Leave the letters with me. I will think about them. And don't worry. Every problem has a solution.'

With TouTou gone Miss Harple returned to her kitchen preparations, but not for long. This time when the doorbell rang it was Miss Scarlett, who lived only a few yards away, in a lane leading off the High Street. Miss Harple did not care for Miss Scarlett, whom she regarded as a malicious gossip, but she could be kind and gentle in the presence of distress, and she saw that Miss Scarlett was upset. She sat her down now in the little sitting room crowded with knick-knacks, and asked her what was the trouble.

'I have had such a shock. This morning earlier I was in Payne's the chemist, I went in to get some indigestion tablets, but also because – I wonder if you have heard the story about Elfrieda Payne and the grocer's boy, it seemed to me that he, I mean Mr Payne, was looking very *tense*, and when Elfrieda came down the stairs. . .'

'Miss Scarlett, I do not want to know about Mrs Payne and the grocer's boy. Something has upset you. You were going to tell me about it.'

'Yes, my tongue runs away with me. I got my tablets, turned round to go out, and came face to face with Colonel Mustard.'

'The man who has taken a short lease on old Mrs Cunningham's house now she's gone to live in Malta. I have met him once or twice, he seems pleasant enough.'

'Oh yes, he *seems* pleasant. But his name is not Colonel Mustard, and he is a swindler. He called himself Commander Salt when I knew him, and persuaded me to invest in his company. It was called Electric Car Electrics, they were going to make very cheap electricity out of old newspapers soaked in sea water, which would run a new electric car. He said I should make a fortune, but he disappeared and I never saw a penny of my money back. Oh, it was such a shock.'

If Miss Harple thought that a fool and her money are soon parted, she did not say so. She gave Miss Scarlett a cup of tea and one of her home-made scones, found out by a few adroit questions that it was unlikely Miss Scarlett would have a case for legal action against Colonel Mustard, spoke soothing words, and said she would speak to the Colonel. She reflected that there were several fools with money in Mayhem Parva, but she did not say that to Miss Scarlett.

Colonel Mustard, alias Commander Salt, alias Group Captain Fairweather, did his usual hundred morning press-ups, ran round the garden half a dozen times, ate a hearty breakfast which he cooked himself, said 'Top of the morning to you' to Mrs Middleton the cleaner, and retired to his study to look through the draft prospectus for Uniworld Military Disposals, a company which according to the prospectus was being formed to buy out-of-date military equipment in European countries cheap, and sell it to the Third World. As the Colonel read through the draft he talked to himself.

'Agents all over Europe – old uniforms, cooking equipment, armoured cars, all sorts of electrical gear, out-of-date planes – going for a song, my dear sir, going for a song – no question of military use, m'dear madame, planes converted for commercial use, armoured cars turned into jeeps, uniforms retailored as dungarees – endless possibilities – you'll see thirty per cent a year on your money – and helping people who need it, shouldn't consider taking it on otherwise.'

The Colonel made a few amendments, stood up, looked at himself in the glass, admired the soldierly look, the erect stance, the clipped moustache. 'Ready to go, m'boy,' he said. 'If I'm not much mistaken, there's rich pickings in Mayhem Parva.'

But Colonel Mustard was mistaken.

Miss Harple met her visitor, whom we will call simply the Author, at Mayhem Parva station, which had no waiting room and was hardly more than a halt. He was an awkward shambling figure, who was writing a book about Agatha Christie. Miss Harple had known her well, and had an encyclopaedic knowledge of the works. As they walked back through the village she told the Author of her busy morning, the Vicar's call, Mrs Peacock's visit followed by that of Miss Scarlett, her own call on Professor Plum, whom she had found messing about in his laboratory. The Author listened, enthused about the well-preserved village street, and was suitably impressed by Miss Harple's little Georgian home Mayhem House, the Waterford glass on the shelves and the bits of Minton china in cabinets.

'It will be rather a scrap lunch, I'm afraid,' Miss Harple said when they were sipping dry sherry. 'My maid of all work Marilyn is in bed with a gastric upset, and I must apologize for the place looking so untidy.' In reality it could hardly have been neater. 'And that means, I'm afraid, I shall have to give the Vicar's wife, Emerald Green, a hand this afternoon. There's a tea party at the Vicarage, and Marilyn was going to help with cutting bread, making sandwiches, all that sort of thing. If you'd like to come Emerald would be very pleased, but perhaps you'd just be bored by a Vicarage tea party.'

On the contrary, the Author said, it would be a new and no doubt exciting experience. He wandered round the garden while Miss Harple laid lunch, noting the abundance of roses without a trace of blackspot or mildew, the pretty yellow jasmine climbing up the wall, the weedless grass, the yew tree that separated this tidy garden from the overgrown one next door. After lunch his hostess talked about Agatha Christie, her shyness, her love of true English villages like Mayhem Parva, her endless curiosity about tiny details most people overlooked or didn't notice, her relaxed charm with friends. The Author listened and made notes.

When lunch was over, and they had drunk coffee in a shady part of the garden, Miss Harple went round to lend a hand at the Vicarage, leaving the Author to look round the village before putting in an appearance at the tea party. He admired the old-fashioned coloured bottles in the chemist's window, and the sign outside the butcher that said 'Butcher and Grazier, Home-Killed Pork', went into the well-kept church, was amused by the name of the pub which was called the 'Falling Down Man', went into one of the flourishing antique shops and considered buying a Victorian mother-of-pearl card case, but decided it was too expensive. Then he made his way to the Vicarage, where the tea party was in full swing.

There were little tables with four or six people sitting at them, plates of sandwiches, scones and little cakes, dishes of trifle, ice cream. His hand was pressed by one that seemed damp with oil rather than water.

'You must be the friend of our dear Miss Harple. *So* good of you to come. Now let me see, where can we find room for – ah, but here is the lady herself. Thank you, my dear, I must confess to being a trifle parched.' The Reverend Green accepted gratefully the cup of tea handed him, and wandered away.

'Here you are, then,' Miss Harple said a little sharply. 'Do you like trifle?'

'Well – I think perhaps – not after such an excellent lunch.'

'You'll find chairs in the corner, and there's a place over here.' She led the way to a table where three people sat, and introduced him. 'This is Mrs Peacock – Mrs White – Professor Plum. And here is Emerald with a cup of tea.'

Little Mrs Green said it was nice to see any friend of Miss Harple, and recommended the tuna paste sandwiches which she had made herself. The Author considered his companions. Mrs Peacock sipped her tea delicately, Professor Plum drank his noisily while eating a piece of fruit cake, Mrs White was occupied with a plate of creamy trifle decorated with hundreds and thousands. Mrs White spoke to the Professor.

'This is really delicious, Professor, do try some.'

'Don't fancy it.' The Professor made a harrumphing noise, and said to Mrs Peacock, 'Settling down all right, are you? All very neighbourly here in the village, that garden fence of yours could do with a bit of attention. Quite a handyman myself, if you need one.'

Mrs Peacock murmured that he was very kind, in a voice that sounded extremely refined. Mrs White tittered slightly, leaned forward, and said, 'I hear your laboratory is quite fascinating, Professor, that you make all sorts of wonderful old medicines there. I believe myself that the old remedies are much the best. . .'

She was interrupted by a prolonged high-pitched scream. There was a crash, a sound of breaking crockery. Mrs White stopped speaking to the Professor and said, in quite a different voice, 'Whatever's the matter with Colonel Mustard?'

The Author turned, and saw that a tall red-faced man wearing a blue brass-buttoned blazer was on the ground, writhing and crying out unintelligible words. He had pulled over the table as he fell, and lay in a welter of spilled tea cakes and sandwiches. The Reverend Green, Emerald, Miss Harple and a man wearing spectacles were beside him. The woman who had screamed put a hand to her thin chest and cried: 'I had nothing to do with it, it was nothing I said to him.' Miss Harple took her arm, and said, 'He's been taken ill, Miss Scarlett, nobody's blaming you. Doctor Playden will be able to help.'

The man with spectacles looked up from beside the body, and shook his head. 'I'm afraid not. This man is dead.'

Some time later the Author sat on a sofa in Mayhem House, listening while Doctor Playden and Chief Inspector Haddock discussed the case with Miss Harple. He was amused by the way in which both men deferred to her.

'You're sure you feel up to the mark?' the doctor said. 'I know you've been sleeping badly.'

'I am perfectly well now,' Miss Harple said, with her agreeable touch of acidity.

The Chief Inspector coughed. 'Up to a point it's straightforward enough. There was cyanide in his tea, the question is who put it there. The only other person permanently at his table was Miss Scarlett, though the Reverend Green sat there in between getting up to say hallo to people as they arrived, and chatting with them.'

'And I believe three cups of tea were taken to the table by Emerald, Mrs Green.' The policeman nodded. 'And she just put them down on the table? So it was by pure chance that the cup with cyanide in it came to Colonel Mustard.' Miss Harple paused. 'Unless Mrs Green was the poisoner.'

Doctor Playden protested. 'You surely can't believe that.'

Miss Harple spoke gently, her blue eyes innocent. 'I am simply pointing out the possibility.'

The policeman and the doctor were drinking whisky, the Author and Miss Harple her home-brewed mead. She spoke again, slowly. 'Miss Scarlett had reason to dislike Colonel Mustard, but I don't think any cause to wish him dead. I think in the circumstances I should tell you about it.' She said, and then went on:

'But I have a feeling. . .'

'Yes?' the Chief Inspector said eagerly.

'That perhaps this is only the beginning. There was an old farmer we used to visit when I was a child, and he could always tell the weather after there'd been a storm. The sky might be blue again, not a cloud in sight, but he'd say: "This was only the beginning, the real storm's still to come." I feel like that old farmer. The real storm's still to come.'

Miss Harple, as so often, was right. The Author, curious to follow the case and anxious to talk with her again about Agatha Christie, spent the night in the Falling Down Man, and at breakfast heard the news from the distraught landlord.

'Reverend Green's dead, sir, and that's not all. Ambulances been in and out the village all night, taking 'em to hospital. Doctor's not had a wink of sleep. There be so many taken ill, sir, it's an epidemic like except it's not. They say the Reverend died in his sleep, and I hear tell he was poisoned, they say it was all that tea party at the Vicarage.'

The Author spent the next two days talking to people in the village. He paid a couple of calls on Miss Harple, but there seemed to be always a policeman in discussion with her, either a Sergeant with the autopsy reports, a harassed-looking Chief Inspector, or the Chief Constable himself. She was obviously too busy to talk about Agatha Christie, and seemed disinclined to discuss the case, or cases, with him. The Author paid a visit to Professor Plum's house in the company of Doctor Playden, and saw the laboratory. The Doctor, indeed, was friendly enough to tell him the detailed results of the autopsies on the six victims. It was after he had learned these that the Author paid Miss Harple another and, as it proved, his last visit.

It was late evening, and his welcome was friendly, although not overwhelmingly so. Miss Harple was wearing a blue brocade dress, with a little lace round the neck and a matching piece of lace on her white hair. She looked elegant, but also frail and tired. She apologized for her failure to look out papers she had mentioned about Mrs Christie, but said that she would send them on to him.

'I didn't come to talk about Agatha Christie. I came to talk about the case.'

'The case is solved. Mr Haddock agreed with me that there was only one possible culprit, Professor Plum.'

'But Professor Plum is dead.'

'Precisely. He had always been eccentric, and it is plain that the eccentricity turned to madness. He had the means of making poisons in his laboratory, and had actually produced some of those used. What he did was the work of a madman, and when it was done he felt remorse. Why are you shaking your head?'

'I think there is a different explanation. Would you like to hear it?'

'It has been a long day. Will the explanation take long?'

'A few minutes.'

'Talking is thirsty work. I know you enjoy a glass of mead. And perhaps you would like a biscuit.'

The Author watched as she filled two glasses from a decanter, and placed one beside each of their chairs. When she left the room to fetch the biscuits he changed the glasses. On her return he began to talk, aware of his similarity to a detective in an Agatha Christie story gathering the suspects together to explain the case. Here, however, he had an audience of one.

'There were six victims. Colonel Mustard, who died at the tea party, Miss Peacock, the Reverend Green and Professor Plum, who died during the evening or early night, Miss Scarlett who died in her sleep, and Mrs White who died early on the following morning. Each died of a different poison. Colonel Mustard drank tea laced with cyanide, Mrs Peacock an infusion of hemlock, the Reverend Green was poisoned by taxine and Professor Plum by gelsemium. Miss Scarlett took an overdose of chloral hydrate, and Mrs White was poisoned by arsenic.'

'She was an exceptionally tiresome woman.'

'It's interesting that you should say that. She was the only one to suffer a prolonged period of pain before death.' Miss Harple looked at him sharply, then sipped her mead. The Author drank a mouthful of his.

'It would seem at first glance that the killer was somebody with a passion to try out the effects of different poisons, chosen at random. Nothing at all appeared to link them. But that was not the case.'

The Author waited as if for questions, but Miss Harple did not speak.

'The link was Agatha Christie. All of those poisons were used in her stories. Cyanide of course quite often, most notably in *Sparkling Cyanide*. Coniine, which is derived from spotted hemlock, was used in *Five Little Pigs*, taxine in *A Pocket Full of Rye*, gelsemium in *The Big Four*. One of the victims in *Ten Little Niggers* took an overdose of chloral hydrate, and arsenic was used in a story called 'The Tuesday Night Club'. The murderer, then, was somebody with an expert knowledge of the Christie canon, something that ruled out Professor Plum, who hardly had a work of fiction in his house.'

'But he made coniine in his laboratory.'

'Quite true. Doctor Playden told me he was in hopes of it being adopted as a remedy for asthma. You were friendly with him, often visited the laboratory. I think you took a phial with you on one visit, and filled it from his jar of coniine.'

'And where do you suggest I found those other exotic poisons?'

'Two of them from your garden. Gelsemium is derived from yellow jasmine, which grows up your house wall, and taxine comes from the berry of the yew tree. I noticed a fine specimen at the bottom of the garden. Cyanide is an old fashioned way of getting rid of wasps, and arsenic of rats, although of course they have to be extracted with some care.'

'Chloral hydrate is not easily obtainable.'

'Doctor Playden prescribed it for you because you told him you were sleeping badly. You saved it up, and then with your usual thoughtfulness gave it to Miss Scarlett as a sleeping draught. I remember that after our discussion when Colonel Mustard died, you said you were worried about Miss Scarlett, and went round to see her.'

Miss Harple straightened the lace round her neck. 'And I suppose you think I gave little Marilyn something to upset her stomach, so that I replaced her as Emerald's assistant at the tea party?' The Author nodded. 'You are really very ingenious. Ingenious but ridiculous. Nobody will believe this nonsense. Have a biscuit.'

He shook his head. 'When I tell the Chief Inspector about the yellow jasmine and the yew tree I think he'll take notice.'

'You really suggest I put those various poisons into the teacups?'

'Yes. You carried round most of the cups and some of the cakes. It wouldn't have been difficult to give them to the right people.'

'Arsenic in tea would taste distinctly bitter.'

'Of course. I should have mentioned that. You knew Mrs White liked trifle, and copied the Christie story in which the arsenic was in the hundreds and thousands on top of the trifle.'

'There is one thing you have forgotten.'

'I don't think so.'

'The three teacups were taken to Colonel Mustard's table by Emerald Green, not by me. I couldn't possibly have known he would take the cup containing the cyanide.'

'Oh, that was clever. But then of course you took that from Agatha Christie too, and adapted it for your own purposes. There is a story in which the poisoner wants a victim and doesn't care who it is, anyone in a group will do. And you didn't mind which of the three at their table took the cup with cyanide, because all of them were going to die. The other cups contained the hemlock and the taxine.' He yawned. He felt very tired.

'I congratulate you. You were perfectly right.'

'Thank you.'

'You may have been puzzled by my motives. I simply wanted to preserve the reputation of this unspoiled English village.' Miss Harple leaned forward and looked at him intently. The Author found it hard to meet the gaze of those icy blue eyes. 'Colonel Mustard had plans for inducing our more credulous residents to invest in his companies, and they would have been ruined. Mrs Peacock had a past which – I won't dwell on it, but she was really not the kind of person we want here. I did my best to get her to leave by sending some letters suggesting she was carrying on an entirely fictitious affair with Professor Plum and telling her she would be happier back in London, but she insisted on staying here. A pity – I rather liked her. Miss Scarlett I did *not* like. She was a busybody, mischief maker, tale teller, really no loss. Neither was Mrs White, who always thought of herself as the merry widow, which meant that she set her cap at any eligible man she met, in a way I found most distasteful. The Reverend Green's conduct was scandalous – I shall say no more than that. And Percy Plum. . . ' Her voice, which had been jarring as a clatter of steel needles, softened to little more than a whisper. '. . . was part crazy, but part a wonderfully clever scientist. I was very fond of Percy.'

'Then why. . . ?'

'Because of his discovery.' Miss Harple looked down at the carpet, her manner almost coy. 'In his experiments Percy had stumbled by chance on what crime writers have feared might exist for years, the undetectable poison. He told me the secret, and of course it is safe with me, but the silly fellow insisted it should be made public. Can you imagine the result for books like Mrs Christie's? It would no longer be possible to write them. Why didn't I use the poison, you may ask? That wouldn't have been fair play, would it? And when we try to imitate crime writers we must always observe fair play.' She broke off. 'You worked things out very well, but you made one mistake. Shall I tell you what it was?'

The Author nodded. He found it hard to keep his eyes open.

'You failed to notice that when I left this room to get the biscuits I could see what you were doing in the looking glass placed just over there, beside the bust of Agatha Christie. I had expected you to take the precaution of changing the glasses, and had prepared my own glass of mead accordingly. Of course, if you had not changed the glasses I should have knocked over my own by accident.'

'You mean. . . ' The Author tried to rise, but found that his legs refused to obey him. He saw Miss Harple now as through a mist.

'"To cease upon the midnight with no pain" – a beautiful line, I always think. It is a minute to midnight now, and I think I can trust you with the secret of the undetectable poison. The three elements are. . . '

Those were the last words the Author heard.

Julian Symons has a vivid recollection of interviewing Agatha Christie. She disliked giving interviews, said 'I suppose as it's you it will be all right', and really unbent when she saw his fear that the tape recorder wasn't working. The result was an interview more candid than most. Apart from his claim to fame as one of the rare Christie interviewers, Julian Symons has just received the Cartier Diamond Dagger for half a lifetime of crime.

ALL'S FAIR IN LOVE

SUSAN MOODY

The Grand Hotel
Chorlington Spa,

September 16th, 192-

Dear Mr Williams,
Re: Reginald Barnes, Policy No. 526/34-BN

As requested, I am writing to keep you informed of the current situation here. Reginald Barnes, Policy No. 526/34-BN (hereinafter the Subject) duly left Blackheath in a taxicab, evincing every appearance of difficulty, the affected limb apparently giving him much inconvenience and his back evidently paining him considerably. I followed in a second cab as far as Paddington Station, where I deemed it unnecessary to 'skulk' any further since we would be travelling to Chorlington Spa on the same train.

Naturally I sat in a Ladies Compartment, while he settled himself into a 'Smoker', but I took every opportunity to pass along the corridor and observe him. At no point did he seem in anything but the acutest discomfort.

At Chorlington, we were met by a species of small motor omnibus belonging to the spa hotel: it transpired that we were not the only guests arriving by that particular train. Indeed, one of them I had already noticed during the journey, an unpleasant little man, rather too emphatic as to spats and moustaches, with a distressing tendency to stare. I took him for some kind of foreign tradesman and was therefore surprised to find him stepping aboard the 'bus with myself and the Subject – though in Mr Barnes's case, it was not so much a question of stepping as of hoisting, which he did with much groaning and swinging of his left leg and in fact, owing to the steepness of the vehicle's steps I doubt if he would have managed it at all without the help of the little tradesman.

(I cannot forebear at this stage from pointing out that I myself remain convinced of the genuineness of the Subject's claim. Only a very suspicious mind could think otherwise. The fact that he took out a policy for personal damages in the amount of seven thousand pounds only three weeks before sustaining a fall from his horse is surely no more than coincidence. Certainly my dear father would have thought so. But that, I suppose you would say, is why *he* is now in an early grave and *you* are running the business he laboured so hard to build up.)

But I digress. . .

The other passenger to join us was a good-looking young man possessed of what I can only describe as an open and manly countenance. I assumed he was recently returned from overseas, in view of the fact that his face was considerably sunburned and there were a number of labels attached to his luggage indicating that he had sojourned at various hotels in Luxor, Cairo and Alexandria. An archaeologist, perhaps. Or with the Foreign Office. We shall see.

The hotel itself seems pleasant and well-ordered. I am glad your original notion of my keeping watch on the Subject in the guise of a chambermaid came, in the end, to nothing. It is bad enough to be employed as an occasional insurance claims investigator (although I have pointed this out to you before, I cannot refrain from repeating that I find it trying in the extreme to consider that had my poor father taken out one of his own policies, I would not be in my current financial predicament and obliged to take work where I can find it); to be, in addition, forced to dodge around the country *spying* on people is totally alien to my nature. This is the third time you have asked me to pose as something other than I am – or would have been, had poor Father been less dilatory – and quite frankly I hope the need will not arise again.

Thanks to your ingenuity in previously discovering the Subject's destination for this week, I have duly been allocated the room next to his, though I feel bound to say that for a single woman, I have been placed in a most embarrassing position by your telephone requests for confirmation that this had been done. The hotel clerk gave me the most odious leer as he handed over the keys, and the chambermaid who accompanied me to my room smiled in a manner I can only describe as 'knowing'. It is obvious that they imagine me to be in some way infatuated with the Subject. Need I say that I find this idea totally repellent?

I will write to you further tomorrow.

Yours, etc.

Sarah Pierce (Miss).

P.S. Don't forget that you are supposed to be escorting Miss Lamberton to *Chu Chin Chow* tomorrow. I trust you enjoy the evening, though I think it doubtful – but you have already heard my views on the kind of women who use peroxide on their hair. I will not bore you with them again.

The Grand Hotel
Chorlington Spa,

September 17th, 192-

Dear Mr Williams,

Re: *Reginald Barnes, Policy No. 526/34-BN*

Since you asked me to spare no details, I shall give hereinunder as full an account as possible of the events, trusting that you will not find my description too tedious.

Yesterday, having written my preliminary report to you, I

completed my ablutions, unpacked my bags and made my way downstairs to the Palm Court Lounge, a pleasant glassed-in room which contained, in addition to a number of palms and some comfortable wicker furniture, a bar and a trio of ladies playing Strauss waltzes in the corner. As you have repeatedly pointed out that it is important to 'look the part', I had no hesitation in ordering a cocktail from the barman (I shall naturally present an itemized account of expenses upon my return to London) before taking cognizance of my fellow guests. I record what I have learned of them below, in no particular order.

1. FRANK ELLIOT, single, 31. Just returned home from some years in Egypt, where he was, as I surmised, serving with the Foreign Office. A most charming person.

2. Mrs MAY SAUNDERS, a widow, early 50s, here with her niece, who is

3. JANE GARDINER, single, 28.

4 and 5. CELIA and CHARLES PLAYFAIR, a brother and sister taking the waters in order to alleviate the effects of sharing a damp house in the Scottish Highlands with their uncle. They are both in their late 20s and seem very pleasant, though personally I do not much admire people who seem content to live off family wealth – but, as you yourself often remark, chance would be a fine thing.

6. The Rev. LAWRENCE HILL, 40ish, rector of a small parish in Gloucestershire, accompanying his mother, who is

7. Mrs EMILY HILL, in her 60s. I have no hesitation in saying that Mrs Hill seems to me to be the most unpleasant woman I have ever had the misfortune to come across. The way she orders the servants around is one thing; among a certain type of person such behaviour passes for social distinction, but to bully her son in the way she does is exceedingly distasteful. She is one of those women about whom one finds oneself remarking that it's a wonder no one has strangled her. Why her son suffers her treatment of him without remark, I really do not know – I certainly should not bear it for a moment were I in his shoes.

8. The man I had taken for a tradesman turns out to be from Belgium and called Pierrot or something similar. A most suitable name: a seaside promenade concert would be a more fitting setting for him than an hotel such as this. Personally I have never been able to abide men who dye their hair. As for waxed moustaches. . .

9. The final guest is a Major ARTHUR COTTERILL, formerly with the British Army in Cairo. In his early 40s, I should judge, with one of those brick-red complexions that so often occur in fair-haired men forced to live for long periods in tropical climates.

What I find particularly interesting is the fact that they all seem to be interconnected in some way. For instance, Mrs Emily Hill was apparently in Cairo at the same time as Major Cotterill, and even vaguely remembers meeting him there. The father of the Playfair couple was also in Egypt – a banker, I believe – and Mrs Hill knew him well. Mrs Saunders was apparently at school with Mrs. Hill many years ago, and so on.

There seems, by the way, little doubt that the Rev. Lawrence HIll, who apparently knows Miss Gardiner through mutual friends in Exeter, is deeply smitten with the young woman. Quite delightful to see, really. It is a situation which Mrs Saunders gives every impression of wishing to promote. A woman of Miss Gardiner's age (the same as my own) needs to be loved – more than that, she needs to be given every chance to fulfil herself through those two finest and most honourable of states: matrimony and motherhood. Denied them, there is no saying what she might do.

The Subject continues to give every appearance of a man suffering from chronic damage to the back, as stated on his Claims Form. Incidentally, although last night before retiring I spent some time with the toothglass provided by the management pressed to the wall, I could hear nothing that gave me any suspicion that Mr Barnes is not what he seems. He undressed with a series of muttered oaths, groaning horribly every now and then, and finally climbed into his bed with every indication of pain. Even without the toothglass, I could hear him through the wall at various moments during the night, which were most disruptive of slumber.

I fear I would be failing my duty if I did not also add that Frank Elliot was most attentive to me, both during our sessions in the baths this morning, throughout our enforced wallow in some evil-smelling kind of mud, and at the picnic which the management laid on for its guests in the afternoon. You will be pleased to know that he has invited me to join him for cocktails this evening: it will keep the Agency expenses down and I know how much store you set by *that*. (May I point out, before I present my expenses claim, that a cocktail or two in the evening should be considered as nothing more than the barest recompense for the agonies I have endured in the line of duty. Sulphurised mud is absolutely *disgusting* and though I showered with extreme thoroughness after being allowed to emerge from the depths of the mud-pits, I fancy I smell it about my person even now.)

I will write to you again tomorrow.

Yours sincerely,

Sarah Pierce (<u>Miss</u>)

P.S. I hope your evening with Miss Lamberton was a success and that she was dressed in a more fitting garment than the one she chose to wear when she turned up so unexpectedly at your mother's house the day Father and I were invited for Sunday lunch.

The Grand Hotel
Chorlington Spa,

September 18th, 192-

Dear Mr Williams,

Sensation!

I can hardly believe it, but Mrs Hill – of whom I wrote to you yesterday – was discovered this morning dead in bed! Strangled!

Naturally we were all shocked beyond words, and I for one was extremely thankful to have the strong arm of Mr Elliot to lean on, since the news, coming so hard on my description of her in yesterday's letter was something of a shock to me personally. I felt almost as though I had brought this death upon her myself, though kind Mr Elliot took both my hands in his and pointed out that I could not possibly have done so. He has a most comforting voice.

(Incidentally, Mr Barnes groaned so much throughout the night that I was unable to get even a wink of sleep. I am convinced you are mistaken about his 'putting it on'.)

After breakfast, we were summoned one by one to a small anteroom for the purpose of being questioned with regard to the murder. Apparently the Pierrot person is a detective of some kind and while we waited for the arrival of the police, he had consented to make some preliminary enquiries. Upon discovering that I was proficient in Pitman's shorthand, he asked me to take notes for him: I agreed to do so, on the understanding that I myself had been eliminated from his enquiries.

'So charming a young lady could not possibly be responsible for such an ugly deed,' he replied, bowing in an odious manner towards me. (It is just the sort of patronizing attitude towards the fairer sex that I most despise – and one of which you, ~~Robert~~ Mr Williams, could never stand accused.)

'I really cannot see why,' I said coldly. 'Some of the most famous murderers have been young women.'

'Ah,' he said. 'You are a student of criminology?'

'No, although I have read a great many detective stories and even toyed with the idea of writing one myself,' I returned. 'It is simply that I should prefer to be eliminated from the list of suspects on rather stronger grounds than those of my supposed charm.'

'Do not worry, Mlle Pierce. You have an alibi,' he said.

'Indeed?' I raised my pince-nez and stared at him through it in the manner you always refer to as resembling an indignant swan's.

'Your next door neighbour,' he continued. 'Mr Reginald Barnes has already testified that you snored most of the night, making it impossible for him to sleep.'

I will not go into what reply I made to this. I most certainly do not snore, but there was no point in saying so. Dandified little horror that he is! I much prefer a certain 'disorder in the dress' myself, such as Frank Elliot has – or yourself for that matter (and goodness knows you could never be suspected of dyeing your hair: no one in their right mind would elect for such a vivid carrotty red if they had any choice in the matter).

In the course of his investigations, Pierrot seemed far more interested in the past than in the present. He said to me between interviewing the two Playfairs that the *why* was so much more important than the *how*. There certainly seem to be some impressive whys in this case.

He picked on the same fact that I reported in my last letter, namely that all the people here seem vaguely connected with each other or with Mrs Hill – except for myself and the Subject. And Mr Elliot, of course. Remarkable as it may seem, given such unexceptional people, Pierrot was able to establish fairly solid motives for murder in each of them – hypothetically, of course.

Take the Playfairs: he learned that until their return from abroad three years ago, their uncle had not seen them since they were small children. Suppose (said he) that Mrs Hill knew they were in fact not the Playfairs at all, but a couple of imposters or confidence tricksters and she had threatened to expose them. Might they not wish to eliminate her?

He was equally cavalier with Rev. Hill, letting him leave the room with considerable reluctance.

'He is greatly in love with the beautiful Miss Gardiner,' he said. 'And the mother, she stood in his way. Also, of course, he had the easiest access to the lady.'

'Surely you cannot suspect her own son, a man of the cloth!'
I cried.

'In love, Miss Pierce,' he replied, 'All is fair. Except murder.
I do not approve of murder.' (As if the rest of us did!)

Then there was Major Cotterill. It transpires that he has just
accepted an appointment as mathematics master at a major
boys' public school. He seemed most unwilling to explain why
he had left the Army, so much so that personally I began to suspect some misdemeanour of an unmentionable nature. Pierrot
agreed, saying that it could well be something that Mrs Hill
knew about and intended to reveal to his new employers, thus
leaving him without means of support. 'And it is easy to see that
the good Major is none too well off,' he said. 'His shoes are in
need of soling, and his shirt-cuffs are frayed. To lose this teach-
ing job might spell disaster for him.'

Jane Gardiner might well be guilty too, according to his theory: for the same reasons as her lover. (If she is, I know how she
feels. At 28, one does begin to experience a certain feeling of
being 'left on the shelf,' which is distinctly unpleasant, particularly when all one's friends are already married.)

As for Mrs Saunders, she stated that Mrs Hill was a horrible
bully during their schooldays and, as far as she knew, had continued to be so for the rest of her life. She said she had known
Mr Hill well as a young woman; I deduced from the way she
coloured up, that perhaps there had been a certain *tendresse*
between them before Mrs Hill swept in and married him herself.
I pointed this out to Pierrot and he agreed, adding that some
men – not himself, of course! – are weak. (I don't hold with
weak men, but I do recognize that they exist. You yourself are
a very strong personality and I will admit that I admire you
for it.)

Frank Elliot was the last to be questioned. I am not ashamed
to say that my heart skipped a beat as he came through the
door, so handsome and upright, his fair hair shining. How amaz-
ing it is that on such short acquaintance, two people can feel

such closeness to each other – but you will know how I feel since you apparently experienced much the same rush of affection for Miss Lamberton (if that indeed is her real name) after only one meeting in the saloon bar of the Duke of Wellington public house – though you would be wise, in my opinion, to ask yourself what sort of a woman frequents such establishments on her own.

However...

'Mr Elliot, do you play bridge?' was Pierrot's first question – as indeed it had been to everyone.

'A little,' he replied. 'I much prefer poker.'

'Do you indeed?' said Pierrot. 'And might one learn where you acquired that complexion?'

'I spent some years in Africa,' said Frank (as he has asked me to call him), 'and when I returned to England decided to take the long way home. I had never seen the Pyramids, for example. Since I intend to settle down,' (here he gave me such a *meaning* glance that I almost blushed), 'I thought I should seize the opportunity while it offered.'

Pierrot wagged his egg-shaped head: 'And have you ever met either of the Hills before?'

Frank vigorously denied it. When he had gone, I said: 'Mr Pierrot...'

'Poirot,' he said, sounding somewhat annoyed. 'Her-cule Poirot,' enunciating as though I were an idiot child.

'Mr Poirot, why do you ask each one if they play bridge?'

'Because whoever carried out this murder is someone with a cool nerve, a steady hand and a mind that can swiftly calculate the odds,' he responded. 'These are all characteristics of the person who strangled Mrs Hill. I am convinced that this was not a premeditated murder – why otherwise kill her here? No. It occurred here for one of two reasons: either Mrs Hill recognized the murderer and threatened to – how you say? – blow the gaffe on him or her. Or else the murderer, coming upon her unexpectedly here, decided that she constituted a danger that must be eliminated immediately.'

'Do you have any idea who the murderer might be?' I asked.

'*Zut!*' he said. 'Even Hercule Poirot cannot work the miracles. I need more information before I can be certain. But I will tell you this – *everyone of the people we have questioned this morning has lied to me.*'

'How do you know?'

'I am the greatest detective in the world,' he said. (Typical of a foreigner, isn't it? No Englishman would be so conceited.) 'I judge from little things: the way the eyes open, the breath comes more quickly, the manner in which the hands behave. Hands are difficult to control. But – 'he raised his finger in a most dictatorial fashion: 'Hercule Poirot does not mind lies, *for out of lies comes the truth.*'

'I'm sure I hope so,' I said. 'I don't like the idea of being locked up in a hotel with a homicidal maniac.'

'Whoever committed this crime is not insane,' said he. 'Far from it. He – or she – is not only ruthless but in full possession of their wits.'

In the evening, I put on my plum crêpe de Chine – the one you said I looked so well in when we went to see *Aïda*. Frank Elliot certainly seemed to like it. Naturally our company was a little subdued. The Rev. Lawrence Hill sat on a sofa with Miss Gardiner, his eyes red with what I assumed was weeping. Mrs Saunders sat at a low table with the two Playfairs and Major Cotterill, playing a quiet hand of bridge together. The Subject read the newspaper, uttering stifled cries whenever he changed his position. As for Frank and I, we sipped cocktails together and spoke of the future, but I cannot pretend that we were as gay as we might have been in happier circumstances. I think we were all relieved when it was time to retire. I asked myself which one I considered most likely to be the villain and decided that Major Cotterill was the obvious suspect.

Yours sincerely,
Sarah Pierce (Miss)

P.S. I trust Miss Lamberton continues well. I should be extremely surprised if *she* can take down shorthand.

The Grand Hotel
Chorlington Spa,

September 19th, 192-, immediately following breakfast.

Dear Robert,

Your telegram this morning addressed to Mr. Poirot was quite extraordinary. Of *course* Frank Elliot did not murder Mrs Hill. I have incontrovertible proof that he could not have done so though modesty forbids me saying what that proof is. How could you shame me in such a manner? When it arrived, it was handed to Mr Poirot at the breakfast table and he showed it to the rest of us with eyes that positively twinkled.

'Very satisfactory indeed. I think,' he said, looking at me.

'I beg your pardon?' I took the paper from him and seeing your name, felt as though I could fall through the floor.

'As I have already remarked, Miss Pierce, all's fair in love and war. I believe the plot thickens.'

'I'm afraid I don't follow you.' I said coldly. Naturally I was forced to pretend that I knew nothing whatsoever about who could have sent the cable. Really! I have seldom felt more embarrassed.

I will write at greater length when I have recovered myself.

Yours, Sarah.

P.S. What *would* Miss Lamberton say if she knew of your hot-headed action?

The Grand Hotel
Chorlington Spa,

September 20th 192-

Dear ~~Robert~~ Mr Williams,
Re: Reginald Barnes, Policy No. 526/34-BN

Please forgive my shaky hand, but I have just lived through a night such as I never hope to experience in my life again. As you can imagine, the atmosphere in the hotel last night was extremely sober. The thought that we have among us a cold-blooded murderer was enough to dampen the spirits of even the most ebullient. I myself was reduced to imbibing rather more of the contents of the barman's cocktail shaker than was wise, in the hope of falling more easily asleep upon retirement. Certainly even the stoutest of hearts might have trembled, upon contemplating the peril involved in spending the night alone, when any one of us could well be the next victim. When Frank Elliott offered to spend the night on guard in my room, I am not ashamed to state that I decided to accept his protection, despite the apparent immodesty of his suggestion.

Having undressed in the bathroom and wrapped myself in my peignoir, I employed the toothglass again, in order to check up on Mr Barnes. As before, he groaned and cursed his way through his toilette and heaved himself, with every appearance of difficulty, into bed. I repeat that I am convinced of the soundness of his claim.

Upon Frank's entering the room, I arranged myself upon my bed with the eiderdown tucked up to my chin. If he was to be my companion through the night that was still to be endured, then let it be with the utmost propriety.

I fear that I dozed off, despite my trepidation. This must be due to the presence of a strong and – dare I say it? – loving companion, affording me a sense of security. It must have been around two in the morning that a dreadful scream pierced the silence of the hotel and I started up, feeling my hair (becomingly put up for the night – not my usual practice, but I would not wish Frank to see me in curling papers. That is a privilege preserved for husbands and he is not mine - not yet.) stand on end. Frank, too, rose to his feet from the chair where he had been watching over me and the two of us rushed out into the corridor. There lay a body, immediately apparent as that of

Major Cotterill. Blood still streamed from the back of his head, which had clearly been shattered by a terrific blow. Had it not been for the strong arms of Frank Elliott, I would have fallen fainting to the floor at so horrid a sight, but luckily he was there (as I hope he always will be) to support me.

I am sending this to you by first post. Poirot, who emerged from his room in a dressing gown of vulgarly patterned silk, has informed us that the police will not allow us to leave even if we should wish to. Naturally I am upset at being forced to remain in this House of Death, but at least it provides me with further opportunities to comply with your demands and keep up my observation of the subject.

Yours, in horror,

Sarah Pierce (Miss – for the moment).

It was after the excellent lunch provided by the Grand Hotel, Chorlington, that Hercule Poirot, returning from a short stroll along the esplanade, was unexpectedly witness to what appeared to be an abduction. He was fascinated to see the strong-willed and inquisitive young woman who had made herself known to him as Miss Sarah Pierce being bundled into a low-slung sports car by an expostulating young man with a full head of vivid red hair.

Hastening nearer in order to offer assistance, the Belgian detective's shrewd glance saw at once that Miss Pierce, far from being overcome by her ordeal, gave, in fact, every indication of enjoying it. Indeed, while the red-headed young man continued to exclaim in an excitable manner, she caught Poirot's eye and winked at him. On the other side of the road he could see Mr Barnes, the unfortunate gentleman with the bad back, standing in a doorway and watching the *contretemps* with considerable astonishment.

'Blasted Frank Elliott,' the young man was saying. 'I'm not leaving you here with him another moment longer. If the police want you to hang about then they'll have me to reckon with.'

'Robert,' Miss Pierce said. 'Please let go of my arm. You are acting in a manner that can only be described as headstrong, and you have already wrenched one of the buttons from my raincoat.'

'I don't care,' cried Robert. 'I shan't let go until you give me your solemn promise to give up any idea of this Elliott person. You've only known him a few days, whereas the two of us have been close for years.'

'But you have never given any indication of caring for me,' Poirot heard Miss Pierce murmur. 'Indeed, I was under the impression that it was Miss Lamberton whom you favoured.'

'Hang Miss Lamberton!' said the young man. 'You must have bally well realized that it was only lack of time which stopped me from asking you to be my wife. And if you think that the future Mrs Williams is going to spend another night under the same roof as a murderer, you are greatly mistaken.'

At this point he caught sight of Poirot. Advancing pugnaciously, he said: 'And I suppose you're the famous Belgian detective, are you?'

'I have that honour,' murmured Poirot, twirling the points of his waxed moustaches.

'Found the murderer yet?' demanded the redhead.

'The murderer?' Poirot said, astonished. 'Of what murderer do you speak?'

'Even if you haven't, you can give Mr Frank Elliott a message from me.'

'Mr Elliott?' Poirot's eyebrows travelled slowly up his egg-shaped forehead. 'Who is this. . . '

'Blasted Foreign Office people. Just tell him to keep his bally hands off other people's fiancées in future, will you?'

'Are you proposing, Robert?' Miss Pierce said, from the front seat of the car.

'Yes, I bally am.'

The expression on Miss Pierce's face lingered with Poirot as he watched the sports coupé zoom off in a cloud of smoke.

Slowly he walked up the steps and into the hotel, waiting politely as Mr Barnes negotiated the revolving door. Mr Barnes seemed to be highly amused by something; Poirot could not decide what, unless it was the fact that in the past ten minutes his back problem seemed to have improved considerably. Indeed, watching him walk at a fast clip towards the bar, Poirot reflected that one would scarcely have been aware that anything was wrong with him.

Poirot himself went into the Palm Court Lounge where the Rev. Lawrence Hill, and his so-delightful mother were waiting for him to join them in a hand of bridge. Shortly afterwards, Major Cotterill arrived to take up the four.

Although he played with his customary skill, Poirot was not entirely happy. Something was niggling at him. 'Frank Elliot,' he said to himself, as Mrs Hill dealt the next hand. 'Frank Elliott. Do I know this name?'

Excusing himself, he got up and went over to the desk where the receptionist sat typing bills. The register lay open. He turned the pages, searching for the name Frank Elliott, but it was not to be found. He stared round the hotel lobby, puzzled. And then suddenly, his brow cleared.

A very determined woman, Miss Pierce. And highly efficient, too. On the couple of occasions that they had chanced to speak, he had been much struck by her air of knowing exactly what she wanted. If he, Hercule Poirot, the greatest detective in the world – as he was often the first to acknowledge – was any judge, whatever her objective, he rather thought she had just achieved it.

Susan Moody has been an assistant orchid grower, Hovercraft purserette, sandwich maker and creative writing tutor at Bedford prison. She has writen seven crime novels starring the exotic Penny Wanawake and recently switched genres with her highly successful suspense novel, *Playing with Fire*.

THE LADY
IN THE TRUNK

PETER LOVESEY

'I packed my trunk. . . '

Inspector Duggan chanted the words as if to a child and pricked up his eyebrows in expectation. He was grinning.

There was no response.

'I said I packed my trunk. . . '

Sergeant George Slim stared at his superior without a glimmer of comprehension.

'. . . and in it I put. . . ?'

The sergeant pressed his lips together in a sheepish smile, and shrugged.

'Come on, man. Don't be so dense. I packed my trunk and in it I put. . . ' There was a gritting of the teeth now. What had begun as a somewhat tasteless attempt to make light of their unappealing task was fast becoming an aggravation. 'The old parlour game. Don't you ever play it, for heaven's sake?' Inspector Duggan demanded. 'I packed my trunk and in it I put. . . '

'We don't play no parlour games in my house,' the sergeant finally succeeded in saying.

'. . . and in it I put a body, a blood-stained poker and a piece of sacking to cover them up.' Making clear his opinion that he was saddled with a nincompoop, Inspector Duggan folded his arms and gave his attention to the real corpse in a real cabin trunk in the luggage room at Itchingham Station.

The find had been notified by Hegarty, the station-master, a man of exemplary efficiency, whose station held the silver rosebowl as the best-kept on the Brighton Line. Today, on this warm July morning in 1927, Hegarty was a troubled man. The presence of a dead body in his luggage room – a body he had personally discovered after his keen nostrils had detected an emanation foreign to the Southern Railway – a *murdered* body – would be no help at all towards his ambition of retaining the rosebowl for an unprecedented third year. Having shown the two police officers what he had found, Hegarty had backed away, and was now outside, inhaling the fresher air on the platform.

'Feeling strong?' Duggan asked the sergeant.

Actually not a vast amount of strength was required to lift the body from the trunk and deposit it on a stretcher. The young woman had been slimly built.

They arranged the limbs decorously. 'You know who she is, of course,' Duggan said in a voice suggesting quite the reverse.

It happened that Sergeant Slim *did* know who she was. As a local man, he recognized the neat features in the still-neat frame of black bobbed hair. The face had not been damaged. The fatal blow must have been to the back of the skull, where blood had dried and caked the hair in a patch that was obvious to the touch. The clothes, fashionable and no doubt expensive, consisted of a lightweight summer coat, red-brown in colour, with accordion-pleated black frills, over a pink georgette dress, white lace gloves, white silk stockings and black patent leather shoes.

'If I didn't know who she is, I ought to be doing another job,' George Slim responded, trying manfully to match the inspector's nonchalance. 'I've seen her hundreds of times in the Wheatsheaf on Saturday nights when they have the dances. She's that singer.'

'Yes – but do you know who she is?'

Duggan was a detective of the old school, not an easy man to work with. His captious style of conversation had seen off numerous detective sergeants in his twenty-five years with the

Brighton CID. The black, stoat-like eyes, angular nose and toothbrush moustache reinforced the cantankerous personality.

The sergeant answered limply, 'I believe she called herself the Singing Flapper.'

'That's a lot of help!'

Sergeant Slim stared down at the dead face as if it might whisper a clue, and then admitted, 'I don't know her real name.'

Duggan clicked his tongue and informed the sergeant that the dead woman was Lady Pettifer.

'A titled lady!' said the sergeant on such a piping note of disbelief that it spared him from sarcasm for several minutes.

Duggan explained. 'She was married to Sir Hartley Pettifer, that old boy who used to drive around Brighton in an open carriage. Remember him?'

'The one who always wore a top hat?'

'Yes. Know anything else about him? Evidently not. He made his fortune out of buying and selling hotels. Lived in a suite on the top floor of the Old Ship. Lived is the operative word. Regularly when he spotted a beautiful woman on the prom, he'd stop the carriage and invite her to sit beside him. Not many refused. And not many could resist the invitation to tea and cucumber sandwiches after the drive.'

'In his rooms?'

'Where else? He didn't have time to waste.' Duggan turned his gaze to the body on the stretcher. 'This one was a fast worker too. She insisted on marrying him. The story I heard is that she was just a minor actress – a soubrette – who happened to be appearing in some musical comedy on the West Pier. She became the fourth or fifth Lady P. – and the one who outlived him. The old fellow hopped the twig last year, and left her everything.'

Slim had heard all this in amazement. Although he was a man of thirty, with twelve years' service behind him, he was still capable of being shocked by the eccentricities of the rich. 'If she was so well off, why did she bother to sing in the Wheatsheaf?'

'It was no *bother*. It was her choice. She was convinced she was another Gertie Lawrence.'

'She wasn't. I heard her.'

'Never mind. She could sing like a drain and no one would argue.'

'She wasn't as bad as all that, sir.'

'The point is that Lady Pettifer *owned* the Wheatsheaf, not to mention six or seven other good hotels, so she could serenade the guests night after night if she wanted. What else did I see at the bottom of that trunk?'

Sergeant Slim leaned over the side and came up with a bloodstained yellow cloche hat.

'Is that all?' Duggan asked.

Slim had another look before confirming that the trunk was now empty.

'Excellent,' said Duggan, obviously savouring his assistant's puzzled reaction before adding in a tone that could only be a provocation, 'Mighty good to have a motive so soon!'

'A *motive*, sir?'

'It's downright obvious, isn't it?'

'Not to me.'

Duggan sighed, shrugged and explained that what was missing was a handbag. No young woman in hat and coat would go out without a bag. From which he deduced that Lady Pettifer had been robbed – probably by someone who knew she was rich. Moreover, the chance was high that her murderer had also robbed her of some jewellery, for none remained on the body, except for her wedding ring, which had been out of sight under a glove – no brooch, ear-rings or necklace.

After that impressive flexing of his mental muscle, the inspector ordered his awed assistant to lead a search of the station and its environs. A vanload of uniformed policemen from Brighton awaited orders in the station yard.

'What exactly should we look for?' Slim asked.

Duggan rolled his eyes heavenwards. 'The handbag.'

'If it was stolen, it's gone, sir.'

'No, sergeant. Your intelligent thief gets rid of it. Takes any money out, and then disposes of the bag.'

Left alone, Duggan covered the body with the sacking and unfastened the attaché case containing his fingerprint kit. Unhelpfully neither the poker nor the trunk responded to the mixture of chalk and metallic mercury that he applied with his camel-hair brush. An hour's work yielded only a few anonymous smudges.

He had more success when he questioned Hegarty. In ten minutes with the stationmaster he established that the cabin trunk, which was brand new, had arrived empty at the station the previous week and was still awaiting collection. Remarkably, its owner happened to be the famous writer, Mr Rudyard Kipling, who lived twenty miles away. Mr Kipling had ordered it from the Army and Navy Stores in London for an overseas trip he was planning, and it had been delivered by mistake to Itchingham instead of Etchingham, Kipling's local station. There was no suggestion that the great man was in any way implicated in the crime.

Kipling's trunk had been left in the luggage office, a room that in reality served as a station glory hole, because little in the way of luggage was ever left on Itchingham Station. Instead, the room contained such impedimenta as a broken weighing-machine, a porter's trolley, a set of obsolete destination-boards, a bicycle, Mr Hegarty's golf-clubs, several brooms, a box of light-bulbs and the set of fire-irons that was removed from the waiting-room in the summer months. The luggage office was kept unlocked during the hours the station was open.

The fire-irons were incomplete. The poker was missing from its hook. Mr Hegarty, sunk in gloom, confirmed that the blood-stained poker found in the trunk matched the set.

'Splendid!' said the inspector. 'The nature of the crime is unfolding. Lady Pettifer was murdered here on the station – probably in this room – some time last Saturday evening after she sang in the Wheatsheaf and was on her way home to Brighton. She was struck from behind with the poker, robbed of her bag and any jewellery she was wearing and her lifeless body was dumped in the trunk. Tell me, Mr Hegarty, were you here on Saturday evening?'

Hegarty's ashen depression flared into sudden alarm. 'You don't suspect me. . . ? Absolutely not. I was off duty by six. I spent the entire evening playing chess with the vicar. You're welcome to ask him.'

Duggan was grinning to himself. 'I was merely seeking to enquire, sir, whether you saw the unfortunate lady.'

Hegarty made it clear that the station had been manned on Saturday night by a booking clerk called Crocker, a conscientious young fellow who had no objection to working late, unlike most Southern Railway employees.

Crocker came on duty at two, and Inspector Duggan interviewed him in the station-master's office. Dapper in Oxford bags and Fair Isle pullover, clean-shaven, and with a confident manner, Crocker impressed Duggan as bright and efficient, the sort of young man who ought to be training as a detective instead of mindlessly sitting at a window issuing tickets for a living. Helpfully it emerged that Crocker's attitude to his work was anything but mindless. He recalled precisely when Lady Pettifer had bought her ticket on Saturday evening.

'She was going for the 11.15 to Brighton, which was unusual for her. Most Saturdays she caught the next one, the 11.45. However, she arrived in very good time, at one minute past the hour. I remember because the church clock was still chiming and it's fifty seconds late by Southern Railway time. I wished her a good evening and issued her with a ticket.'

'She didn't already have a return, then?'

'Not to this station.'

Mr Hegarty intervened to explain that Brighton didn't issue return tickets to the smaller stations along the line. The passengers had to purchase a ticket for each journey.

'I understand.' Duggan turned back to Crocker. 'Did the lady seem at all distressed?'

'Not that I noticed. She had a friendly smile for me, as always.'

'You knew the lady?'

'She bought a ticket from me every Saturday. She sang with the band at the Wheatsheaf dances.'

'That much we know,' said Duggan. 'Do you happen to remember what she was wearing?

'Her yellow hat and brown coat.'

'A necklace?'

Crocker thought for a moment and then said decisively, 'Pearls.'

Duggan arched his eyebrows. The motive of theft looked even more likely now. 'Presumably when she paid for the ticket she took the money from a purse.'

'Quite correct. In a black patent leather handbag.'

'You're certain you saw a handbag?'

'Positive. I just described it.'

'You're being very helpful, Mr Crocker, and I hope you can help me even more. When Lady Pettifer went on to the platform, was anyone else already waiting there?'

'Almost certainly not. Nobody else had passed through the booking hall since the previous train had left.'

Duggan was thinking what an unshakable prosecution witness this young man was going to make. First, there was the burdensome matter of finding an accused. 'And after she had bought her ticket, did any others arrive?'

'Only two.'

'To catch the 11.15?'

'Yes.'

'Did you happen to recognize either of them?'

'Both,' answered Crocker. 'They're regulars on Saturdays, just as she was. They both come from Brighton to attend the dances. One is the bandleader, Maxie Sands, and the other is a lad known as Leftie. I can't tell you his surname, but he's well known in Brighton as an amateur boxer, hence the name.'

'I dare say we'll find him, then. These two – Sands and Leftie – were the only ones to follow Lady Pettifer on to the platform?'

'Apart from myself.'

'*You* went on to the platform?'

'To meet the train.'

Again, Hegarty found it necessary to explain station procedure. 'Crocker here was the only member of my station staff left on duty. Doubling up is quite normal late at night, when not many people are using the station. As well as issuing tickets, he whistles the trains out and collects the tickets from passengers arriving.'

Duggan commented, 'I wouldn't call that doubling up. I'd say he was a general factotum.' He put another question to Crocker. 'So you must also have seen who boarded the train?'

'Yes, it's a bit of a rush, as you can imagine,' Crocker explained. 'I can't leave the booking office until the last possible moment in case someone arrives late wanting a ticket. I got to the platform in time to see Mr Sands and Leftie stepping aboard. There was no sign of Lady Pettifer. Now, of course, I understand why not, but at the time I presumed she'd boarded the train quickly, before the others.'

'The train entered the station before you went on to the platform?'

'That is correct. When I hear it arrive, I pull down the hatch in the booking office, pick up the whistle and the lantern and go through the staffroom to the platform.'

Duggan summed up in the workmanlike style that had taken him so far in the CID. 'So it comes down to this. To your knowledge, one of those two must have attacked Lady Pettifer and robbed her before they boarded the train. You say Sands was the first to buy a ticket?'

'The first after Lady Pettifer.'

'Are those tickets numbered in sequence?'

Crocker confirmed that they were. Because they were the last three tickets issued on Saturday night, and a fresh batch were started the following day, he was able to supply the numbers. Lady Pettifer had been issued with ticket 512, Sands the dance-band leader, 513, and the boxer called Leftie, 514.

'In case you needed to see them,' said Mr Hegarty, 'I telephoned Brighton to see if the tickets were collected that night. They did – and here they are.' He held out tickets 513 and 514. 'Sands and Leftie certainly completed their journeys.'

Late the same afternoon – like some explorer who had discovered the lost city of the Incas – Sergeant Slim made his way triumphantly along the railway track at the head of his line of helpers. He was carrying a black patent leather handbag.

'You don't have to hold it by the handle,' Duggan told him without gratitude. 'It makes you look effeminate. Where did you find it?'

'Three hundred yards along the track, sir. It was lying on the embankment. The reason I was holding it by the handle, sir, was that I spotted some fingerprints on the shiny surface.' Even before he had finished speaking, Slim found himself wishing he'd found some better pretext for mentioning the fingerprints. Duggan preferred to make his own discoveries.

'Show me,' said Duggan acidly, producing a magnifying glass. He examined the bag. 'I wouldn't call these fingerprints. Smears is what I'd call them. You couldn't prove anything with these. See for yourself.'

'Yes, they are rather smudged, sir.'

'Wouldn't surprise me if you made them yourself,' Duggan commented loudly enough for Slim's team of helpers to hear. 'Let's look at the size of your hand. Your right, man – not your left. Can't you see it's a right-handed set? Press your fingers against the bag. It's all right. I know what I'm doing. Give me a set of prints above these others and we'll compare them.'

Slim obeyed. It was manifestly clear that the first set of prints had been made by a smaller hand than his own.

'She took her bow before we began the last waltz. That's a good ten minutes before the end.'

'She didn't sing the last waltz?'

Sands winced. 'Perish the thought!'

'Why do you say that?'

'The last waltz is meant to be romantic. Dimmed lights and cheek-to-cheek. She was always so far off key that she ruined every number. Most of the time the lads would be doing their best to drown the sound, but you can't battle it out like that in the last waltz.'

'You sound unimpressed by her singing.'

'I have every right to be. Three nights a week she inflicted herself on me and my lads. We're a good band. You wouldn't have known it when she started her caterwauling.'

'Why did you put up with it?'

'We're trying to scrape a living at this. We need every engagement we can get. Lady Pettifer owns – I should say owned – most of the decent hotels along the south coast, but you wouldn't think it from the money she paid. And now if you'll excuse me, I have a one-step to perform.' He picked up his baton and left the room.

The detectives followed him out. Through the strains of *Horsey, Keep Your Tail Up*, Sergeant Slim remarked to Duggan that Sands had seemed a decent type, and was rebuked for making a classic error. Some of the meanest murderers ever to have come before the courts, Duggan informed him, had been amiable fellows to meet. When Slim rashly remarked that a man with a love of music couldn't be wholly evil, Duggan reminded him that George Joseph Smith had given a rendering of 'Nearer My God to Thee' on the harmonium shortly after drowning one of his brides in the bath, and the infamous Charlie Peace had been a virtuoso of the violin. Maxie Sands was the obvious suspect, the first person to have followed Lady Pettifer on to the platform on the night she was murdered. 'The blighter hasn't told us anything yet, but I'll have him over a barrel in the next interval,' added the inspector. 'Just watch me.'

The dance ended, the floor cleared and the law swooped.

'Where precisely was Lady Pettifer standing when you arrived on the platform?' Duggan demanded, metaphorically rolling out the barrel.

'I've no idea. I didn't notice her.'

'What do you mean – "*didn't notice her*"? She was the only other person there.'

'She must have stepped into the ladies' waiting-room,' Sands said defensively.

'I don't want your opinion,' Duggan told him. 'I can form my own, and I think I have. Did you see anyone else before the train arrived?'

'Only one other. He came a few minutes after me. A big fellow. The one they call Leftie. He often comes to the dances. Does a very smooth tango. He's heavily in demand as a rule.'

'A gigolo?'

'I'll put it this way: he usually ends the evening with a rich woman.'

'But not last night,' said Duggan.

Sands looked impressed. 'How did you know?'

'You just told me he was alone on the platform. How long was he in your view before the train arrived?'

'Not much over a minute. Maybe two. No more.'

'Did he go into a waiting-room, or the luggage office?'

'Not while I was there.'

'You're certain?'

'Absolutely. May I go now? It's time for my foxtrot medley.'

The interrogation over a barrel had ended flatly, if not feebly, and Duggan was quick to explain why, as soon as he and Sergeant Slim had left the dance-hall. 'Of course I knew he couldn't possibly be the murderer the moment I clapped eyes on him. Do you know why? I don't suppose you do,' he went on uncharitably, without giving Slim an opportunity to answer. 'Did you notice his right hand?'

believe you didn't mean to kill her. I suppose she turned her back on you when you asked for money. I'm willing to consider manslaughter rather than murder, but you'd better be straight with me, and truthful, or I'll see you dead-headed, Wallflower.' He placed a hand on Hooker's shoulder.

It was an improvident gesture. The boxer swung his left fist upwards. It struck Duggan's protruding jaw, thrust forward to reinforce the threat. Duggan straightened, curled and crumpled, striking his head on the concrete floor. He lay still.

Sergeant Slim bent over him and looked for signs of consciousness.

Leftie Hooker remarked, 'I shouldn't have done that.'

'But you did,' said Slim, and there was a hint of admiration in his voice.

'Are you going to arrest me?'

'Not yet,' said Slim. 'I'm going to fetch a doctor.' He left.

In the two days that Inspector Duggan was required to pass in hospital, Sergeant Slim put the finishing touches to the Case of Kipling's Trunk, as it was known to the press. Then he visited the hospital.

Duggan was sitting up in bed, arms folded, chin as far out as ever, apparently to demonstrate that nothing had changed. 'You arrested Hooker, I trust,' he said at once.

'Yes, sir.'

'And charged him?'

'Yes, sir.'

'What with?'

'Assaulting a police officer.'

'And. . . ?'

'That's all, sir. I did consider charging him with resisting arrest, but I thought you wouldn't want to make too much of the arrest.'

'What do you mean? I got my man. We've nothing to be ashamed of.'

Slim coughed. 'Actually you didn't get him, sir. Leftie Hooker is innocent of murder.'

'*Innocent?* The blighter attacked me.'

'But he didn't attack Lady Pettifer, sir. Somebody else attacked her.'

Duggan sagged appreciably, reclined against the pillow and looked more like the convalescent he was. 'Not Maxie Sands? Surely not Maxie Sands?'

'No, sir. Mr Sands was telling the truth. He and Leftie both told us the truth when they said they didn't see Lady Pettifer on the station platform that night. She didn't go for the 11.15 train. After her last song, she must have spent some time in her dressing-room. She went for the late train, the 11.45.'

'But there's a serious flaw in this,' said Duggan, showing more colour. 'She had ticket 512. We found it – I found it – in the handbag. The others had tickets 513 and 514 and caught the 11.15.'

'Right, sir – but have you considered who issued the tickets?'

'Crocker? You suspect Crocker, the booking clerk, of misleading us?'

'Of murder, sir.' Slim made a rapid summation of the facts. 'He put one ticket aside, knowing Lady Pettifer generally caught the last train and was the only passenger. Then he issued the next two tickets to Maxie Sands and Leftie Hooker, who caught their train. When Lady Pettifer arrived, Crocker issued her with the ticket, followed her on to the platform, struck her with the poker and robbed her. He hid the body in the trunk, to await an opportunity of disposing of it. Just to make it look as if a passenger had killed her, he walked along the line and threw the handbag on to the embankment.'

Duggan said faintly, 'What made you think of Crocker?'

'The prints on the handbag. Leftie's hand was larger than mine – much too big to match the dabs we had.'

'Those prints won't satisfy a jury.'

'A confession will, sir. I reasoned that Crocker wouldn't want to keep the jewellery for long, so I put a tail on him and he tried selling a diamond necklace – he lied about the pearls, incidentally – to a dealer in the Lanes this morning. The man is no professional. He didn't know where to look for a fence. He coughed the lot when we collared him.'

After a pause, Duggan said, 'Clever. Deucedly clever.'

Sergeant Slim permitted himself the gratification of a smile. 'Thank you, sir.'

'I mean that trick with the tickets,' said Duggan. 'It takes a rare intelligence to outwit me.'

Peter Lovesey has published fourteen detective stories of which the best known are probably his Victorian mysteries featuring Sergeant Cribb and Constable Thackeray. These were successfully televised with Alan Dobie playing Cribb. *Time Magazine* once called him 'charming, chilling and wickedly clever'.

JACK FELL DOWN

H R F KEATING

''Twas on the Isle of Capreee that I found her. . .'

Blithely ignoring the rocking of the little steamer in the lurching Mediterranean swell, the girl with the sun-catching cap of peroxided hair sitting hatless on the wooden bench right in the vessel's prow lifted her voice in sudden bubbling song. A blurred blueness in the distance, Capri, indeed, was the little wallowing tub's destination.

'Really,' exclaimed in heavily scandalized tones one of the few other passengers braving the last gusts of a salt-laden sirocco up on deck, an Englishwoman in an ample frock loud with different coloured daisies. But, finding her exclamation had produced no reaction in the only other passenger not comfortably below, save in the stern for a scatter of peasants returning with emptied baskets from Naples, she moved nearer along the ship's greasy rail.

Her target was an excessively tall gangling gentleman, not very suitably clad for the Mediterranean in a suit of gingery wool with the trousers ending in tight bands round the calves. He was leaning against the rail smoking a cigarette and staring with an air of melancholy towards the distant island.

'Not a very lady-like performance,' the ample, beflowered lady pronounced, with a look of pinched disapproval in the direction of the girl in the prow.

Briefly lifting his cap, the ginger giant produced, in foreign-accented English, a decidedly non-committal reply .

The large lady was not to be put off, however.

'Tell me,' she said, leaning forwards with a smile at once coy and overwhelming, 'I must know. Are you Mr Sven Hjerson, the famous Finnish detective? I mean, you must be. I saw your picture in the paper here just last week. You've been helping the Vatican in some mysterious business or other, haven't you?'

'Well, madam, I must make some congratulations to you. You have, as they are saying, done a fine observation.'

'Knew I was right. Generally am. Buckley's the name. Arabella Buckley. Miss. You on another case, eh? The Corpse on Capri, ha?'

'No, no,' Sven Hjerson was quick to reply. 'It is just that after much brainwork in Rome I have thought to give myself a little holiday on this famous Capri Island.'

'Sight too famous nowadays, if you ask me,' Arabella Buckley pronounced. 'All the fault of that dreadful song. How that girl can bring herself to sit there singing it I can't imagine. You know who she is, don't you?'

'No, I have not such pleasure. And, madam, I would. . . '

'She goes by the name of Jilly Jonathan. She's one of those, what-d'you-call-'ems, stars. A star of the screen.'

'The cinema is not a place I am very much attending.'

'No, nor me. Frightfully vulgar. But one gets to know about these people somehow. Well, I suppose in the case in point. . . ' Miss Buckley directed a vigorous glare towards Jilly Jonathan, face lifted to the sun, cheerfully carolling the sentimentally sad words of the song. 'Engaged to the Earl of Woodleigh, you know. They announced it just a couple of weeks ago. On holiday out here with him now. Excelsior Hotel in Naples.'

'And it is there that you also are staying?'

'No, no. Can't afford a place like that. Simple *pensione* for me. Appalling Italian food, of course, but beggars can't be choosers, what?'

'You are unable to get good vegetables?' Sven Hjerson asked with sudden anxiety. 'In Rome I was in the similar predicament. But I had heard that in the South things are better.'

'Oh, the vegetables are all right, I suppose. It's no porridge at breakfast that gets my goat. Coffee and rolls. What nonsense.'

'Then you think that on Capri I shall be obtaining good vegetables?' the detective inquired. 'You see, they are so important for the uttermost functioning of the brain.'

'Well, never stayed on the island myself. Just visited it once. Last Sunday, as a matter of fact. Same day as Lord Woodleigh and that – and his fiancée.'

'They are travelling together, just themselves?' Sven Hjerson asked with a sudden flicker of interest.

'Oh, no. Good gracious me, no. Woodleigh's too much of a gentleman, of course, for anything like that. Though I dare say she. . . No, there's a whole party of them. Woodleigh, the girl, the Hon. Peter Horbury and Mrs Lettice Horbury. He's Woodleigh's cousin, and his heir, of course, unless that's the older Horbury brother who ran off to Australia years ago and has never been heard of since. And then Woodleigh's secretary even came out last week, so I gather. Some trouble at home, and he sent for her. No, whole thing's perfectly above board.'

'You are most well informed, madam,' Sven Hjerson said, a little drily.

'Oh, well, you know how it is. Interesting people and all that.'

At the prow Jilly Jonathan abruptly stopped singing and jumped to her feet. She made her way, still seemingly dancing to the tune, the huge crocodile-skin handbag on her arm swaying heavily in time, to the door down to the saloon. Hauling it open, she thrust in her peroxided head and called out something.

A moment or two later a man who, from his lanky form and fine-boned features, could only be her fiancé, Lord Woodleigh, emerged, evidently doing his best to overcome a certain reluctance.

'Darling,' Jilly Jonathan said, her voice ringing out for all to hear, 'don't fug away down there. It's super up in the sun. And, look, Capree's getting nearer and nearer.'

'Capri, old girl,' Lord Woodleigh said, giving the name its Italian rather than its popular song emphasis.

'Oh, well, what's it matter how you say it? The thing is it's there. And this time we're really going to get to see the Blue Grotto. You can't go to your stuffy old church today. Not when it's not Sunday.'

Lord Woodleigh smiled at her, plainly overcoming a natural reticence.

'Oh, my dear,' he said, 'you'll really have to get used to me going to Mass. Every Sunday, without fail. And on Holidays of Obligation, too.'

'Well, okay. But this isn't a – what-did-you-call-it? – holiday of obliging. It's a real holiday. Time to do as you like. And fancy telling me that there was an interesting stoup in that old church on the island.'

'It's what the guide-book said, my darling. They are used in Catholic churches to hold holy water.'

'Yes, but I thought it must be some arch or something that everybody had to stoop to go through. I didn't think even that would be very interesting, but I liked the idea of old Peter having to bend himself for once.'

'Now, you're not to make fun of Peter. He's always been a bit on his dignity, I suppose, but that's the way he is. Comes of half expecting to inherit the title and half not, I dare say.'

Jilly Jonathan gave a quick little frown.

'I think actually,' she said, 'he's terribly jealous.'

'Jealous?'

'Of me, darling. After all, I came along when he must have thought you were safe to be a bachelor for ever and ever, and now he'll never be a lord and everything.'

'Well, that will depend on whether we have children, angel. If we don't, although now you get the estate you can't, of course, inherit the title.'

'But I would still be a lady, wouldn't I?'

Lord Woodleigh's long ascetic face broke into another ice-cracked smile.

'Yes, my dear, from the moment we're married you'll be Countess of Woodleigh.'

'And if you. . . Well, if you were to sort of pop off, I'd go on being a countess, wouldn't I? And shouldn't it be an earless anyhow? And, darling, don't pop off, will you? Ever? Ever?'

Again Lord Woodleigh smiled. Almost grinned.

'Haven't I told you?' he said. 'A dozen times at least. The wife of an earl is a countess, and if that earl dies his wife becomes the Dowager Lady Blank. It's really quite simple.'

'But, sweety pie, I am – what's it you keep saying? – a bear of very little brain.'

'But a very nice little bear all the same.'

'Brazen hussy.'

Arabella Buckley hissed out the words, but Sven Hjerson thought it very likely they had been carried by the sticky breeze as far as the couple in the prow.

He was unable to observe, however – as he would have liked to do in his ever-observant way – just what the expression on Jilly Jonathan's pretty face might have been. At that moment, emerging from the saloon below as if propelled from a circus cannon, there appeared a distinctly grotesque figure. He was, beyond doubt, an Italian, swarthy in complexion, crowned under a battered panama with a mop of grease-shining black curls, plump with much pasta. But he had chosen to dress in what he may have conceived to be a British manner. He wore a blazer, not unlike the one Lord Woodleigh wore except that instead of discreet brass buttons it was decorated by no fewer than five enormous, tinselly affairs. In place of the modest flannel bags Lord Woodleigh had on, this fellow had a pair of white trousers, much too short for him, stained heavily on one side and showing beneath a pair of socks in a hideous approximation to a Scottish tartan. These eventually were mercifully lost in brown and white 'correspondent' shoes.

'Milord, milord,' he shouted, hurling himself towards the pair in the prow. 'Milord, you are, yes, yes, yes, wanting hotel on Capri? Yourself and the pretty lady, yes? One bedroom only. Yes, yes, yes?'

Lord Woodleigh gave him a look that would have quelled in an instant any insolent groom or keeper.

'Certainly not,' he said. 'Go away.'

He might have been obeyed. Except that Jilly Jonathan burst into unstoppable giggles.

'Oh, Jack,' she managed at last to get out. 'Do let's take up the offer. If only as a joke, to tell people at home when we get back.'

'No, really. It would hardly be a joke in very good taste.'

'Oh, milord, milord. Make that very good joke, yes? Very good joke. One room only. Very, very pretty lady.'

Now something more than a quelling look appeared on Lord Woodleigh's fine-bred features. Cold anger.

'Listen, my man,' he said. 'The guide-book warned us about hotel touts of your sort, and unless you make yourself scarce I shall put you into the hands of the Carabinieri.'

The threat was enough. More than enough. The tartan-socked tout positively scuttled his way to the vessel's stern.

By the time the boat reached the island Sven Hjerson had still not succeeded in shaking off the ample, daisy-sprinkled form of Arabella Buckley. From the yet more gloomy expression on his normally lugubrious face it was evident that he had resigned himself to her companionship at least as far as his hotel perched up far above the sea.

So it was without surprise that he found himself sharing with her one of the tinny, open-sided cars of the creaky old funicular that saved tourists the toil of climbing the seven hundred and more steep stone steps up from the Marina Grande.

As soon as the linked train of little open cars began its steeply angled ascent she clutched the Finnish detective by the arm.

'Mr Hjerson,' she gasped. 'Did you notice?'

'It is my business always to make notices. But, alas, madam, I do not in the present know what it is you are asking if I am seeing.'

'That Italian. That what-d'you call-'em. Tout. He's on the funicular with us, in the next car with Miss Abernethie.'

'Miss Abernethie? She is the lady I have seen? Very middle-age, hair grey, clothes most plain, pince-nez spectacles, expression always disapproving? Lord Woodleigh's secretary he has sent for?'

'Yes, yes, that's her. But don't you understand about that – that tout?'

'Madam, what should be understood?'

'Why, that he's here because of Jilly Jonathan. He's trying to lay his filthy hands on her, I haven't a doubt. And perhaps she. . . You must have seen how struck he was with her. Very, very pretty lady, all that sort of beastly foreign stuff.'

'Well, but, madam, if the fellow is a tout – tout, is that the word? – for one of the hotels here, is it not likely he would need to be ascending like us?'

'Ah, no, you see, no. The thing is that it costs 40 lira to go up now, but if he had waited just one hour more, till the 11 a.m. departure, he would have had to pay only two lira. It said so in the guide-book.'

The Finn considered.

'Yes, madam,' he said at last, 'I am granting that his conducting of himself is not what might be expected. But, you know, there may be many other reasons why it is important for him to get to the top so quickly. It does not have to be that he has conceived what the French are calling the *coup de foudre* for Miss Jonathan.'

'You can tell that,' said Arabella Buckley, 'to the Marines.'

It was an exclamation she might have had to clarify. But at that moment their creaking conveyance gave a sudden fearsome jerk and came to a dead stop.

Once again Miss Buckley clutched Sven Hjerson's arm.

'I knew it wasn't safe,' she jabbered. 'I knew it the moment I saw it last Sunday. These Italians, you can't trust them, you know. Certainly not with anything mechanical. That's something it takes a sturdy British workman to understand.'

Sven Hjerson's lugubrious face lit up in a brief smile.

'Then I am able to give you a reassurance, madam,' he said. 'This funicular is looked after by an Englishman. You can rely upon the observations of Sven Hjerson for this. I noted him working on the machinery while we were waiting to ascend. He was dropping one of his tools and let forth a number of obscenities. His voice was what is called, I am understanding, Cockney or perhaps Australian.'

'Yes,' said Arabella Buckley. 'Yes, well, that is reassuring. Only...'

'Yes?'

'Well, if he was repairing the machinery, it can't have been safe in the first place, can it?

Then Sven Hjerson took his revenge for the past tiresome two hours.

'Madam,' he said, 'you are right. We cannot be certain. Definitely not safe.'

His mischievous words, however, were to prove within a very few minutes appallingly prescient.

The funicular had resumed its climb, apparently smoothly enough. Arabella Buckley had released her grip on the Finn's long, ginger-suited arm. Perhaps with some reluctance. They sat in silence then looking out to either side of the steeply tumbling rocks interspersed with dry, hard Mediterranean shrubs.

But, almost at the end of the ascent, there came a new series of alarming jerks and they juddered to a halt once more. At once there came, clear in the sunny air, a long piercing scream.

The tall Finnish detective acted with a turn of speed altogether surprising to Miss Buckley. In an instant he had vaulted over the side of their car and had begun swinging himself along towards the head of the train and the car occupied by Lord Woodleigh and Jilly Jonathan.

They were no longer in it.

The side of the car opposite the landing stage, rustily flimsy at best, had fallen or been pushed away, leaving a jagged edge all round. Sven Hjerson clambered aboard and cautiously peered over.

'Nothing,' he called at once to the others, whose view of the top car was obscured by the tall backs of their seats. 'But one cannot see greatly far down. Perhaps they are well. It is not so long till some bushes are there. I see to the side a railing also. Perhaps it has stopped their descent. I cannot make out.'

The remaining passengers – there were not many of them – had in the meanwhile managed to make their way, by scrambling from the outside of one car to the next, to the safety of the solid wooden landing stage. They stood there in a frightened cluster.

'I am going to make the climb downwards,' the Finn called to them. 'Help will be needed. Would some gentleman like to assist me?'

'Yes, yes. Let me. I'm his cousin, Peter Horbury.'

The Hon. Peter Horbury appeared to be some ten or twelve years younger than the earl. There were traces of the same fine-boned look about him, but his features were already well masked by what was likely in the course of time to become a solid layer of self-indulgent fat.

Nevertheless he seemed willing enough to accompany the Finnish detective in the dangerous climb down over the tumbling rocks to where his cousin and his cousin's pretty, peroxided fiancée lay. Perhaps dead. Perhaps, taking into account the comparative shortness of the descent, only injured.

In the event it took the two of them, scrambling and sliding downwards beside each other, faces to the rocks, only some five or six minutes to reach the spot where the railing which Sven Hjerson had noticed further along had in fact stopped the couple's fall. But it had stopped Lord Woodleigh in the most horrible of ways.

His head must have fallen almost directly on top of one of the tall spikes that surmounted the old iron rail. He had not been impaled, but the spike had been driven far upwards from near his throat before his body had slumped clear. There could be no doubt at all that he was dead.

Jilly Jonathan had been luckier, or less appallingly unlucky. She was lying not far from her fiancé, eyes closed, deathly pale but apparently hardly injured. The tall Finn and Peter Horbury together raised her up and in a moment or two her eyelids fluttered open.

With unexpected tenderness Sven Hjerson told her what had happened.

'Oh, my God, my God,' she said, 'I was showing Jack the view out there, and I leant over pointing to something and then suddenly the whole thing seemed to tilt and. . . '

She broke off, and Sven Hjerson felt her body slump again in his arms. But by the time he had gathered up her handbag and Lord Woodleigh's camera, which had come to rest nearby, she was able slowly to make her way with them to the nearest point where the accident could be reported.

Some two hours later the whole party sat, exhausted and silent, in deckchairs on the terrace of Sven Hjerson's hotel, sipping half-heartedly at cups of abominable tea and looking without seeing anything at the wide sweep of the Bay of Naples spread out far below them.

Jilly Jonathan was pale but had calmed down after the bout of hysterical weeping that had overcome her once they had got her to the hotel. Peter Horbury sat beside her, still looking tousled from his exertions among the rocks. Next to him his wife, a tall rangy woman whom Sven Hjerson somehow saw even here as being astride a hunter, was leaning forward tapping the tips of the fingers of each hand one against the other. Beside her, chair drawn a little back, Miss Abernethie sat, her face rigid with disapproval, though of what precisely there was no telling. And, to Sven Hjerson's concealed annoyance, Miss Arabella Buckley had contrived to make herself one of the group, her ample form straining the faded green canvas of a chair firmly set among the others.

Into the Finn's head there had strayed, not to be expelled, the words of an English nursery rhyme that a child had once recited to him. *Jack and Jill went up the hill to fetch a pail of water, Jack fell down and broke his crown and Jill came tumbling after.* The childish words went through and through his mind, blotting out all coherent thought. And he felt, obscurely, that the terrible accident needed to be given coherent thought. As much and as deep coherent thought as he was capable of. But it had been days since he had managed to obtain a good, large dish of fresh-cooked vegetables. His famous brain was stupified.

Perhaps this was why, uncharacteristically, he burst out aloud with the thought that at last chased the nursery rhyme momentarily from his mind.

'No. No, no. That car could not have tipped over of itself. Jack and Jill went up the hill, yes, and Jack fell down with Jill tumbling after also; But it was in no manner a simple fall. There must have been a push.'

Arabella Buckley was the first to recover from the shock of that strange outpouring.

'Mr Hjerson,' she said, 'are you. . . Well, are you sure? I mean, don't you . . . Well, don't you sometimes expect to find mysterious deaths wherever you go?'

Sven Hjerson nodded slowly.

'Yes,' he said. 'Yes, that is a good supposition you have made, madam. I would not have thought you. . . But, no. No, it is not right. Sven Hjerson is always making observations. He has trained the eyes to do it. I was telling you, was I not, that I was seeing with exactness what the English workman was doing while we were waiting to ascend. I know how the funicular is operating. Exactly. And I am repeating. Jack and Jill did not tumble down the hill without somebody giving a push.'

'But. . . But. . . ' Peter Horbury brought out. 'But that means. . Well, that means. . . '

'Murder, Peter,' his wife snapped, leaning forward in the saddle. 'That's what Mr Hjerson has the effrontery to be claiming has happened.'

'Madam, there is no effrontery. Yes, Lord Woodleigh has been murdered, and Miss Jilly Jonathan has been a victim beside him. Sven Hjerson has said it.'

'In which case,' Arabella Buckley pronounced sturdily, 'there's only one thing for it. The what-d'you-call-'ems. The police. The Carabin-somethings.'

It was perhaps an hour later that the island's police chief left them with a clicking heels bow. Despite his almost complete lack of English and the poor Italian the others possessed, several things had emerged.

Only a handful of people, it had been established, had been near enough to the leading car of the funicular to have been able to give it the fatal extra push that had sent Woodleigh and Jilly Jonathan tumbling down the steep hillside. These were Peter Horbury and his wife who had been in the little car immediately next to Lord Woodleigh's, and Miss Abernethie, who had been in the next car suffering the presence of the tartan-socked hotel tout. 'I am afraid I took pains to look out at the other side so as not to see him,' she had said. 'But he was there. He was very definitely there.'

'So it could have been he who slipped over the side and did it,' Arabella Buckley had promptly declared.

'Yes,' Sven Hjerson had been constrained to agree. 'It would have been possible for him, I think. Just possible.'

He had given Arabella Buckley a quick glance then.

'Just as it might have been possible for you also, madame,' he had said. 'I, too, was regarding the view on the opposite side from yourself. I could not in the court of law swear that you had been under my observations the whole time we were making the ascent.'

But the others, with the abominable tout in their sights, had been quick to fix the blame on him. The Carabinieri chief had left at once with a promise of finding the man within the hour, to which he added, *sotto voce*, a pledge to get the truth out of him by whatever methods might be necessary.

Sven Hjerson was not, however, willing to let this convenient solution put an end to his own investigation.

'Ladies and gentlemen,' he said when the police chief's hurrying back was out of sight, 'let us not make ourselves deceived. Is it so likely that that man, however much he may have been struck by your beauty and gaiety, Miss Jonathan, would have at once decided to assassinate your future husband?'

But Arabella Buckley, with a murderer who was not 'one of us' almost under her thumb, was not going to let him go so easily.

'Dash it all,' she said, 'Lord Woodleigh spoke very sharply to the fellow when we were on the boat. And these Italians are fearfully hot-headed. Everybody knows what foreigners are like.'

There was a chorus of agreement. It served to make the Finnish detective rather sharper than he might otherwise have been.

'No,' he said. 'Let us please seek for more stronger motives.'

Round the semi-circle of chairs quick looks flicked from face to face.

'Yes,' Sven Hjerson went on, 'it is in fact, I am thinking, that all those people who might have given that not very well balanced car the one push needed have also possible reasons for wishing the death of Lord Woodleigh. And of you also, Miss Jonathan.'

He gave Jilly Jonathan a brief bow from his enormous gangling height.

'Well, I say, that's a bit rich, don't you know,' Peter Horbury said indignantly.

'Nonsense, Peter,' his wife pounced down on him as if he were a hound that had misbehaved. 'The man's quite right. You've got a perfect motive. After all, you're the Earl of Woodleigh now.'

'Good lord, so I am.' For a moment or two Peter Horbury contemplated his newly elevated status. 'But, I mean to say, I did always think I would inherit one day, with Jack being such a confirmed. . .'

He broke off, blushed and tried not to look at Jilly Jonathan.

'And you, madam,' Sven Hjerson turned to Peter's wife. 'You are now – I heard the belated Lord Woodleigh explaining this myself – you are now Countess of Woodleigh. It is a great honour.'

The new Lady Woodleigh looked as if she might take her riding-crop to him if he so much as uttered another word.

'Choose to think that would be a reason for sending old Jack into the next world if you like,' she said. 'But I'm sure there are others with better reasons for wanting to get rid of him.'

'Don't see who you mean,' Arabella Buckley said, a blood-red blush rising up in her cheeks. 'I mean, I've hardly met any of you, let alone. . . '

'I am thinking,' Sven Hjerson said, 'that Lady Woodleigh the new, is meaning someone else, not you, Miss Buckley.' He turned in his chair a little. 'I am thinking, Miss Abernethie, she is perhaps wondering, like myself, why you were sent for to Naples in the middle of the new-engaged couple's holiday. Is the trouble at home that I am hearing of, perhaps, that someone had been – what is the expression? – boiling the books?'

'No. No. It's a lie. I haven't. . . Why should. . . Oh, you are all so beastly. Beastly.'

Miss Abernethie jumped from her chair, scuttled in the direction of the broad flight of steps leading to the road outside, tripped clumsily over Jilly Jonathan's big crocodile-skin handbag, fell to her feet, scrambled up again, pushed the heavy bag aside with a cry of rage that came oddly from her dumpily respectable self and ran off out of sight.

'Quick, quick, after her somebody,' Arabella Buckley shouted, her prejudice in favour of foreign murderers seemingly suddenly abandoned.

Poor overweight Peter Horbury, the new Lord Woodleigh began to heave himself from his deckchair and then sank back into it.

'Oh, she can't get off the island,' he said. 'No need to go chasing about.'

He turned to Sven Hjerson.

'Perhaps, my dear fellow, since you're some sort of detective, you'd try to get through on the telephone to the Carabinieri. They should pick her up without any trouble.'

But Sven Hjerson appeared not to have heard. He had made no attempt to pursue the fleeing secretary and was sitting as if in a trance staring somewhere between the chairs occupied by the new Lord Woodleigh and Jilly Jonathan.

'Yes,' he said eventually. 'Yes, Sven Hjerson sees it all. It is nothing so ever to do with that Australian or Cockney mechanic.'

'I should jolly well hope you do see it,' Lady Woodleigh snapped. 'Damn it, the dreadful woman's run off. It should all be quite evident enough by now.'

'No, no,' the Finnish detective said, shaking his head as if to rid himself of the last remnants of misunderstanding. 'No, you see, Lady Woodleigh, it was not Miss Abernethie who was responsible for the death of Jack who went up the hill. Perhaps she has boiled some books, but that is another matter altogether. No, the murder of Lord Woodleigh was conceived here on Capri, I am believing. Perhaps because something called a stoup in a church was not so interesting enough as he had thought.'

'What on earth,' Arabella Buckley said, 'has the stoup to do with murder?'

'I will tell you. Last Sunday the belated Lord Woodleigh and Miss Jilly Jonathan could not see the famous Blue Grotto on this island because Lord Woodleigh insisted to go to Mass in a church here. It was this, I am thinking, that made Miss Jonathan realize that if the marriage she was about to enter into with a man much different from herself, and older also, would not go well, she would never from a Catholic be obtaining a divorce. So she decided to make away with him.'

'But that's ridiculous,' Arabella Buckley bounced out. 'I mean, the girl wasn't even married to him yet. She'll be left with nothing now.'

She looked across at the film star, not with a great deal of pity. Jilly Jonathan was sitting just as she had been ever since they had come out on to the terrace. Still as a stone.

'No, that is wrong,' Sven Hjerson went on in his level, accented tones. 'You heard so much as I did, Miss Buckley. On board the steamer the two of them were talking about what would happen to the title if Lord Woodleigh was to die before they had any children, and Lord Woodleigh said – Sven Hjerson's ears heard it – *although now you get the estate*. Now, he was saying. And about something as important as so much land and money he would speak with correctitude. So he has already made his will, yes, leaving all already to his future wife. That is the motive.'

'Well, yes,' said Lady Woodleigh. 'But that doesn't mean she killed him. She survived the fall down the hill. He might have done, too. Not much worse than a tumble in the hunting field.'

'No,' Sven Hjerson said, 'you have not thought about the wrong handbag.'

'What wrong handbag, for heaven's sake? Man's a fool.'

'Yes, for some time even Sven Hjerson was a fool. He saw that handbag. He was even carrying it, and thinking how heavy it was. But he was never saying to himself until one moment in the past that it was much peculiar that a girl as pretty and as fashionable with her peroxide hair as Jilly Jonathan was carrying on holiday a big, crocodile-skin handbag. He was never saying to himself in that heavy bag what should there be?'

At this he leapt from his chair in one long gingery streak, seized the bag and without ceremony upended it.

Out on to the stones of the terrace there fell a thick metal spike, not at all dissimilar to the blood-smeared one on which Lord Woodleigh had not fallen, out of sight for a few vital minutes from anyone looking from above.

'A clear case of premeditated murder, the conception made here last Sunday, the spiky weapon obtained from somewhere, the risk taken,' he said. 'Once more Sven Hjerson has triumphed. Without also fresh vegetables.'

HRF Keating, President of the Detection Club, is best known for his ingenious and inventive 'Inspector Ghote' novels. He is also a respected reviewer and critic, ex Chairman of the Society of Authors, and editor of *Agatha Christie: First Lady of Crime*.

EXPERTS FOR THE PROSECUTION

TIM HEALD

It was a golden day in a golden age. Golden lads and lasses had just breakfasted on golden toast, a little blackened at the edge in some cases, spread with golden shred or golden syrup. Now they tripped merrily to a schoolhouse of golden Cotswold stone burnished by a golden English sun in a bright blue heaven inhabited by a golden English God.

All was right with the world.

Up to a point.

Sergeant Bramble had just returned from the Manor House upon his bicycle. The sergeant was stout and pink and, after the exertion of a mile-long bicycle ride, seemed stouter and pinker than usual.

'Well I'll be jiggered!' he exclaimed to himself as he bent to unfasten his clips, 'I'll be jiggered and no mistake.'

And so saying he went into the tiny village police station with its distinctive blue lamp and the lettering chiselled into the stone above the doorway which said 'King's Magnum Parva Police Station'. A handwritten note stuffed into the bootscraper said 'Two pints today, please.'

Inside he filled a kettle and lit the gas-ring. The *Daily Express* had arrived in his absence and its front page confirmed what he had already heard from Mrs Pettifer up at the Manor.

'Baronet vanishes,' it screamed. Good headlines did scream at you in those days. 'Baronet vanishes! Clubs abandoned at 15th green. "Seemed perfectly normal to me," says Major.'

Sergeant Bramble turned his attention to the kettle. When it had boiled, whistling with a tinny Woolworth sibillance, he warmed the pot-bellied black teapot, spooned in two piles of thick tarry Indian leaves, left them awhile as he had a scratch of the back, then poured the dark brown liquid into a plain white cup, with saucer, added milk from a bottle plus two sweetening spoonfuls of caster sugar. Only then did he return to the newspaper.

Routine in his life was everything and he would be jiggered if anything – even the abduction of Squire Blacker – would interfere with it. The article was by Percy Hoskins, the greatest crime reporter of his or any other age, Percy who walked with Commissioners of Police and thieves and villains, who drank champagne at the Caprice, had an apartment in Park lane, was an intimate of Lord Beaverbrook, yet kept the common touch. Sergeant Bramble allowed himself the luxury of a fleeting smile. Perhaps, who knows, the great Hoskins might yet grace King's Magnum Parva with his presence.

Sergeant Bramble drank some tea and wondered where Constable Quince had got to. Constable Quince was new to the job and, in Bramble's estimation, unsuited for it. He seemed to think that a policeman's lot should be to deal in drama. He wanted excitement. He aspired to 'The Flying Squad'. He talked, misty eyed, of 'The Yard'. He wanted to be a detective. He was a fan of Sexton Blake. He was a pain in Sergeant Bramble's bottom and the sooner he could recommend that Quince be transferred to somewhere more metropolitan, where robbery with violence might occur, the happier Bramble would be.

'Dratted nuisance that Quince lad!' thought Bramble, and started to read the paper. This he did with difficulty, partly on account of his bad eyesight, partly because of what in later years would come to be referred to as 'a learning disability' or 'mild dyslexia'; and partly because he simply wasn't much of a reader. He didn't actually have to run his finger along the line in order to make sense of it, but he did like to mouth the words as he got to them.

'Fears were growing last night for the safety of Sir Vivien Blacker, Bart. of the Manor House, King's Magnum Parva who vanished from his home yesterday. Eton and Sandhurst educated Sir Vivien, 28, was last seen yesterday morning at Royal Wrigglesworth Golf Club. "Sir Vivien often played a round before breakfast," said Major Ernest "Tiger" Bagshot, 43, Secretary of Royal Wrigglesworth, "But my suspicions were aroused when his black labrador, Bonzo, appeared at the clubhouse at approximately ten o'clock. The dog seemed distressed and there was no sign of his master."

'Major Bagshot accompanied Bonzo to the 15th green where he found a ball and a complete set of Henry Cotton "St Andrew's" clubs lying, abandoned. Sir Vivien's mashie niblick was in a bunker approximately forty yards from the hole.

'Sir Vivien is the eleventh baronet and is the only surviving son of Sir Tregarron Blacker, the celebrated big-game hunter who died in the sinking of the *Titanic*, together with his wife, Lady Mabel. Extensive searches revealed a series of tyre marks along the fairway leading to the15th and there are fears that Sir Vivien, reputed to be one of the seventeen richest men in the country, may have been kidnapped and held to ransom.

'Our Social Correspondent writes: "Sir Vivien Blacker is a leading member of London Society whose name has been linked with many of our most nubile heiresses. A familiar and dashing figure on the polo field and the Cresta Run, he is universally popular in all circles being blessed with great charm, a ready wit and debonair good looks. Unmarried, his heir is his second cousin, once removed, Mr. Alfred Blacker who is believed to live in Hobart, Tasmania, where he was last heard of working as a Real Tennis professional.'"

Sergeant Bramble was so engrossed in mouthing along with the *Daily Express* that he did not notice the opening of the door. It was only when it shut with a rusty creak that he realized that he had company.

'Sergeant Bramble?'

The query, for such it was, emanated from an elderly lady who appeared to be clad entirely in shawls. Her complexion was pink and white and her eyes were very wide and of an astonishingly china blue hue. She seemed vaguely familiar.

The sergeant deliberated for a moment and then spoke in the soft but unmistakable burr of deepest Mummersett. 'I am he,' he said.

'Then, Sergeant,' said the little old lady, 'your troubles are at an end.'

'Saving your presence ma'am, but I bain't got no troubles.'

'Oh now, dear me, Sergeant, let's not beat about the bush.' The lady raised an admonitory finger in rebuke and the sergeant observed, to his surprise, that despite it being a hot summer's day, she was wearing what appeared to be mittens. 'I have come,' continued the old lady, 'about the Case of the Missing Baronet.'

'You'm don't want to be believing what they do write in they newspapers ma'am,' exclaimed the sergeant, but his visitor was not listening. 'It reminds me of my dear father one day at Sandwich,' she was saying, 'when we were picnicking on the sands and we had arranged to meet him at the nineteenth hole. Imagine mother's distress when she discovered there was no such thing! But never fear, sergeant. I shall find the body in a jiffy and we shall apprehend the guilty party before the day is out.'

Sergeant Bramble was about to remonstrate when they were interrupted by Constable Quince wheeling his bicycle.

'And this must be Constable Quince,' said the old lady. 'How do you do, Constable?'

'Very well, thank you Ma'am,' said Quince amiably.

'How did you know this man's name was Quince?' asked Bramble with a hint of incredulity.

'I make it my business to know such things, young man.'

Bramble was forty-five and had not been thus addressed for

almost a quarter of a century.

'Which,' continued his visitor, 'is why I am able to assist you with your enquiries.'

'What enquiries?' asked the policeman.

'Why,' she exclaimed, 'your enquiries into the murder of poor Sir Vivien.'

'But. . . ' Bramble began, but she silenced him with a glare from the astonishing blue eyes. Strange, thought Bramble, that such an apparently dithery old lady should be able to look at you like that. Bloody terrifying. If you asked him she ought to be put away for she was plainly off her trolley.

'And now, Sergeant, I must be about my business. I shall begin with the dog. If you have any need of me you may enquire of my nephew the vicar.'

And so saying she gathered up her shawl, adjusted her mittens and scuttled from the room.

'Phew!' exclaimed the sergeant, producing a red and white spotted kerchief from his trouser pocket and mopping his fevered brow.

'What was all that about?' asked Quince.

But before Bramble could answer, the door opened and another stranger entered. He was a small man, distinctly foreign in appearance, with a rigidly waxed moustache and an egg-shaped head which he carried rather to one side. He seemed somewhat breathless but his intelligent eyes twinkled with amusement.

'Allo, messieurs, I have arrived as you would have it, in the Nicholas, n'est-ce pas?' he said.

'I'm sorry sir, I'm not entirely with you.' The placid equilibrium of Sergeant Bramble's existence was suddenly being put at risk.

'Oh ho, m'sieur,' said the little man, 'I was not, as your expressive idiom puts it, born on the preceding day.' His eyes flashed and he presented his elegant moustaches. 'It is correct, is it not, that your seigneur is vanished into the air. Pouf!' He slapped his palms together like a conjuror. 'Comme ça. Without the merest trace.'

'Well. . . ' Sergeant Bramble made as if to speak, but the foreign person silenced him with a glance that would have iced coffee. 'The answer,' he said, 'lies perhaps in your game of golf. Our friend played, I think, off a handicap of trois. Also perhaps we should think a little of the monnaie. Was our friend Sir Vivien as rich as he pretended? Perhaps there was trouble with the gaming table? But I shall call first at the Manor and present my card. Never fear, messieurs, we shall have this mystery solved in time of nothing at all. Should you wish advice from the world's greatest detective you may enquire for me at the Rose and Crown. It is there that I am putting up.'

Saying which he passed jauntily from their ken, shutting the door behind him with a flourish.

'What's all that about, Sarge?' asked Quince.

'It means,' said Bramble wearily, 'that we are under siege from the great detectives. We just have to hope your aristocracy don't read the *Daily Express*. Otherwise we'll be up to our necks with toffs in monocles and deer-stalkers all of 'em trailing manservants and frightening the cows and horses by blasting around in they great green Bentleys they all drive.'

'Cor,' said Quince.

'I'll warn Mrs Pettifer they're on their way,' said the sergeant, 'Then you'd better keep an eye on the old lady and I'll watch the froggie geezer. Make sure they don't create too much mischief. I do reckon they have till sundown. Then we'll have it all sorted out.'

'Sorted out?' said Quince. He looked astonished. 'We're going to sort it out ourselves?'

Bramble nodded. 'We'll sort it out, my son. In our own good time. Now let me ring Mrs Pettifer.'

The 'phone rang for a very long time and when Mrs Pettifer eventually answered she sounded quite put out.

'Oh, Sergeant,' she said 'Thank heaven it's you. I've got this tiresome woman here asking endless rude questions. She keeps wanting to know if I play golf. She even had the audacity to suggest that I might have been 'carrying on' with Sir Vivien. The idea! She says she's some sort of detective. But she doesn't look like a detective.. She says she's called on you already and she's helping you with your enquiries. I tried to talk to her sensibly but she just wouldn't listen.'

'Oh dear,' said Bramble out loud. Privately the words he used were 'I'll be jiggered. Silly old bat!'

He and the housekeeper continued to converse for a few minutes and finally he said, 'Very well, Mrs Pettifer, sherry at six.' He spoke the words 'sherry at six' with a hint of menace, rather as if he had said 'pistols at dawn'.

When he replaced the receiver he regarded his subordinate for a moment and then smiled. 'Now, young Quince,' he said, 'you've always wanted a spot of real detective work to do. So I tell you what. You get on your bike and find that old lady what were in here just now and you don't let her out of your sight. Don't you let her know what you're up to, mind. Just you do prevent any serious mischief. And I'll do the same for the foreigners.' He put down the empty tea cup with surprising force. 'I don't hold with foreigners,' he exclaimed, 'leastways not here in King's Magnum Parva. Foreigners may be all right abroad but we don't want none of them and their ways here.'

And without more ado the two officers fastened their clips about their ankles, wheeled out with velocipedes and were on their way.

Bramble spotted his quarry entering the post office some ten minutes later. The small foreign person was walking as jauntily as ever, though Bramble realized that he did so with a pronounced limp. Bramble decided to follow, and when he entered the office, which was also the village shop, he found the stranger in earnest coloquy with the postmaster, one Algy Brind.

'It is, ma foi, a matter only of the little grey cells, m'sieur', he was saying. 'Your baronet is kidnapped. Now if he is kidnapped, what may we deduce? That a person has done so in order to extract the monnaie. And how will this be done? In order to make such an extraction a message must be conveyed. And how better would a kidnapper do such a thing than to send a letter by his Majesty's Mail. In such matters it is the most obvious things which are the most important and which stare at you from under the nose without being perceived. And so I must ask you again to allow me to inspect the morning's mails.'

'Oh, Sergeant Bramble!' Algy was obviously relieved by the arrival of the law. 'This person says he's acting on your behalf and he wants to inspect all the mail. Ingoing and outgoing. I've explained that it's the King's personal property until safely delivered to the addressee, but he doesn't seem to understand.'

'Now then, now then,' Sergeant Bramble spoke in reassuring country tones, 'what seems to be the problem?'

'Pas de problème,' the peculiar foreign person gave a dismissive shrug and Sergeant Bramble caught a strong whiff of musky eau de cologne. 'Our friend here does not seem to appreciate that the world's greatest detective is conducting a criminal investigation and that he is not to be thwarted. Now that you are here he will hand and deliver.'

'You can't do that there here, I'm afraid,' said Bramble affably. 'His Majesty's mails are not to be interfered with. This isn't France.'

'You mean Belgium.' The small man's eyes flashed and he looked awfully cross. 'Ma foi, the world's greatest detective is not to be interfered with either. We are in the presence of very great evil, my friends, and the little grey cells must not be denied.' He paused. 'Did Sir Vivien perhaps purchase a licence for his dog from this office?'

'I'm not at liberty to divulge,' said the postmaster.

The detective looked from one man to another and flexed his moustaches. 'My friends,' he said, 'you will regret this very much.'

Meanwhile in another part of the village Constable Quince had run his quarry to earth in the vegetable garden of the Manor. She appeared to be taking herb samples. Constable Quince hid in the potting shed and lit a Woodbine. Presently the old lady came towards him, entered the shed and sniffed knowledgeably at a tin of weedkiller. Constable Quince had retreated behind a stack of deckchairs and extinguished his cigarette. Much good it did him. She had spotted the cigarette smoke from afar and now she could see his feet protruding from under the canvas.

'Smoking is not good for the lungs. Nor the complexion,' she said. 'Size nine boots, Constable. Unless you have a good reason for standing over there I should come out and get some fresh air. It is a very clement day.'

The constable emerged sheepishly.

'Do you play golf, Constable?' she asked.

'Can't say as I do,' he said.

'If Sir Vivien had reached the fifteenth green at the time of his abduction and Bonzo arrived in the clubhouse at ten o'clock, we can assume that Sir Vivien himself must have begun his round at, shall we say, about half past eight.'

Since this clearly required an affirmative the constable nodded.

'And as it takes half an hour to drive to Royal Wrigglesworth we must assume that Sir Vivien's Lagonda would have driven through the village at about eight.'

Again the constable nodded. The little old lady seemed pleased at this. She had evidently decided that the policeman was a handsome as well as an agreeable fellow.

'Are you a married man, Constable?' she enquired.

The constable said he wasn't.

'Nor,' said his interlocutor cryptically, 'is Sir Vivien. Perhaps this is a case of cherchez la femme. But come let us go to the garage.'

Thus the day proceeded. The two great detectives prowled up

and down the village street dogged by the two official police-men. Sergeant Bramble and Constable Quince very quickly gave up trying to understand what it was that the experts were looking for. It was perfectly clear to all four of them that the forensic skills, the intellectual abilities, the sheer weight of grey cellular matter, the brutalizing experience of countless similar quests, possessed by the real experts was infinitely greater than that of the mere professionals. This was a case of Gentlemen versus Players in the golden age when such distinctions still applied and when it was obvious to anyone with an eighth of an intelligence that no paid journeyman could ever begin to com-pare with the rapier-like 'amateurs' who flitted with effortless superiority, solving one crime after another with a brilliant insouciance which was the dismay of the criminal fraternity, the envy of the constabulary, and a source of immense satisfaction to most of the upper middle class, especially those with an apti-tude for the *Times* crossword.

So when the great lady detective drew a hair from her head and stuck it across the lock on the front door of Sir Vivien's motor car, Constable Quince said nothing. And when the great gentleman detective got hold of the village postman and sub-jected him to an interrogation which ranged from what he had eaten for breakfast to whether or not he possessed a wireless set and if so what he had listened to on the previous morning, Sergeant Bramble maintained a stoic countenance.

At luncheon all four of them fetched up in the saloon bar of The Rose and Crown. A great detective might have considered this an astounding coincidence were it not for the fact that the hostelry was the only place in the whole of King's Magnum Parva where a lady or a gentleman might obtain a meal. And even then it was only a matter of sandwiches or pickled eggs.

'Aha, my friend,' said the great gentleman detective, 'To pickle an egg in the English fashion is a chose extremely curi-ous. Today I would die for one of Mère Poulard's omelettes aux fines herbes. But tell me, the English lady who sits with the peculiar gloves drinking sherry wine with your colleague. She is not, I think, a native of King's Magnum Parva.'

'No,' said Sergeant Bramble, 'she's a stranger in town. Just like yourself.'

'Ma foi! That is a suspicious circumstance.' And the diminutive Belgian pursed his lips and frowned into his half pint of Old Parsnip Ale.

At the far end of the room the object of his attention was exhibiting a reciprocal interest.

'Tell me, Constable,' she said, sipping her drink with maidenly primness, 'the small gentleman lunching with your sergeant. He is not, I think, quite English?'

'Dunno.' The constable's speech was impeded by corned beef sandwich. When he swallowed he said, 'Leastways he bain't from these parts.'

The old lady smiled to herself, a secret smile that implied that the final clue in her private internal crossword had slotted into place.

'Dear me,' she said, 'one is surprised to find foreigners in a place such as this. That moustache is not an English moustache, the flower in the button-hole is from some foreign field and I fancy he does not care for his pickled egg. There is also something about him which suggests that he is not unacquainted with evil.' She gave a shudder. An involuntary shudder but a shudder nonetheless.

The police remained silent in the face of such speculation. It was plain that the two great detectives were discomfited by each other's presence. And both Bramble and Quince were relieved when their respective charges had finished lunch and set off again on their quest.

'Wild geese, mon vieux, is what you presume me to chase,' said the gentleman to Bramble, 'but I assure you the stable door is bolted.'

'Oh dear, oh dear', said the lady, 'Nothing, but nothing, is ever what it seems.'

And so, in the end it was time for sherry at the Manor House.

That sense of dénouement, of the safety catch being taken off pistols, of seconds leaving the ring, was almost palpable. The police were baffled. Never had they seen so much enquiry, so much question and answer, so much deployment of grey cells at one extreme and of gut intuition at the other. Yet they were not downhearted.

For all was *not* as it seemed.

Mrs Pettifer made a charming surrogate host in the absence of her master. She greeted the ill-assorted quartet with genuine warmth and friendliness. Nevertheless the atmosphere was somewhat fraught. It was clear that the true purpose of this meeting went a great deal deeper than mere small chat.

It was the foreigner who broke the ice.

'Eh bien, my friends,' he said, brushing a crumb of cheese straw from the lapel of his immaculately pressed suit, 'it is time to make the beginning. For in the beginning, as the bible tells us, is the end. And while it may be that the tragic case of the disappearing baronet is one that appears to defy all logic, it is not a case that defies the world's greatest detective. It is a case which, I am afraid to tell you, has its own beginning and middle and – alas – an end too.'

Here, Mrs Pettifer began to interject but the small gentleman silenced her with a flap of the wrist which was altogether not very gentlemanly and proved too much for the great lady detective who made a more purposeful interjection of her own.

'This is very interesting,' she said, 'but I'm afraid that it is nothing more than a performance. It is a very clever performance – what they call in theatrical circles a *beautiful* performance. But it is still no more than a performance. Not real. This person claims to be a great detective and yet he has detected nothing, nothing at all. He has asked questions all over the village, but none of the answers have solved this dreadful crime. And I can tell you why. It is because the villain of this piece is none other than he himself.'

There was a sudden silence. You could have heard a pin drop if anyone in the room had dropped one. Eventually the little man cleared his throat.

'Very ingenious,' he said, 'The classic smokescreen. As soon as the villain is about to be unveiled what does she do, she throws the sand in the face of her pursuers. In the chasse, messieurs, mesdames, the beast is at its most dangerous when it is cornered. N'est-ce pas? This little old lady is not so innocent as she seems. Indeed she is not innocent in the least.' And pointing a trembling finger at her he said in a steely voice of condemnation, 'Madame. J'accuse.'

Even as he uttered the words a strange noise could be heard from beyond the French windows. At first Sergeant Bramble thought it was one of the latest Atco motor-mowers but it seemed to be coming from above them.

Mrs Pettifer spoke. 'I think,' she said, 'that you are about to have your problem solved. Come with me.' And so saying she led the way on to the terrace with its beautiful scents of honey-suckle, rose and jasmine. As they stood there looking east they were able to discern a small buzzing winged shape heading towards them over the immense Capability Brown park.

'An aeroplane!' said Constable Quince.

'Well I'll be jiggered,' said Sergeant Bramble.

The small bi-plane wobbled over the oaks and the elms, banked at the north end of the ha-ha and started to descend towards the huge lawn which ran, treeless along this side of the house between terrace and park. It was a perfect landing. The plane bumped to a halt, the engine coughed and died, and two figures in leather flying helmets swung out of the open cockpit and came towards them arm in arm. One was a dashing, debonair young man; the other was a beautiful elegant girl with high cheek-bones and eyes of the purest grey.

'Hello auntie!' called the man as they neared the little party.

'Hello uncle!' echoed the young woman in a foreign accented voice waving cheerily.

'Mon dieu!' said the little man, not apparently sure whether to be terribly angry or frightfully cross, 'Nicole!'

'I might have known it,' said the old lady, 'Vivien's such a naughty boy!'

The couple tripped up the terrace steps and embraced their respective relatives with affection.

'Nicole and I are getting married,' said Sir Vivien, 'and we wanted you to be the first to know. Mrs Pettifer, I think you can bring out that magnum of the widow now.'

'Saving your presence sir,' said Sergeant Bramble, 'I tried to explain that there was nothing amiss and that you'd be back in time for supper with Miss Nicole. But they wouldn't listen.'

Nicole giggled. 'That's exactly what we expected, Sergeant. We knew that the one way to get the world's two greatest detectives to come here would be to stage a mysterious disappearance. Of course that nice Mr Hoskins at the *Express* was in on our secret.' She turned to the two detectives. 'We telephoned Mrs Pettifer from Paris. And she told Sergeant Bramble.'

'I must say Nicole's a proper Amy Johnson,' said Sir Vivien. 'She put the old kite right down in the middle of the fairway. Super piece of flying, darling.'

Mrs Pettifer came out on to the terrace with a tray, glasses and a big bottle of champagne.

'Paris?' said the foreign detective.

'What better place for an engagement party à deux?' said the baronet, pouring out wine. 'Pity we had to leave Bonzo behind, but we knew he'd be good at raising the alarm.'

'Mes enfants,' said the small Belgian person, "chers collègues, I am enchanté by your successes. Mme Pettifer, my man Georges, I think, has consulted with you on the subject of the wines. And the cooking also. You, my poor dear lady,' and he turned here to the other great detective, 'have as one says "raided the vegetable garden". We have established, have we not, that the public house is not worthy of a celebration dinner. So, with your agreement, Sir Vivien, your aunt and your uncle will entertain you at dinner chez vous.'

'My dear Vivien,' said his aunt, 'I do commend you on your herb garden as well as on your choice of bride. Your dear new uncle-in-law whom I was fortunate enough to encounter on the morning train from Paddington agrees that it would be nice if our friends from the constabulary were to join us.'

'But auntie. . . ' The baronet was incredulous.

'But uncle. . . ' His fiancé likewise.

'You see dears,' said the old lady, 'no one, least of all a great detective, believes what they read in the newspapers.'

'Which reminds me,' said her friend. 'We took the liberty of asking our friend Percy Hoskins to join us for dinner. He should be hear in a trice, for his departure from Paddington was scheduled, I believe, for nine minutes before five.'

There was a short silence now in which anyone with good enough hearing to detect a pin-drop would have detected the sound of hundreds of little grey cells jostling and barging each other in frantic efforts to arrive at a perfect understanding of the day's events. And then everyone raised their glasses in a spontaneous salute to the happy couple, to the perfect English village, to exotic foreign ladies, to the belle cuisine, to love, to life and above all, of course, to great detectives and their creator.

Tim Heald's most plausible link with Dame Agatha is that his own crime novels were adapted for TV by Trevor Bowen, who later went on to do the same thing (with rather more success) for the Dame. He has only seen 'The Mousetrap' once.

A FÊTE WORSE THAN DEATH

PAULA GOSLING

Colonel Feather's card tricks were not going well. Peggy Mitchell, seated at the rear of the Variety Tent, sighed in sympathy as, one after another, the right card failed to appear from or disappear into the deck. Colonel Feather's face was getting red, and he was beginning to perspire.

The small audience had begun to fidget on their rickety folded chairs. A child's piping question about the next 'act' – a professional juggler currently on the variety bill in a nearby town – was hurriedly hushed, as much by the Colonel's glare as its mother's whisper. The Great Whirlo and his potential fan would have to wait – Colonel Feather was a determined man, and this was his moment. Once again, he shuffled the recalcitrant deck, smiling too broadly, compelling their attention.

Peggy stood up and slipped out of the tent into the bright August afternoon. They had been so lucky with the weather; a clear sky, and a soft breeze that kept everyone comfortable. The colourful draperies of the various stands and tents billowed and flapped gently, as the denizens of Little Tuckett strolled about on the freshly clipped lawns of the vicarage garden, taking in the various delights on offer.

She waved to old Mr Pinkney, who was patiently manning the second-hand bookstall. Hemmed in by idle readers, and knots of little boys scrabbling through the boxes of *Beanos*, *Magnets*, and *Boy's Own* annuals, he waved back with a weary smile. Mr Venables was overseeing the bran-bin, frowning like an irritated camel. Right next to him, Mr Doran was grinning maniacally as he handed out squishy tomatoes for the parish-ioners to throw at their young vicar, trapped in the 'stocks'. She beamed at her husband, bravely facing the barrage of produce, and winced as a particularly juicy specimen caught him right on the chin. Poor daft lamb, she thought, affectionately.

'Oh, Mrs Mitchell! Mrs Mitchell!' The thin, over-dramatic shriek was all too familiar. Peggy turned.

'What is it, Peony?' she asked, with practised calm.

'The water, ma'am, it's *still* off. There's none for the tea urns or the washing up or. . . ' her voice dropped dramatically. 'Or for the toilet, neither. There's a queue built up. People are com-plaining.'

'Oh dear.' She peered around at the various exhibits, squint-ing into the sun. 'I'm sure I saw Mr Clancy around here, some-where.'

Peony sniffed. 'Probably in the beer tent. He has an awful thirst since he come back from serving in Egypt. Maybe he thinks being a Sergeant in the Engineers makes him too good to work for ordinary folk. He was supposed to come, yesterday, and never showed up. Old pisser.'

'Peony!' Peggy was shocked.

The girl was unrepentant. 'Well. . . you'd think a man with so many kids would make an effort, wouldn't you? Unless maybe they're not all his.' She giggled.

'That's quite enough,' said Peggy, attempting a stern ap-proach to her audacity. 'I've told you before – if you want to keep your place at the vicarage, you can't go around saying such unchristian things. You know Mr Mitchell doesn't like it.'

Peony looked suitably chastened, but there was a glint in her eye that told Peggy there was plenty more she *could* say, and *would* say, if it weren't for the fact that she adored the Vicar with a passion that bordered on the obsessive. It was only by issuing rather unconvincing threats of his disapproval that Peggy could keep the girl in line.

It was not easy for a spirited young woman like Peggy to be

the wife of a country vicar. When she was eighteen and had actually been accepted at Chelsea Art School, she had been determined to be somebody wonderful, somebody famous, like Amelia Earhart or Margaret Mead. But her girlish dreams of adventure had somehow melted under the gaze of a handsome young curate who arrived, one bright morning, at their local church. They had married within a year. David was a hale and hearty kind of cleric, and for a while she cherished hopes of missionary work taking them into some exotic foreign clime. His rather surprising decision to accept the modest living of Little Tuckett had put an end to that.

Sighing over lands and wonders lost, she had accepted the inevitable. She had been brought up a good Church of England girl – she knew the drill. And being married to David made up for a great many afternoon teas and Women's Institute meetings.

But organizing and overseeing Little Tuckett Church Fête had lowered her resistance. The problem of the cut-off water supply – it had been off since eight that morning – had made it much worse. Her patience in equally short supply, she found herself exasperated, not for the first time, by Peony's snide tongue. But she stifled her annoyance, and smiled – the very model of a good vicar's wife.

'Well, I'm sorry everybody's moaning at you, Peony. Tell them I said the water will be fixed, soon. If I can't find Mr Clancy, maybe David can coax it to work.'

She went to find her husband, and discovered him still laughing and ducking the tomato barrage, naked from the waist up but liberally coated with a kind of raw ketchup. He was a totally happy – if less than salubrious – man. It seemed a shame to disturb him, but. . .

'David?' she called, over the laughter and teasing of the good-humoured crowd. 'The water's still off. It's causing problems.'

'Talk about Mysterious Ways,' he grinned. 'I was wondering when I was going to be let free to do the work of the Lord.'

'You mean the work of Mr Clancy,' said Peggy, as he stood up and took the towel she gave him. 'And if you think you're going to get all that off without a shower, you're wrong.' She handed him another towel. 'Hurry up – I gather people are standing in line for the loo.'

'Ah – now that *is* serious,' he said, picking up his shirt and reluctantly easing it over the traces of tomato pulp. 'I'll attack the pipes with my new hammer.'

David's approach to practical problems harked back to his days on the rugby pitch, often with similarly injurious results. 'I'll see if I can locate Mr Clancy,' she said, in some alarm.

She went over to the Cookery and Refreshments Tent, but was stopped at the entrance by a pale-faced Constable Perkins.

'I'm afraid there's been a bit of bother, Mrs Mitchell,' he said. 'Maybe you ought to wait outside, here.'

'Why? What's happened?' she asked trying to see past him.

'Well – it's Councillor Phipps,' the constable said, in a low voice. 'He's dead – dropped right down in the middle of the cake-tasting. Doctor's looking at him now. It's a shame, happening right here at the fête and all. But we don't want to cause a fuss, now, do we?'

Unfortunately, a fuss proved to be unavoidable.

'Poisoned,' Dr Padgett said, standing up.

There was a shriek from the group of six women who stood back against the side of the tent. 'No!' Maxine Venables held her hands clasped before her as if in supplication. 'I never,' she gasped. 'I never.'

Dr Padgett looked puzzled. Mr Catlett, Chairman of the Judging Committee, spoke low in explanation. 'He'd just tasted Mrs Venables' cake and was cutting into Mrs Feather's. He was doing the cake judging for us, as he always does, every year. Bit of a gourmet, he was.' Mr Catlet, a plain and practical man himself, pronounced it to rhyme with poor-net. 'Said it were very nice, very nice indeed – and then he choked, went a funny colour, ripped his collar open, waved his arms a bit, and dropped down dead. Very shocking, it was.'

'I never did it! I never!' Mrs Venables insisted.

'All right, woman, all right,' said Dr Padgett testily. 'I said he was poisoned – but not necessarily by your cake. Did you change your recipe? Use a new brand of anything?'

Mrs Venables drew herself up. She was a tall blonde woman, slightly overweight but still handsome.

'Not a bit,' she said. 'Coffee gâteau, mine was, an old family recipe. All pure ingredients from the cleanest kitchen in Little Tuckett – ask anyone.'

'Well, you can see the colour of him,' Dr Padgett muttered to Constable Perkins. 'It will mean tests, of course, but from his appearance and what Catlett described, I'd say cyanide. It was very quick – he still has bits of various decorations and cherries in his mouth.'

He turned and looked at the display of cakes on the long table. There were six of them, five with small slices taken out and the sixth with the knife still in it. Miss Pinkney's was a chocolate layer cake with cherries, angelica leaves, and pink sugar roses on it. Mrs Doran's was a Victoria sponge with toasted almonds and walnut halves carefully arranged on the top. Mrs Clancy's was a marble cake frosted white and decorated with chocolate curls and chocolate creams. Mrs Yardley's was a plain sponge, but had been lacily covered with swirls and dollops and curlicues of golden buttercream icing dotted with candied violets. Mrs Feather's cake was a simple white confection, quite plain in comparison with the others. But then, Mrs Feather had never needed anything to brighten up her baking – she was a superb cook. Mrs Venables' cake was – as she had said – a perfect coffee gâteau, smoothly frosted in caramel, with three cherries on the top. A fourth cherry had been in the slice the Councillor had just removed and eaten.

'There was a cherry on your cake, too, Dorothy,' Mrs Venables said, accusingly, to Mrs Feather.

'Yes, I know there was,' said Mrs Feather in a soft, sad voice. 'That packet of cherries was the only decoration I had on hand. I haven't been doing much baking lately.' She sighed. 'But I woke up in the middle of the night and couldn't get back to sleep, so I decided to bake a cake, after all. I hardly had anything in the cupboard so I had to make do. . . ' She trailed off, embarrassed.

'He could never resist a cherry,' said a soft voice, and they all turned. Mrs Phipps stood there, quiet, plain, dressed in dove grey, with a handkerchief clutched in her hand. In the excitement, everyone seemed to have forgotten her – which was not unusual. Her husband had always been the centre of attention wherever he went – large, handsome, charming: a vote-getter by trade and inclination. There were tears on the unremarkable face of Mrs Phipps, but she had made no sound, from the minute of entering the tent until now.

'Oh, my dear,' said Peggy, going to her. 'I'm so sorry, so very sorry. Come up to the vicarage and I'll make you a cup of . . . ' Then she remembered the water problem. 'Come and sit down,' she said, and led Mrs Phipps to a chair by the useless tea-urn.

Constable Perkins, who had been enjoying himself at the fête, 'patrolling' the exhibits, had only by chance come into the Cookery Tent at the vital moment. He'd kept the curious out while the doctor made his examination. Now he drew himself up and Took Control. He gazed at the women, and the small group of people who had been in the tent when the councillor actually collapsed. Fortunately, most of the crowd had been drawn to the main attraction of The Great Whirlo in the Variety Tent at that particular point in the afternoon. There were no teas being served and, anyway, everybody in Little Tuckett knew that either Mrs Clancy or Mrs Feather always won the Cake Competition.

'I'll want nobody leaving until I say so,' said Perkins. There were murmurs of both assent and dissent. Some protested they had to get home, but their tone was half-hearted. What supper preparations could compare with this rare excitement?

'And nobody touching anything,' Perkins went on, in a loud voice. 'Nothing – is that understood?' He glared at Mr Catlett, who quailed before this rare intimidation from a man who was normally jovial and kind.

'Touch nothing,' Mr Catlett echoed. 'I quite understand.'

'Now, I am going to make a list of those present,' Perkins continued. 'And we shall eventually want to take statements from everyone – in particular, the six ladies who baked these cakes.'

It did not take long. One by one the members of the crowd trickled out into the fête, carrying with them the news of Phipps's death. ('And maybe murder!')

Gradually there arose a faint humming from outside the tent as people gathered to talk and speculate, so it seemed as if those left inside were surrounded by a swarm of curious but not unfriendly bees.

Constable Perkins was torn between keeping an eye on the scene of the crime – and perhaps making a brilliant arrest – or calling up reinforcements. But common sense, coupled with the prospect of the time and paperwork involved in interviewing the hundred or so people who'd been through the Cookery and Refreshment Tent during the past few hours finally defeated his hope for personal glory through brilliant deduction. 'I shall have to report this to my superiors,' he finally said, when only Peggy Mitchell, Mrs Phipps, Mr Catlett and the six cake-bakers remained in the tent.

Mr Catlett was deputized to 'keep an eye on everything' while Perkins went up to the vicarage to make his 'phone call. Voices were raised outside as he progressed through the crowd, but he told everyone to 'move on' and 'go home', instructions which, of course, were ignored. They stayed outside – but they stayed.

The six competitors sat at the tea tables, together but strangely separate – each gazing at her hands or off into the distance, and never at one another. Peggy and Mrs Phipps sat together, slightly apart from the rest.

Peggy was determined to be sympathetic. The trouble was, Mrs Phipps didn't seem to need sympathy. She was perfectly calm, perfectly quiet, and had nothing to say, other than a reiteration of her previous statement, to wit, 'he could never resist a cherry'.

Was this common knowledge, Peggy wondered? She asked Mrs Phipps, as delicately as she could.

'Why else would there be so many fal-lals and thingamajigs on those cakes?' the widow said, wearily. 'They were all out to catch Henry's eye. The fancier something looked, the better he thought it tasted. Cherries, chocolates, walnuts, and anything in silver paper – Henry always wanted the best of anything and everything. Thought it was his due. I'm glad he's gone – I can do what I like, now.' It was the voice of a woman released, in more ways than one, from a life of obedient acquiescence to a stronger personality. It was also the voice of innocence, Peggy thought. For if Mrs Phipps been clever enough to manage her husband's murder, then she was too bright to make such uninhibited admissions, even to a sympathetic vicar's wife, other than in the knowledge that she'd nothing to hide. Peggy glanced across at the six women seated nearby.

She had learned, over the past five years, that a vicar's wife is expected to be sympathetic, helpful, and above reproach. To her credit, whatever other social solecisms the inexperienced Peggy might have committed during their stay in Little Tuckett, she had never betrayed a confidence. Once they'd realized this, the villagers came to her often with their problems. She had soon learned that almost everybody has something they want to hide, and something they're eager to share. A great deal of gossip about the village and its inhabitants had thus come her way, from every direction. It gave her a rather unique 360-degree view of the place.

She knew of at least one reason why each of these six women would have been glad to see Handsome Henry dead. Miss

Pinkney's father had been nearly bankrupted through a failed business venture with Phipps. Some said this loss of funds was what lay behind a recent broken engagement between the rather unattractive Miss Pinkney and the third son of a titled but impecunious family. Then there was the question of the paternity of Mrs Clancy's last child: Mr Clancy had only just returned from Egypt after a two-year posting, and – as Peony had pointed out – the child was only 14 months old. Mrs Doran's husband had been a loser to Phipps, both at golf and in the bedroom. Had he discovered it, or was she afraid he would? Doran's short temper and long memory were famous in Little Tuckett. Mrs Feather's daughter Imogen had a brief, unhappy affair with Phipps, only last Christmas, and had subsequently left the village to care for an elderly aunt in Scotland. Some said she'd left with a broken heart. Phipps's latest conquest – he rarely went long without excitement – had been the childless and bored Mrs Venables, whose cake was the last he'd tasted, and whose husband was the local chemist.

Oh dear, Peggy thought – the local *chemist*.

And Mrs Yardley? What about Mrs Yardley – oh, yes. Of course. Mrs Yardley's husband had lost his job recently, and Phipps held the mortgage on the little cottage they were so proud of. They'd been in it only a year, but Mrs Yardley had lavished as much effort on it as she had on her beautiful cake. Had Handsome Henry tried to foreclose – or, seeing how pretty Mrs Yardley was, had he suggested an alternative form of payment?

Peggy thought she knew of at least another ten people who would not really be mourning the death of Henry Phipps. There could be as many more – dozens more – about whom she knew absolutely nothing at all. As manager of the local estate agency and building society, Handsome Henry got around. Had an enemy completely unknown to Peggy travelled to the fête in Little Tuckett with the express purpose of bumping off the fulsome Phipps? If one such had done the deed, she could be of no assistance in the enquiries.

But if it was a *local* person. . .

'Dear me,' she murmured.

'I beg your pardon?' asked the Widow Phipps. Peggy saw with some dismay that she wore the distant smile of a woman reviewing her late husband's insurance position.

The tent flap drew back, and David Mitchell entered, cleaned up and resplendent in dog-collar and cardigan. Apparently the water supply had been restored. Peggy got up and hurried over to him. 'David,' she whispered, drawing him aside. 'I'm afraid I know rather a lot of people who wanted to kill Mr Phipps.'

'Oh, so do I,' he said, gravely. 'Heaps. Including me.'

'What?' She was shocked.

'He's been pressuring me to sell the land next to this house,' David said. 'The very land on which he now lies dead, in fact.' He glanced over at the mound of tablecloths hastily borrowed from the tables of the unused tea-stall, under which the body of the late Councillor Phipps was now reposing.

'But – it belongs to the Church.'

'Of course. But both the vicarage and the church itself are in desperate need of repair. A word from me to the Commissioners might have swayed the sale in Phipps's direction. He had a tame developer all poised to move in. Kept saying something about building a parade of really modern shops. He went on and on about it until I could cheerfully have strangled him.'

'Well, fortunately for you, he was poisoned,' said Peggy, in some relief.

'Doesn't matter – I could have done it,' said David, pointedly. 'In fact, from what Perkins was just telling his inspector on the telephone, anybody might have slipped into the Cookery Tent before the judging and put a poisoned cherry into temptation's way for Henry Phipps.'

'Only somebody who knew his weakness for them,' said Peggy.

'You usually have to know someone quite well to hate them,'

David observed. 'And a lot of people knew him very well indeed, believe me.'

Peggy was all too aware of that. Questions of Morality and Christian Virtue aside, she didn't really blame all the women Henry Phipps had conquered for succumbing to his wiles. Life in a small village could be deadly dull, and Henry had been absolutely charming when he chose to be. The difficulty was, he'd chosen to be charming so very, very often. Why, even Peggy herself had been one of his targets – until he realized there was no chance for him there. If David had ever learned of the things Phipps had said to her, he would probably. . .

'Oh dear,' she said, again.

They stared at one another in dismay, the sad, small wickedness of their friends and neighbours strewn around their minds like dirty confetti from a party long past. Henry Phipps had been the chief celebrant at this particular form of 'get-together', and now someone had brought his priapic revels to a rather spectacular end.

Constable Arthur Perkins was a phlegmatic man, resigned long ago to losing his hair and his prospects for promotion as he worked out his years in an area singularly free of serious crime. This was only his second murder in eighteen years, and he was somewhat annoyed by it, coming as it did during the best fishing of the year, and right at the time when his garden was at its peak. Murder, he felt, was a winter occupation – dark deeds were suited to dark months. Not now, and surely not here, in these gaudy summer surroundings.

He glared at the people who surrounded the tent, and they glared back, wanting action. Well, he thought, they'll have plenty of action when my Inspector gets here. Meanwhile – and he crossed his arms as if to underline the point – nobody gets in and nobody gets out.

Leaving David with Mr Catlett, Peggy went back to the table and sat down. 'The police will be here soon,' she said, quietly.

'Constable Perkins is here,' Mrs Clancy said.

'Yes, I know. But there will be a great many more, soon, and they'll be asking a great many questions.'

'Oh dear,' Mrs Feather said. 'And it's so hot.'

That was true enough. With the tent flap closed, the heat had been building up under the canvas. Mrs Feather looked quite pale, and there was a constant and discreet pressing of handkerchiefs to the upper lips and foreheads of all the women.

'Perhaps if we tried to get things straight in our minds now, it might hurry the enquiry along,' Peggy suggested, casually.

'I really don't see what good that would do,' snapped Miss Pinkney.

'Oh, anything to get it settled,' said Mrs Doran, glaring at the spinster beside her. 'I have a hairdressing appointment at four.'

'Well, we could start by working out exactly how and when the cakes arrived.' said Peggy. 'They're not easy things to carry, after all.'

It transpired that each woman had packed up her own cake to bring to the fête. Mrs Yardley had re-used a proper cake box from a city bakery; Mrs Doran, Miss Pinkney and Mrs Clancy had used their usual cake tins; and Mrs Feather and Mrs Venables had used ordinary cardboard boxes. And they'd all packed them up this morning.

'Did anyone help you to get the cakes *out* of their containers for the judging?' Peggy asked. 'I mean, I expect it's difficult to manage without harming them.'

No – each lady had personally placed her cake on the long table – without assistance. But then Mr Clancy and Mr Venables, who had been standing by to offer encouragement, had fallen into an argument concerning position. Mr Doran had moved his wife's cake to the first position, and Mr Clancy had moved it back to the middle, saying the first cake tasted had the best chance, and his wife's cake would be first as it had got there first. Mr Venables disagreed and made some claim about taste-buds and their 'overstimulation'. Mr Clancy was not impressed by this scientific distraction, and said so. Vehemently. Colonel Feather had then expressed a worry that children could easily reach over and scoop up a fingerful of frosting, perhaps spoiling someone's chances, so he and Mr Doran – the latter complaining mightily about his lumbago – had moved the cakes to the back of the table. Agreeing that the cakes should be protected, Mr Pinkney had set up a sort of crêpe paper barrier along the front of the display.

There was one exception. Mr Yardley, according to his wife, had never set foot in the tent. 'He just dropped me off,' she said. 'He had to go to Burford to see someone about a new job.'

'But I saw your husband come into the tent while you were over at the tombola,' Mrs Doran said to Mrs Yardley.

'Oh, you couldn't have,' Mrs Yardley protested.

'Well, I did,' said Mrs Doran, piqued. 'What's more, he was hanging around the cake display, looking rather shifty, if you ask me.'

'Well, nobody asked you,' huffed Mrs Yardley.

Peggy pressed her lips together. Trying to find out who had direct access to the cakes had proved nothing. Apparently all of the husbands – or, in the case of Miss Pinkney, her father – had had the opportunity. Even young Mr Yardley had to be a possibility, if Mrs Doran was right and he had been 'hanging around' the tent instead of pursuing job opportunities in Burford.

Poison was traditionally a 'woman's weapon' – but would a woman bake a cake for a competition and then put poison on it? Hardly likely, since tests would immediately reveal her guilt. But a decoration – that was different. What if it had originally been on one of the other cakes? It could have been switched around by anyone, hoping to lay the blame elsewhere. Or it could have been brought in and substituted. Or even added to others already there. She looked over at the long table. The six cakes sat there, apparently innocent and, oddly enough, still appetizing. In previous years the competition cakes had been auctioned off to benefit the Belltower Restoration Fund – and that had been the intention this year, too – but there would be no bidders, now.

Mrs Doran smiled at young Mrs Yardley. 'Wouldn't be the first time your husband's come back when you didn't expect him, would it?' Her tone was very unpleasant. 'Maybe he's keeping an eye on you.'

'What do you mean by that?' Mrs Yardley demanded, her cheeks flaming.

Mrs Doran just smiled – and it was not a pleasant smile.

'That was unkind,' said Mrs Feather to Mrs Doran in a reproachful tone, as Mrs Yardley began to sniffle.

'I'm not feeling particularly kind at the moment,' Mrs Doran snapped.

'I'm not surprised,' said Mrs Clancy. 'I hear your husband was blackballed when he tried to join the Country Club. Wonder who did that?'

Mrs Doran stiffened. 'That's not true!' she said, but her voice betrayed her.

Miss Pinkney spoke up, her small voice carrying a waspish sting. 'Some people never learn.'

Mrs Doran's lips drew back in a snarl. 'And some people learn just in time. Too bad Henry Phipps happened to mention your father's debts to that chinless wonder you had on the string. That will teach your father to allow your "admirers" to visit the Black Lion.'

Miss Pinkney went scarlet. 'Geoffrey didn't care that we were poor, it was nothing to do with that. I decided I didn't want to get married. In fact, I *sent* Geoffrey away, if you must know!' she shrilled.

'And now somebody has sent Henry Phipps away – for good,' Mrs Venables said, and laughed – or tried to.

'If he'd gone away a long time ago, it would have been better,' said Mrs Clancy wryly.

'There's altogether too much said at the Black Lion,' Mrs

Yardley said darkly.

'And too much heard,' Mrs Venables agreed.

Mrs Feather drew a long breath and let it out. 'I wish you'd all stop this,' she said, rubbing her forehead. 'Has Dr Padgett gone? I have such a headache.' She did look unwell – her face was pale. 'I haven't been sleeping well, lately.'

'Guilty conscience?' asked Mrs Clancy unpleasantly.

'Bad dreams?' Mrs Venables suggested.

'No – it was the telephone. It rang around four o'clock and woke us up. Marcus said it was some idiot wanting the Water Company.'

'There's a burst main at Nether Hassett,' Mrs Clancy said knowledgeably. 'They wanted my George up there, yesterday. He was gone *all* day, and come back late for supper.'

'Hmmphh,' said Mrs Venables. 'Your precious George can't have done much good if the main burst *again*.'

'Perhaps that's why *our* water went off this morning,' Peggy mused.

'Well, they never called him back, and lucky for them,' Mrs Clancy said. 'If it was four in the morning, he'd have told them what to do with their water main.'

'It's usually our number they ring,' Miss Pinkney said. 'Our number's only one digit different from the Water Company's. Father's complained again and again.'

'Well, all I know is, I couldn't get back to sleep,' said Mrs Feather wearily. 'I never can, once I'm woken. My mind just goes on and on. . . ' She looked bleak at the recollection of those dark hours.

'Well, *my* conscious is clear,' Miss Pinkney said archly. 'I sleep like a baby.'

'You surprise me,' said Mrs Venables. 'Considering the Council is planning to close down the Library because you can't keep track of things properly.'

'No doubt *you* take sleeping pills,' said Mrs Clancy. 'Your husband has so *many* potions and mixtures on his shelves.'

'Oh, yes – wasn't there something about a wrong prescription last year?' Mrs Yardley asked. 'Didn't he *poison* someone?'

'How dare you!' said Mrs Venables, going white.

'I think you're all disgusting,' Mrs Doran sniffed. 'And poor Mrs Phipps, with her husband lying there. . .'

Mrs Phipps stirred. 'I don't particularly need your sympathy, Hazel Doran,' she said. She looked at each of the women in turn. 'Or anyone else's.'

'I don't know what you mean,' Mrs Doran said stiffly.

'She means you're all hypocrites,' said Shirley Yardley in an accusing tone. Her eyes filled with tears – whether of shame, frustration, or grief it was difficult to tell. 'You *all* had good reason for wanting Henry Phipps dead.'

'So did your husband,' hissed Mrs Doran.

'So did Henry's wife,' snapped Mrs Venables, stung by Mrs Phipps's collective rejection of their doubtful sympathy.

'I don't deny it,' Mrs Phipps agreed. 'I'm glad he's gone. I'm just waiting to see who I have to thank for it.' She looked around the tent, her pale eyes filled with simple curiosity, and then looked back at Peggy. 'Who do you think I should thank, Mrs Mitchell?'

Peggy shook her head, unable to speak. Suspecting was one thing – accusing was quite another. The heat in the tent, the pinched faces and the angry voices were all becoming unbearable. She couldn't face them a minute longer. Especially not one of them.

She stood up, abruptly. 'If the water is back on, I'll get Peony to make some tea or some nice fresh lemonade. I think we all need cooling down,' she said, and left them to their bitter devices.

'What is it, Peggy?' asked David. Something in her face, in her eyes, in the clenched line of her jaw, had made him hurry out of the tent after her.

'I think I know who did it,' she said miserably.

'Then you must say,' David told her.

'Not until I'm certain,' she said, and went slowly toward the vicarage – and the telephone.

He was still in the Variety Tent, sitting on one of the rickety chairs. Peggy sat down beside him. 'I'm afraid it's going to have to come out, Colonel Feather,' she said gently. 'They'll soon find the evidence they need, once they know where to look.'

He fixed her with a bloodshot eye. 'Evidence?'

'That you killed Henry Phipps.'

For a moment he glared at her, opened his mouth to deny everything, and then slumped in the chair, which creaked in protest. 'Man of action,' he said. 'Always was. See an opportunity, seize it. That's how you win wars.'

And lose battles, Peggy thought. She waited, then spoke softly. 'Was it your daughter, Imogen, who made that trunk call from Scotland this morning?'

He sighed, and shook his head. 'No. It was my sister. Imogen is dead. And the baby, too. It happened very quickly, she said. Haemorrhage, complications. . . .' His bleary eyes filled with tears but he tilted his head back and glared at the top of the tent. 'I couldn't find the words to tell Dorothy, so I said it was a wrong number. Was going to tell her this morning, but when I came downstairs and saw her packing up that cake – when I remembered *he* was going to be there, that I'd have to see his smug damned face, hear that ghastly loud laugh of his. . . I couldn't stand it. I saw the cherry and realized an opportunity was at hand. Had just the stuff in the shed. Should have got rid of it years ago, but hadn't. Fate, perhaps? No? Well, have it your own way. While the wife was getting dressed I took another cherry from the packet and prepared the thing. I planned to switch them when we got here – just sleight of hand, you know. Work of a moment.' He riffled the deck of cards he still held, then faced her. 'I gave him an even chance, of course.'

'An even chance?' Peggy asked, in some surprise.

'Absolutely.' The Colonel apparently had his own rules about such things. 'I put the poisoned cherry there, I admit that. If he *hadn't* eaten it, I would have bought the cake at the auction and got rid of it. But he did eat it, and I thought he would. His own greed killed him, you see. Took what didn't belong to him, as usual. You could say he killed himself, really.'

'I don't think that would hold up in court,' said Peggy softly. Or in Heaven, she thought.

'No?' The Colonel shrugged. 'Well, I shall get a good lawyer. We'll have a go.' He glanced at her. There was no guilt in his eyes – only grim satisfaction. 'How did you know?'

Peggy took no pleasure in the telling. 'I checked with the Exchange about your early morning caller and they said it wasn't local, but a connection from Edinburgh. You hadn't told your wife about it, so I thought it was probably bad news, and that it might have upset you enough to – well, to do something. You see, whoever put that poisoned cherry on the cake must have got sugar on his hands, but couldn't lick them because of the poison, and couldn't wash them because there was no water available. Wiping them might have been enough for most people – but not for somebody who was trying to do card tricks.'

The Colonel looked down. 'Ah, ' he said. 'Sticky fingers.' He smiled at her in wry relief. 'Thank you, my dear. For a while there I thought I was losing my touch.'

Paula Gosling is an American who has lived in England since 1964, and has been described in the *Observer* as 'the deadliest import since they found a black mamba in a crate of oranges at Covent Garden'.

WEDNESDAY MATINÉE

CELIA DALE

The Regent Theatre stood halfway down Shaftesbury Avenue towards the Piccadilly end, convenient for the Trocadero or the Criterion for those who like their after-theatre supper served amid gilt and chandeliers rather than in the garlicky hinterland of Soho. It was a handsome building, much embellished by scrollwork picked out in cream, and topped by a tower something between a lighthouse and a campanile on which was displayed in enormous, twinkling light bulbs.

CISSY SALT AND FREDDY PEPPER
in
RING FOR ROBSON
The Cheeriest Show in Town
with
Marion Conroy   Bunty Baird
Gilbert Forbes   Jack Walker

Beneath this an equally twinkling canopy overhung a pavement inlaid with tiles of lilies and acanthus leaves leading through swing-doors to a foyer rich in crimson carpet, mahogany, plump banquettes, frames of photographs of the cast in this or other productions, a Box Office within whose highly carved confines the Box Office manager or his assistant lurked like priests in the confessional receiving through the pinched grill the whispered wishes of communicants. In the evenings they wore dinner jackets.

As did the House Manager who roamed throughout performances in the foyer or the staircases, the bars of Stalls, Dress Circle and Upper Circle, keeping an eye on programme girls (most of them certainly mature) who, in their black dresses and little aprons, ushered, sold programmes and in the intervals brought trays of tea and biscuits (coffee in the evenings), while in the orchestra pit the band (tuxedoed, although who knew whether their trousers matched) played pleasing music. The crimson curtain, weighted with gilded fringe and tassels, footlights glowing at its hem, promised delights.

Backstage, however, things were different. Round a side street, down an alley strewn with the detritus from Berwick Street fruit market, a scuffed swing-door gave entrance to stone stairs and passages like those of a tenement building. Straight ahead big doors led on to the wings and stage itself; up one flight the star dressing-rooms 1 and 2. Above again numbers 3 and 4 – and the lavatory for all; above again, numbers 5 and 6, and a sort of cupboard where lurked the two understudies and Johnny, the callboy/Assistant Stage Manager. The air was close, soured through with the smell of size, canvas and stewed tea, and, around the entrance cubbyhole of Bert, the stagedoor-keeper, Goldflake cigarettes and the chancey whiff of Flossie, his aged spaniel.

It was a hot August afternoon, a Wednesday matinee.

The smell of rotten oranges from the alley was strong as the swing-doors were pushed open. Bert looked up from his Star.

'Afternoon, Master Conroy.'

'Good afternoon, Mr Bassett.' He was a stout, rather handsome boy of thirteen, grey flannelled, pulling off a school cap.

'Come to see your mum, 'ave you? Act Three's just gone up, so she'll be a while, but Miss Baird's not on yet. Be sure and tap the door, else you'll catch 'er in 'er desserbil. She'd like that, I daresay, but yer mum wouldn't, and can't say as I blame 'er.' He inhaled sourly and broke into a glutinous cough.

'Thanks, Mr Bassett.'

Conroy folded his cap into his pocket and started up the stairs, then pressed against the wall as footsteps clattered down and round the turn came Freddy Pepper himself, big ears and horn-rims that were his trademark, in tennis togs above which his ruddy make-up glowed. He did not acknowledge Conroy, but hurried on down with that glazed look of someone already encased in their next entrance. He had come not from his own No. 2 dressing-room but from the floor above. The door of No. 1, where his wife Cissy Salt dressed, was ajar.

Conroy continued up to the next landing. The door of No. 4 was open, the room empty; No. 3, the room his mother shared with Bunty Baird, was shut, and as he came to it he heard a sharp crack, a yelp and Bunty's voice 'Oh shog off, you silly old fool, beat it!' As he hesitated the door opened and Gilbert Forbes came out in a rush, his make-up smudged on one side of his face, his toupee not quite straight. His tall frame, in its butler's black and white, seemed to vibrate. He glared at Conroy without seeing him and charged back into No. 4, slamming the door.

Bunty, in a rather grubby pink kimono, turned from the mirror where she was padding her face with a caked flat powderpuff. 'Conroy, angel! How lovely to see you!' She twined her arms round him and kissed his cheek. She smelled warm and sweet, like a marshmallow. 'Mummy's on stage, you're just in time to button me up.'

He had known his mother would be on stage and her dresser Jessie in the wings waiting to help her with her quick change, and Bunty alone; but he had not bargained for her not being dressed. He stood, scarlet-cheeked, as she moved towards the screen, throwing off the kimono as she went. She wore peach satin camiknickers and no stockings – it was breath-taking.

From half behind the screen she called, 'Tell me the gossip, darling. How's school?'

'It's the holidays.'

'Of course it is! Silly me!' Garments fluttered over her head and she emerged more or less inside a pleated tennis dress, sailor-collared but daringly short. 'Be a pet and do me up, sweetie. I'm on in five minutes, that old ass slowed me down.'

It was difficult to fasten the buttons down her back as she bent and moved about in front of the mirror, powdering, moistening, curling. Besides, his hands were trembling. She turned, all flaxen and pink and white, haloed by the naked light bulbs round the mirror. She was only a little taller than he.

'What a useful boy you are, darling,' she said softly, 'Good at all sorts of things.' He was dumb as an ox. 'Find me my shoes, there's a pet.'

Dazedly he saw them by the sagging chaise-longue. As he bent to get them she stretched out her leg beside him, smooth and wet-white bare, a shabby pink mule dangling from the toes.

'Put them on for me, Conroy,' she said, leaning back on both hands against the dressing-table.

On his knees he took off the slipper, slid the white high-heeled sandal on to her foot. Her toenails were varnished pink. He felt as though he were going under dentist's gas. . .

The door banged open.

'Why, whatever are you doing, Master Conroy?' Jessie, his mother's dresser, sidled in, a dress and jacket over her arm. He jumped up, scarlet.

Jessie was small and hunched, like a white-haired mouse, hardly visible beneath the garments she carried. She gave Bunty a very sharp look. 'You'll miss your entrance, miss.'

'Keep your hair on, Jess.' Coolly Bunty turned to give a final look in the mirror; then put her fingers to her lips and, as she passed Conroy, pressed them against his. 'You were marvellous, sweetie,' she murmured and was gone.

Marion Conroy was on stage until the final curtain calls and came up the stairs with the rest of the cast afterwards, observing as she did that Pepper went into his No. 2 and shut the door but that Cissy opened it and went in after him, the wide-eyed babyish stare that was the caricaturists' joy quite absent. She entered her own No. 3 to find her son reading a copy of *Playgoer* and Jessie creeping about hanging up costumes. Strictly speaking, Jessie's services were shared with Bunty, but Bunty had no quick changes and was also a slut – her dressing-shelf was a clutter of blunted sticks of grease-paint, dirty powderpuffs, a mangey rouge-stained rabbits-foot, caked make-up towels, and powder over everything.

Besides, Jessie had been with Marion for years, following her from production to production, doing sewing and little chores in between times when Marion was 'resting'. Marion, a ripely handsome woman in her mid-thirties, who had played a season at Stratford-on-Avon and toured as Mrs Tanqueray, was extremely displeased at having to share Jessie, let alone a dressing-room, and particularly with a chit like Bunty; but the Regent was small and naturally the two Star dressing-rooms, 1 and 2, went to Salt and Pepper, that perennial and professionally married pair of comedy-thriller performers whose productions never ran for less than a year – a godsend in a profession where rehearse for three weeks, open and close in two was not unusual.

So Marion, back on the boards after the death of her boring solicitor husband some years ago, compressed her lips and maintained as well as possible the stately calm that so well suited her part as the Balkan Countess whose family jewels were stolen in this season's Salt and Pepper offering (Robson the butler was the master crook, in league with the Countess's French maid). She greeted her son with a nod and relief that Bunty had lagged behind on the stairs, giggling with some others.

'Not a good audience,' she declared from behind the screen as Jessie helped her out of her dress, 'Typical matinee. And some silly woman crashed her tray to the floor just as I made my second entrance – disgraceful!' She emerged in a dressing-gown and sat down to remove her make-up. 'Are you hungry, Conroy? I don't feel I can face more than a snack in this heat. . . '

The door flew open and Bunty danced in. 'Conroy, my pet,

are you still here?'

His mother's voice was cold from behind the make-up towel. 'We shall be going out, Bunty, never fear.'

'Oh I don't care, darling, I shan't be here. I'm going up to Jack's for a bite and a bubbly between shows. It's too much of a fag to go out.' She bounced to the mirror to powder and tweak for a moment, catching Conroy's eye and giving him a wink. Then she undid her dress (she could manage it quite well by herself, it seemed) and let it fall, picking up the kimono from the couch and wrapping it casually around her. 'So don't mind me,' she said sweetly, patted Conroy's cheek as she passed, and was gone.

Marion and her son had an agreeable high tea of poached eggs on toast, tea and cakes, went for a little walk along Old Compton Street and bought some gorgonzola and a pound of cherries before returning to the theatre for the evening show; he was allowed to watch the first act from the wings before making his way back to Putney on his own. There was plenty of time before Curtain Up at 8 o'clock, half the cast had gone out and backstage had a drowsy air about it. Even Bert was not in his cubbyhole, but Flossie was and gave a languid thump of her tail. There were no new notices on the wall-board criss-crossed with tape for messages, and Marion allowed Conroy to push open the big doors and go out into the cavernous darkness of the wings with their slats of scenery fencing the hollow stage, its set furniture dead beneath one working light.

He loved yet feared this place. This empty stage, this empty auditorium beyond, agape like a hollow mouth, had more potency for his mother than ever he and his dry father had; its unreality was more real for her than their reality. He could not comprehend but he could feel it. The smell of canvas, dust and size pinched up his nostrils, a heady mysterious smell, sweet and sour at once. He shivered.

And then, tearing the silence, came a scream.

Dressing-room doors opened, voices questioned, feet clattered on the stone staircases. And on the stone staircase, a few steps up from Bert's cubbyhole, Flossie barking asthmatically from inside, lay Bunty Baird, head down, her pretty limbs ugly in disorder within the flimsy disarray of her kimono, one white sandal still on her foot.

Shrieks, exclamations, curses. Pepper, Cissy, Dorothy, who played the comic char, the Stage Manager Bob, his Assistant and callboy Johnny, all popped out of their various rooms like gophers from their burrows to gather and shout. 'My God!', 'Christ!', 'She's knocked out,' 'Lift her up', 'Don't move her', 'What happened?' Marion pressed Conroy's face into her bosom to hide the sight.

Jack came rushing down from his room on the top floor and threw himself down beside Bunty, cradling her head. 'What happened? Oh God! Speak to me, do something someone. . . '

Freddy Pepper pushed him aside. 'Give her air, for God's sake. Let her breathe, man.'

'She's unconscious. . . '

'She's dead!' from Dorothy.

'No she's not. Move her into Props – gently, be careful. . . ' Gently they lifted the bedraggled form as Bert came lumbering down from the 3 and 4 landing, with Gilbert Forbes behind him, and behind him the trembling form of Jessie, wringing her hands. Pepper and Jack carried Bunty through the doors into the wings and on into the Property Room, a cavern of furniture and baskets of props, rich with the smell of dust and old beer. They laid her on the couch, Jack huddled at her side.

'What happened? Did she fall? Get a doctor! She'll be all right.'

But she was not all right. She had broken her neck.

They stood around her in the stuffy room, aghast. We must get a doctor.' 'Too late.' 'Are you sure?' 'Oh poor little Bunty!' 'The police. . . we must call the police. . .'

'No.' Cissy Salt, her baby face hard and cold as a coin, stood back from the couch and looked round at the trembling tearful group. 'There's nothing we can do for her now and it's House Full tonight. Police would shut the theatre and I'm not having that.'

'But Cissy. . . ' Her husband gazed at her across the body. 'You can't do that.'

'Yes I can. Rita can go on for her, and Jack's understudy can take over as the maid, Rita's part - we'll make it a footman. Half-way through the last act we'll call a doctor, and the police if you like – they won't stop the show then and the delay won't harm Bunty, poor little cow.'

'But the police. . . '

'It was an accident, we all know that. She must have caught her heel and tripped, just rotten bad luck. But I'm not refunding a whole House Full just because the police come in and close the show. It wouldn't do Bunty any good.'

There was a shocked but not altogether hostile silence.

Then Marion, still clasping Conroy to her, spoke. 'It might be as well,' she said majestically, 'if we all said where we were when it happened. Did anyone see?'

They stirred uneasily. Jack, still kneeling beside Bunty and holding her hand to his cheek, said, 'She'd just left. . . ' He was crying. 'We'd been in my room – Ronny'd gone out, he always does between shows. We were – fooling about. I'd got sand-wiches and some gin. We – we knew Ronny'd be back soon, it was near the half-hour, so we tidied up and I kissed her and – gave her a hug. . .' He gave a sob, 'and she went rattling down the stairs to her room the way she always did and then I heard that awful sort of slither and Bunty's scream. . . '

'And where was Gilbert?'

Gilbert Forbes, still in his butler's costume but without the tail coat and his toupee, was standing at the back of the group, his bald head pallid above his painted face. 'I was in my dressing-room.' His voice croaked. 'I knew she'd gone up to Jack's – she always does now if he's alone, makes no secret of it. I'd shut my door, I was reading. I simply heard the scream and went out and looked down – Bert can tell you.'

They all looked at Bert, standing behind Forbes in his old tweed jacket, nicotine-stained moustache drooping. 'Me? I daresay that's right. I was so shook up by the screeching I couldn't rightly say what happened.'

'Why were you up there?' Marion asked sternly. 'When Conroy and I came in you were not at your post.'

'Answered a call of nature, didn't I,' he answered sourly. 'We're not all bleeding camels. I 'as to use the bog on the landing, don't I? I never saw nothing of that Miss Baird, only Mr Forbes standing there like he says, and Jessie right beside him.'

'Yes, yes, Jessie was there,' Forbes said eagerly.

Where was Jessie?

She was sitting crying on the bottom step of the staircase outside Bert's cubbyhole with Johnny, the ASM and callboy, who had his arm round her shoulders. He looked up as Marion, Conroy still clutched to her side, came out through the doors from the stage, some of the others trailing behind her.

'I've only just got in,' he said. 'What a bloody ghastly thing.'

'She caught her heel, she caught her heel,' wailed Jessie.

'Of course.' Cissy was with them now. 'Those ridiculous heels. And flying up and down the stairs full of gin and nooky – no wonder she tripped and crashed all the way down.' Her blue eyes were cold as slate as she turned to her husband. 'It's a pity you didn't run into her, Freddy, on your way to the Gents – I presume you were on your way to the Gents. You might have caught her.'

'And you might have heard her, darling.' Freddy Pepper's voice was sharp. 'I noticed your door was half open – I *presume* you were inside?'

'Cissy, Freddy – if I might make so bold?' Marion stepped forward, statuesque with Conroy held to her side like Medea in her big scene. 'Curtain up is in just over half an hour. We're agreed, I think, that, ghastly though it is, there's nothing we can do for that poor girl at the moment, and that Rita can go on for her. And Dicky can take over as a footman – he may need a few lines changed here and there.' She looked round calmly. 'It will be a lovely surprise for them both when they come in, Rita's chance at last. Then as soon as the last act goes up Bobby will ring for a doctor and say that Bunty's had an accident. And if the doctor wants the police the performance will be over by then and the house cleared before they can possibly get here.' She paused and mostly everyone nodded. 'And all we shall have to do is to stick together and confess that this dreadful accident did happen a little bit earlier and we all felt devastated but there was a full house and we all felt we owed it to the public that the show should go on. Yes?'

There was a grudging, muted agreement, Cissy and Freddy too preoccupied with their personal tensions to dispute Marion's dominance.

'Now,' said Marion, 'some of us must go back to that poor girl and put her decently in order. And get poor Jack away and back to his dressing-room and fit to go on. Thank God for a fixed set and no stagehands, and the electricians aren't in yet. And Conroy dearest, go up to Mummy's room and wait there till I come, and try to pretend that all the dreadful things that have happened are just part of the play.'

She gave him a little push and, in a daze, he followed Dorothy and one or two of the others up the stairs to the room that had been and still seemed to be Bunty's.

He hardly comprehended what had been happening; the reality and unreality merged together like a nightmare or a melodrama. Bunty's death – lively, stupefyingly alluring Bunty who had stretched out her bare leg to him and put her fingertips on his lips – annulled by a group of people because a performance must go on? He was used to contrasts: Mother taking morning tea in bed with an old shawl round her shoulders and her hair pinned up under a boudoir cap, her face sticky with face cream as he kissed her good bye before school; and Mother in full evening dress decked out in false pearls, her eyelashes beaded with mascara, dominating the stage in any play's last act. . . But this – the group decision to put make-believe before reality – he could not take it in. Nor enter that dressing-room.

He sat down on the top step of the landing outside numbers 3 and 4. The concrete was cold to his bottom, and he stared at the stairs down which Bunty had fallen, his throat and his face and his eyes seeming to swell up in a great hot surge of grief. And there, on the third step, upside down in the corner by the wall, was Bunty's other sandal – dainty lacy white straps with the arched instep and the two-inch heel hanging half off.

He focused, stared, reached out and picked it up. It was light as filigree in his hand, the heel held to the shoe only by one fragment of cleanly cut leather. He held it in his hands and began to blub.

'Oh master Conroy, don't! Don't upset yourself, lovie, don't take on so!' He was aware of a shuffle of shoes, thick stockings, a dark skirt, a slightly stale warm odour. Jessie had come out of No. 3 and now sat stiffly down on the step beside him. She put out her hand to take his but at the sight of the sandal recoiled. 'Oh master Conroy, she wasn't worth it! She wasn't a nice girl at all, truly she wasn't. She was after everything in trousers, young or old, she'd have had Mr Pepper in the end, you mark my words, and then what'd happen to the Company? And as to how she behaved to your mother you'd never believe it – cigarettes, mess, gin in the teacups, and never a please or thank-you. Oh master Conroy, don't upset yourself, dear!'

He sobbed and held the shoe.

'Oh master Conroy, don't cry – not a big boy like you. You was big enough for her, I could see, but you're only a baby still really.' Jessie was crying now too, the tears swelling slowly out above the bags and pouches of her face and running into the wrinkles. 'The rudeness and impudence you wouldn't believe, to me and to your mother. She'd even got Bert's back up proper, over his betting and poor old Floss. And there was poor Mr Forbes gaga as a gooseberry over her, never mind she was laughing at him all the time. And Mr Walker behind locked doors between every matinee and evening. But when it come to you, master Conroy, and you hardly out of short trousers. . . '

She looked down at the sandal and with one worn finger gently moved the heel to and fro on its fragile shred of skin. Her tears were easing and she gave a long gurgling sniff, reaching, it seemed, deep into her empty body.

'All the same,' she said, 'all I meant was for her to break a leg.'

Celia Dale's first novel was published in 1943 and she has since written ten others. In 1986 she won the Crime Writers' Association/Veuve Clicquot Short Story Award. Many of her short stories have been heard on radio and adapted for television.

SPASMO
LIZA CODY

It was Nanny who told me the rotten news. Nanny and rotten news seem to go together if you ask me.

'Magnus's mother has been to see your mother,' she said. 'Poor Magnus has chicken-pox, so you can unpack that suitcase, Andrew. Your trip to Cowes is off.'

She isn't my Nanny. She's Annabel's. She has a black hairy mole on her chin, and I hate her.

'It's very bad luck,' Nanny went on. 'But don't look at me like that. And don't throw your suitcase on the floor. . . now you'll have to pick everything up.'

She didn't understand.

'Temper!' she said. 'If you carry on like that, Andrew, I'll have to tell your father.'

Nobody understood.

I would have to have my tenth birthday party in the rumpus-room with the girls. The summer holiday was ruined. No yacht. No Cowes. No Magnus. It was absolutely and completely spasmo.

Nobody cared.

It was all right for Annabel – she's only six, and as long as she can feed sugar to the milkman's horse every morning she's happy. Little sisters are spasmo. So are big ones: Claire was going to the south of France. *Her* friends didn't go and get chicken-pox. They were all too old for that, and too superior.

Magnus, I thought, was a spasmo, spotty piece of ele-phant dung. If he was ill, bad luck, but why did he have to ruin everything for me?

'Don't kick the rug,' my mother said. 'It's Persian. Don't be so selfish, Andrew. Think of poor Magnus.'

Was Magnus thinking of me? Was Magnus's mother? If she chose to stay in London to nurse spotty Magnus instead of taking me sailing she was worse than everyone.

'It's spasmo,' I said. I must have said that several times already because Ma fixed me with a glittering stare and exclaimed, 'If you say that word once more, Andrew, just once more, I'll send you to the Science Museum again . . . with Annabel.'

I should have known better. Ma was always at her most unreasonable on do-days, and I must have known it was a do-day because not only did we have extra help in the house, but Nanny had been co-opted into the kitchen to make pastry.

'She has cold hands,' Ma explained. 'That's why her pastry is better than anyone else's.'

You didn't have to tell Claire, Annabel or me about Nanny's cold hands; we had suffered from them most of our lives, but what that had to do with pastry was what Father described as a 'female mystery'. He seemed to know a lot about female mysteries and I wanted him to explain. But he never had the time. We didn't see a lot of Father that year because he was in the Government.

'He wanted something in Dominions,' I heard Ma tell one of her friends. 'And he's not the most cultural man, but I expect he'll accept all the same.'

Of course he did: it made him more important. But, although it was something to tell the others at school, secretly I thought he was important enough already. All my life I have suffered because of Father being important.

'Don't disturb your father, Andrew,' Nanny would say, 'he's an important man.'

'Spasmo,' I said.

'And don't say that word. It's not the sort of thing the son of an important man should say.'

'Spasmo, spasmo, spasmo,' I said, under my breath.

'Go to your room!' ordered Ma. She was counting silver ice buckets for the do. What did she need ice buckets for? All she had to do was look at the champagne the way she looked at me and you'd be able to skate on it.

'It's your own silly fault,' Claire said. 'You think people have nothing better to do than listen to you.'

I might have guessed I'd get no sympathy from Claire. She's always sucking up to Ma.

'What's this one for, anyway?' I asked. 'We had a do only last week.'

'Don't call it a do,' Claire said. 'It's a reception.'

'What for?'

'Don't you listen to anything? It's for the Berlin Dance Company.' Claire was excited. I could tell because she was nibbling her fingernails and then trying not to. Now that she was sixteen she had to have long fingernails. You wouldn't think Claire could get any sillier, but she did.

'The exquisite Kezia Lehmann!' Claire said, and sat on her hands. 'They say she's the youngest prima ballerina ever to dance at the Coliseum.'

That was not really Kezia's name. It's just that I could never remember it afterwards, and anyway everyone seemed to pronounce it differently. At the time I was not even listening properly.

'Ooh, a belly dancer,' I said to annoy Claire.

'Everyone says she's exquisite,' Claire said dreamily. She wasn't listening either.

'Spasmo,' I said. Magnus could have made one of his rude jokes which would really have got Claire going. That might have been fun. But Magnus had boring chicken-pox and Claire ignored me.

'A bus-load of boring belly dancers,' I said, and pranced around the room. 'Another boring foreigner. I bet she's a Jew.'

'You're not supposed to say that,' Claire said primly. And she added something po-faced about toleration and talent.

It was the dullest reception ever. It's always the same. You stand by the window with a pathetic glass of lemonade while all Father's secretaries drink champagne and try to make conversation with hoards of people who don't know enough to speak English. Ma and Father shake hands with everyone and look as if they are having a wonderful time. Claire, Annabel and I are supposed to help distribute the food, and let me tell you, at some of these do's it's like feeding a pack of hounds. These foreigners are so greedy there's never anything left over for supper. I don't know why Ma and Father make us come.

I considered slipping away to chew a mouthful of toothpowder. I could work up a good froth and then make my entrance doing an impression of a rabid dog. That might wake the foreigners up.

Actually I quite like the Germans. Their soldiers really look like soldiers. I'd like to have a pair of boots like a German officer. Just think, if Magnus and I went back to school in boots instead of those horrible lace-up shoes, the big boys would have to watch out. Even Father says the Germans are not a bad lot really.

Claire appeared at my shoulder. 'That's her,' she said, tearing at a hangnail.

'Who?'

'Kezia.'

'She doesn't look very exquisite to me,' I said. She was no taller than I was and she wore a grey thing that looked like a schoolgirl's dress.

'Everyone says her extensions are spectacular,' Claire informed me. She pointed her right toe. Claire was wearing stockings instead of socks that summer, and her legs looked funny.

'She hasn't got any extensions as far as I can see,' I said. In the grey dress Kezia looked as flat-chested as Annabel.

'Not only are you ignorant,' Claire said icily, 'but you are also a filthy-minded little toad.' She went away.

I looked around, and it seemed that everyone was looking at Kezia. A lot of them were pretending not to, but somehow she was the centre of an invisible circle. She wasn't saying anything, but Ma smiled at her as if she had done something very clever. It was so unfair. How could Ma look like that at someone who couldn't even speak English? And why was a country like Germany interested in anything as spasmo as ballet?

'You are not interested in the ballet, I think?' someone said, and I turned around. He was tall, and he looked as if he might be good at something decent like cricket. Except he was a German and they don't play cricket.

I was about to say ballet was spasmo, but I stopped myself.

'Girls are interested in ballet,' I said instead. I did not want any stranger thinking I could be keen on anything my sister was stupid enough to find interesting.

'Ah, the manly sports,' he said, and smiled. He was quite friendly really – for a foreigner. And he was the only one not swooning over Kezia Lehmann.

'You should come to my country, perhaps. *Our* young men are better entertained.'

'Sailing?' I asked. I am big for my age and I didn't mind if he thought I was a young man. It was about time. He wouldn't make me have my birthday party in the rumpus-room with the girls.

'Of course, sailing,' he said. 'And much, much more.'

'Could I have a pair of boots?' I asked. He was being much more friendly than Father who hadn't spoken a word to me all evening.

While we watched, Annabel wormed her way into the circle around Kezia with a plate of smoked salmon sandwiches.

I was thinking how funny it would be if I had switched the smoked salmon for ham. Everyone knows that if Hebrews see ham they fall writhing to the floor and all their teeth drop out.

I was going to tell my joke to the nice German but he had

started talking to someone else.

Kezia refused a sandwich but she smiled at Annabel, and – I could hardly believe it – Annabel curtsied. All the grown-ups smiled in that boring way they have when little girls are being exceptionally sick-making. Annabel, taking advantage as usual, wanted to know how to curtsy properly, and Kezia showed her. All the grown-ups clapped their hands. Claire pushed forward. It was absolutely disgusting and shameful to see what fools my family made of themselves in public.

Just then one of Father's secretaries, who was standing right behind me, said, 'Such purity of line, do you notice, even when she's only showing that sweet child how to curtsy.'

She thought Annabel was a sweet child! That's how much she knew.

'They say she is on borrowed time,' someone else said.

'They say her family is being held hostage to her good behaviour. Utterly tragic.'

That was the limit – what did she know about tragic? 'They say she goes like a stoat too,' I said loudly. That is what Magnus says about girls he doesn't like and it's very funny. But I never expected the reaction it got coming from me.

Everyone stopped talking. Father spun round, took three steps towards me and smacked me on the ear. I was stunned. You shouldn't hit children on the head: Father says so himself. But he did it, right in front of a roomful of people. Tears filled my eyes. He didn't even notice. He grabbed my elbow and dragged me to the door.

'What for?' I cried. 'What have I done? I like stoats.'

Everyone was watching. 'Out,' Father said in his quietest voice. 'You've disgraced yourself once too often, Andrew. And this time you've disgraced us too.'

I caught sight of Claire, bright red in the face, looking as if she were about to burst into tears. What did she have to cry about, I thought as I stumbled through the door. Trust Claire to act as if she were the centre of attention. Although, at that moment, I could have done with a little less myself.

'What have I done?' I repeated. 'I only said. . . '

'I know exactly what you said,' Father almost whispered, 'and unfortunately so does everyone else. Go straight to your room.'

'But what am I going to do? It's spasmo in my room all by myself.'

Father looked as if he might hit me again. He said, 'A public insult deserves a public apology. You can think about that, all by yourself in your room. Because, believe me, Andrew, there *will* be an apology.' He just turned his back and walked away, leaving me in the hall.

'I hate you,' I shouted. 'You're a bully. You shouldn't hit boys.' The back of his neck went pink but he didn't come back.

I went upstairs, but I didn't go to my room. I sat on the gallery floor and watched through the balusters. When those silly women went to the downstairs powder room, I saw them go. I know what they do in there. They can't fool me with that 'powdering my nose' act. Even that spasmo Kezia has to have a wee. I thought about it and it made me feel a bit better. I thought about writing a letter to *The Times* and telling them about an important man who beat up his children. That made me feel good too. Magnus would have to take notice. His mother might take me away to live with her. She's a lot nicer than my mother because she doesn't have any stupid daughters to distract her. Magnus's mother understands me. It's so unfair. Magnus has a far better time than I do. It's probably because his father isn't important. When Magnus wants something he gets it, and his parents listen to him when he talks.

When I grow up, I thought, I'm going to join the Socialist Party and become a spy. I could make a floor plan of Father's study, and I'm good at listening behind doors. I bet if I told those Germans downstairs what I knew about Father's job they'd sit up and pay attention. You don't think all those men downstairs are what they say they are, do you? Half of them are spies and secret policemen. Everyone knows that. I could give them the key to Father's safe and they'd be so grateful they'd have a pair of boots made specially for me.

German secret policemen are funny. They wear black suits with baggy knees and look like wrestlers. I bet they're very strong. I'd like to see Father go a round or two with one of them. That'd teach him something. Bullies are always cowards.

I was beginning to feel quite happy again. I screwed my wet handkerchief into a ball. I was about to throw it at one of the maids as she passed beneath me with a tray of glasses, but just then Claire came out of the reception room.

She was saying, 'You can come up to my room if you like. I've got a lovely mirror. It's much better than downstairs.'

Annabel appeared too, tugging that awful Kezia by the hand. 'See my room too!' she squealed. 'I've got a camel. A big camel. It's the biggest one you ever saw.' And all three of them made for the stairs. That made me move in a hurry. I scuttled backwards and hid behind the curtains. Magnus and I call girls the 'Lower Breed', along with servants and foreigners. That made Kezia a 'Lower Breed' on two counts. Apologize to her! I'd rather eat cold fat.

But a good spy is supposed to take risks, so after a while I tiptoed along the passage to Claire's door and peeped in. There were my two sisters consorting with the enemy. She was sitting on Claire's bed with Annabel beside her and Annabel's disgusting camel on her knee. She was pretending it could speak German, chattering away in gobbledegook, and making Annabel scream with laughter. What really made me sick was Claire, who was kneeling behind her, brushing her hair. Downstairs you couldn't see her hair because it was all screwed up in a knot. But now it stretched all the way down her back and Claire was making it shine like black oil. Claire said, 'I wish I had long hair. It's beautiful. I wish you could stay here for ever. I'd brush your hair every day.'

Kezia said, 'I wish too, I could stay forever.' She looked sad. Girls are always trying to make you feel sorry for them, but they can't fool me.

'It must be quite difficult for you,' Claire said, brushing, brushing, brushing the long black hair. It made me feel funny looking at that hair, and I didn't like it. So I didn't hear what Kezia said next.

But Annabel squeaked, 'Why can't you stay with us? You could have Nanny's room, next to mine.'

Well, if that meant Nanny leaving I could almost support the idea. Nanny is definitely a 'Lower Breed', but she doesn't act as if she knows it. Except Nanny would never leave. In fact I think she will live forever just to spite me.

'Is it your family?' Claire asked. What did Claire care about families? She is such a hypocrite.

'Everything depends on me,' Kezia said, and I nearly laughed out loud. Girls think they are so important.

'I must go down now,' she went on. 'I am watched, you see.'

You didn't have to tell me that. Everyone downstairs had been gawping at her. I made ready to slip away down the passage. But Claire said, 'I wish there was something I could do to help.'

A silence followed that, so I sneaked another look. Claire and Kezia were looking at each other and saying nothing. You'd have thought they were best friends or something, except that girls don't have proper friends the way boys do. And besides, they had only just met. But Claire is like that: one minute she knows nothing about a subject like ballet, and the next she's a world expert. You should have heard her when she got that craze for Vegetarianism and Bernard Shaw.

'I think you are sincere,' Kezia said next, and I had to stuff my handkerchief in my mouth. Anyone who thinks Claire is sincere must have a brain smaller than a mouse dropping.

'There is something you can do,' she said. 'It is a small thing, and for you there is no risk.'

'What is it?' Claire asked, eyes wide.

'I have written a letter,' Kezia replied in a whisper. 'There are friends of my family who are refugees in America. Perhaps they can help us. I cannot send this letter because I am always watched and I must never be a disloyal German.'

That finished me off. The girl must have cracked. 'Disloyal to letter boxes,' I said to myself and went down the passage where I could laugh without being heard.

If there's anything that is totally spasmo it's girls.

From my place on the gallery I could keep a watch on Claire's door and on what was happening in the hall below. People were beginning to leave. Not the foreigners, though. They always stay till there's nothing left to eat or drink.

Father came out. He was saying goodbye to a wrinkled old man, all smiles and handshakes. But then he turned towards the stairs and his face went grim and cold. Obviously he had remembered me. I made straight for the curtains, and he went by me without noticing. He walked past Claire's room and turned the corner. He was looking for me.

When he was out of sight I pushed the curtains aside and ran downstairs. If I could stay hidden until Kezia and the rest of the foreigners had gone, I would be all right. Father's study was locked, so I dashed to the kitchen. I don't think Father has been in the kitchen in his life.

But I had forgotten about Nanny. She caught me on my way to the back door. 'Can't you see we're all busy, Andrew?' she said. 'No one has time to attend to you. You're supposed to be making your guests feel welcome.'

'They're not my guests,' I told her. 'They're all spasmo.'

'Don't you use that word,' she said. 'Now get along and behave yourself.' She forced me back into the hall, where I was bound to run into Father.

There was nothing for it: I would have to run away. I had nearly got to the front door when Father appeared at the top of the stairs.

'Andrew!' he shouted in that horrible voice which means you're supposed to do what he says instantly. But I opened the door and bumped into one of the German secret policemen who was smoking on the top step.

'Help me,' I said. 'He'll kill me if he catches me out here.'

'Kill?' the German said, like a parrot.

'Andrew!' called my father from inside.

I had a brilliant idea. 'He's going to kill me,' I said, 'and I want to change sides.'

'Sides?' The German was so stupid.

'You know, be a refugee,' I said.

'Who wishes to become a refugee?' A tall thin man came out of the shadows at the bottom of the stone steps. I ran down to meet him, but when I got there I saw that he had narrow eyes and a mean mouth and I didn't like him one bit. I tried to run past him but he grabbed the collar of my coat.

'Who wishes to become a refugee?' he repeated. His voice was mean too: mean and foreign.

'Not me!' I cried, trying to pull away. 'It wasn't me. It was Kezia. It's all her fault.'

'Kezia?' His eyes were so narrow they looked like gun-slits. He pinched my arm.

'That hurts!' I shouted.

'What have you done with Kezia Lehmann?' He pinched my arm harder – just above the elbow where it really hurts.

'Let go of me!' I yelled. 'You've got it all wrong. It's that ballet dancer. She's upstairs with my sisters. She wants to stay forever . . . she's, she's disloyal.'

'Andrew!' Father appeared above me on the top step and I wrenched myself out of the man's nasty fingers. I ran away as fast as I could along the pavement. I can run as fast as Magnus when I try. I expected Father to chase me, but when I reached the corner and looked back he was just standing there talking to the thin man. They seemed to be arguing. I'll never go back, I thought. He's not a proper father: he'd rather talk to a foreigner than come and find his own son.

I had to walk all the way to Magnus's house in the dark

because I didn't have any money. And by the time I got there I was very cold and hungry. You would have thought Magnus's mother would have been nice to me but I bet Father had already telephoned and told her lies about me, because she made me wait in the hall until Nanny came to collect me in a taxicab. Father didn't even send the car. It was humiliating.

Of course I was sent to bed without any supper. What else would you expect after the rotten day I'd had? But anyway, the foreigners wouldn't have left much. I don't see why we can't have a proper meal after a do. They go to all that trouble to feed strangers and then expect their own family to do without.

There was one good thing, though: in all the fuss I hadn't had to apologize to Kezia. I'd got out of that because by the time I got home she was gone. There was no one there but the family. Ma had gone to bed with a headache, and Father was shut up in his study making telephone calls. That was quite a relief too.

Claire wouldn't speak to me. I tried to tell her about the horrible man on the doorstep but she wouldn't listen.

The next day I overheard her telling Mother about how that spasmo ballet company had cancelled the rest of their performances and gone home. She said it was tragic because of Kezia, and the way she went on you'd have thought it was all my fault.

The way I see it – if I had saved the world from a lot of boring belly dancers I ought to be congratulated.

But nobody ever sees things the way I do. It was going to be a rotten summer. Totally spasmo.

Liza Cody won the John Creasey Award in 1980 for her first novel, *Dupe*. Since then she has gone on to write a whole series of books featuring her heroine Anna Lee.

A LITTLE LEARNING

SIMON BRETT

SIMON BRETT WRITES:

A few years back, I bought an old desk at an auction and, when I got it home, found that the drawers had not been emptied by its previous owner. He, from the papers I found there, I deduced to have been an academic of some kind. In a miscellaneous pile of documents, I came across the following essay. It seems to have been submitted as part of his doctoral thesis by an American postgraduate student named Osbert Mint. Keen that the fruits of his scholarship should be made available to as wide a readership as possible, I have made strenuous efforts to trace Mr Mint. These efforts have proved – regrettably — to be unsuccessful, and the essay is therefore printed here for the first time without its owner's permission.

THE LITERARY ANTECEDENTS OF
AGATHA CHRISTIE'S HERCULE POIROT

There is a popular misconception in academic circles that the works of Agatha Christie are simply popular *jeux d'esprit* which have no connection with the mainstream of English literature. This attitude both belittles the quality of the author's work and also underestimates the wide reading and research which went into the creation of her most famous character. Hercule Poirot did not spring fully-formed into life on Page 34 of his first adventure, *The Mysterious Affair at Styles*. His genesis was part of a much longer creative process and must be seen as the culmination of eleven centuries of English literary history.

Though Agatha Christie was properly reticent about the breadth of her reading, it is clear to the informed student of her works that they reflect a much broader and deeper literary frame of reference than is usually admitted to this particular author. My essay will trace the pattern of references to other literary sources of which the author herself was sometimes no more than subliminally aware.

Though there were clearly classical influences on Agatha Christie's work – most obviously in the collection *The Labours of Hercules* – they are not within the province of this study, particularly since the subject has been expertly covered by other scholars.[1] It is my intention to trace only the English language sources for the creation of Hercule Poirot.

The first unarguable influence on Agatha Christie's writings can be found in one of the Digressions in *Beowulf*. The killing in Hrothgar's meadhall described in the ensuing passage was clearly the origin of the many Country House murders which were to feature in Hercule Poirot's investigations. (The language of the extract has been modernized to render it accessible to the general reader. Those fluent in Anglo-Saxon may prefer to consult the original text.)

'Felled on the floor   limp lay the earl,
Blood from the blade   blackening his back,
While all the warriors,   muddled with mead-drinking,
Snored in their slumbers,   lost like the daylight
That darkness has doused.   One of their number,
A murdering bondman –   hated by Hrothgar
(Bringer of boons,   mighty meat-giver)
And by He who made heaven   (granter of goodwill,
Holy helper) –   unfairly faked sleep.
Wakeful eyes worked,   lurking behind lids,
Knowing that another,   whose sword he had stolen,
A goodman not guilty,   a worthy warrior,

Would be caught for the killing –   unless
One much wiser,   a righteous unraveller,
A reader of runes,   a conner of clues,
Might see through the slaying,   righting its wrong,
And finger the fiendish one.'

Though it might be fanciful to assert that this passage heralds the arrival of Hercule Poirot on the literary scene, it is clear that the Digression prepares the way for the development of the whodunnit form, and particularly of the private detective, 'the righteous unraveller', whose task it will be to solve the murder[2].

Granting that the *Beowulf* reference, though tantalisingly close to unambiguity, cannot be unequivocally accepted as a primary source for Hercule Poirot, the directness of the next reference brooks no denial. It is indeed remarkable – and perhaps a comment on the tunnel vision of many in academic life – that no previous scholars have looked for the Belgian detective's literary antecedents in the most obvious of sources, the Medieval Mystery Play. The very word 'Mystery' could not provide a much heavier clue, and I am bold to assert that Agatha Christie's inspiration to write mysteries featuring Hercule Poirot sprang directly from her reading of the following extract from the Harrogate *Third Shepherd's Play* in the Hull Cycle ('as it hath been divers time acted by the Guild of Chandlers and Gardners upon the Feast of Corpus Christie'):

*The three Shepherds wake to find the fourth Shepherd, Mak, lying
    still beside them.*
1 *Shep.* Now by good Saint Loy – and eke by Saint Beth,
    Why ye lie here, boy, so barren of breath?
2 *Shep.* Aye, why curl up coy, so still on the earth?
3 *Shep.* Oh, gone be our joy – for that stillness be death!
    He is dead!
1 *Shep.* Now deep is my dole, for lost is his life!
2 *Shep.* And taken his soul – how sad be this strife!

3 Shep. His purse it be stole. We must go tell his wife.

1 Shep. In his back there's a hole! It was made by a knife!
How he bled!

2 Shep. Someone foully hath played, some forsaken swine
This murder hath made – by evil design!

3 Shep. At whose door be it laid? Who's the cause of the
crime?

1 Shep. Let's see whose be the blade? By the rood, it be mine!

2 Shep. So then thou must be blamed!

1 Shep. Nay, by our lakin's grace! I slept right through the
night!

3 Shep. Then why scratched be thy face? Why these signs of a
fight?

2 Shep. Why be blood in this place? On thy sleeve it be
bright.

1 Shep. Now, by Saint Boniface! What ye think be not right!
I've been framed!
Oh, would one come, that could prove me guilt-free!

2 Shep. Soft, now what be this hum? And this light that I see?
An angel appears to them.

3 Shep. 'Tis an angel! Be dumb! Nay, drop to thy knee!

Angel Nay, look not so glum! I am come to ye three,
As the scripture foretells.

2 Shep. How his bald head doth shine! Like an egg it be
round!

2 Shep. His moustache be so fine, I am nigh to a swound!

1 Shep. Show this guilt be not mine! Let the killer be found!

Angel Aye, that villain malign I will catch and confound –
With my little grey cells[3]!'

The next unarguable literary reference which Agatha Christie
must have responded to is found in John Skelton's *Speke,
Parrot*. This poem is generally agreed to be made up of material
from different dates and there are considerable textual differ-
ences between manuscript versions. The most telling one, from

the point of view of this study, was found only as recently as 1893 in the Brestimont Collection. It is actually entitled *Speke, Porot* and contains the following significant variants of the first three stanzas:

'My name is Porot, a byrd of paradyse,
　　By nature devysed of a wonderous kynde,
Daintily dressed, so dylycate and precyse,
　　Blessed with a quyte exceptyonall mynde;
　　So men of all countreys by fortune me fynd,
And send me greate crymes to investygate:
Then Porot the culpryt wyl incrymynate.

Cravat curyously clynched, with sylver pyn,
　　Properly parfumed, to make me debonaire;
A myrrour of glasse, that I may prene therin;
　　Mustaches ful smartly with many a divers care
　　Freshly I dresse, and make blacke my haire.
Then, Speke, Porot, I pray you, full curtesly they say;
Porot hath a goodly brain, to ferrit out foul playe.

With my backe bent, my lyttel wanton eye,
　　Fancye and fresh as is the emrawde grene,
About my neck a sylke scarfe do I tye.
　　My lyttyll leggys, my spats[4] both nete and clene,
　　I am essentyale on a murdre scene;
Oh perfecte Porot, the lyttyl clever sluthe,
The clewes wyl trace, and always fynde the truthe.'

The evidence in this extract is conclusive, and it can therefore be definitively stated that Agatha Christie's source for the character of Hercule Poirot was *Speke, Parrot*.

But the author's debts to English literature do not stop with John Skelton. In her development of the character of Poirot, she was clearly influenced by her reading of Sir Philip Sidney's

Astrophel and Stella, and particularly of the following sonnet:

'CXI

Why I haue ask'd you here

O Fate, O fault, O curse, O crime of bloode!
What caitif could haue caused so foul a showe?
What coward turn'd my smiles to sighes of woe?
What joye-killer haue forced my teares to floode,
And caused Loue's flowres to perishe in the budde?
What trecherie hath brought this man so lowe,
Stabbd deeper e'en than Cupid's darts can goe,
That from his hart the beat no more shall thudde?
Were Stella's eyes the motiue for this crime,
Or stolen rubies, iuorie, pearle and gold?
I might! – nay, will! – if you should graunt me time –
The secret of this heauy case unfold.
To shewe the villain and to make all clere
The reason is why I haue ask'd you here.'

There are so many other examples of literature from the Tudor and Stuart period which influenced Agatha Christie that it would be invidious to mention any of them[5]. I will therefore move next to the Augustan Age and another undeniable source-work for the expansion of the character of Hercule Poirot, Alexander Pope's *Essay on Detection*. Almost every line of this surprisingly underrated poem is relevant to the subject in hand, but I will limit myself to the following short extract:

'As in the World's, so in Detection's laws,
All force respects the Universal Cause,
Which Logic's enemies does but confuse,
Confounding those who will not heed the clues.
For, from the first, a mighty endless chain
Links clue to crime, and crime to clue again.
One all-connecting, naught-excluding line

Draws Logic's threads within its grand design;
As when a bloodied sword, by Vulcan's skill
Framed to inflict on man the greatest ill,
Be found imbedded in some chilly corse,
Inhuman stabbed with more than human force,
The first thought is to find and clap in jail
The owner of the sword. Of more avail
Might be to check the angle of the blow
And whether struck from left or right to know.
If from the left, you wrongly would indict
The owner of a sword who used his right.
The true Detective to such ploys is wise,
Nor lets the smallest thing evade his eyes.
Though falsely led, his true mind does not stray,
But follows through its thesis all the way,
Nor does forget, but mightily esteems
That One Great Truth: 'All is not what it seems.'

That Agatha Christie's reading was wide-ranging cannot now be denied, but, even so, the source of one of Hercule Poirot's favourite ploys – almost, it could be said, his trademark, the gathering together of the suspects at the climax of one of his investigations – is surprising. It was only after extensive reading through the writings of many authors that I came across the work which undoubtedly gave the author this particular inspiration. Here, from a late volume of *The Scots Musical Museum*, is the poem which clinches my argument. Though published anonymously, it is undoubtedly the work of Robert Burns:[6]

'CA' THE BURGIES TAE THE BOGGIN CHORUS.

Ca' the burgies[a] tae the boggin[b].
Whaur the willie-paugh[c] be troggin[d].
Seel[e] a' windies[f] wi' the woggin[g],
    My dearie-oh, my dork[h].

When Macporrit[i] gang a-spoolin[j],
Wi' his ganglins[k] in his troolin[l]
He waur mair a skilfu' doolin[m]
    Wi' a' ca'in'[n] roon his ha'!
And his baughit[o] of the hintree[p]
Was sae bree[q] on ilka wintree[r]
That he niver freemed[s] his fintree[t]
    Till he spoffer'd who doon tha'[u]!
    Ca' the burgies tae the boggin, &c.'

a Suspects	b Library	c Detective
d Waiting	e Guard	f Exits
g Police Force	h Possibly a reference to Hastings?	
i Poirot?	j Investigating	k Grey cells?
l Brain	m Detective	n ?
o Analysis	p Case	q Acute
r Occasion	s Sipped	t Tisane
u Till he had told them whodunnit		

I have now supplied sufficient evidence of Agatha Christie's erudition and remarkable range of source-material to silence the most sceptical critic of my thesis. And I think I should definitely be awarded my doctorate as soon as possible.

OSBERT MINT, April 1967

NOTES:

1 Cf. especially Britt-Montes' *The Oresteia: Did Clytemnestra REALLY Do It?* (Scand. Dagblat, Vol vii, pp. 152-157, 1932) and Bent Istrom's *The Death of Aeschylus: Who Dropped the Tortoise?* (Christiana Review, March 1947, pp. 474-523).

2 It has long been a matter of regret amongst *Beowulf* scholars

that this particular Digression is not resolved and that the identity of the true murderer is never revealed. Tom St. Brien's solution (*Grendel's Mother Did It*, Gunterrheinischer Festschrift, 1924), though initially persuasive, cannot ultimately be regarded as other than conjectural.

3 Academic opinion has long been divided over the precise meaning of this line, which is seriously obscured in the original manuscript of the play. Professor Ernst Tombi of Geneva University has argued persuasively that the line should read, '*When my little goose calls*', though has unfortunately offered no convincing reason as to why. Enthusiasts of Agatha Christie will be in no doubt that the line should be printed as above.

4 There seems to be no justification for Bo Mitstern's reading of '*spots*' in this context.

5 Scholars who wish to pursue this topic further are recommended to read the seminal works of Sir T. Bemton, *Christopher Marlowe's Mean Streets* and *The Metaphysicals: Who-Donne-It?*

6 Ms N. Briotte's questioning of this attribution on the premise that 'the poem does not contain enough hatred of women to be authentic Burns' can be confidently dismissed as feminist claptrap.

APPENDIX I – THE NAME 'POIROT'
The much-bruited suggestion that Agatha Christie selected the name Poirot randomly is patently ridiculous. Apart from its assonantic association with the heavily symbolic 'parrot' (discussed more fully above in reference to Skelton's *Speke Parrot*), the name also reverberates with nuances from the French language. The 'poire' or, in English, 'pear' is an obvious subliminal

reference to the distinctive shape of the detective's bald head. That shape is again shadowed in the French word 'poirée', which means 'white beet' and conforms with the frequently-mentioned pallor of the detective's complexion.

Though 'poireau', the French word closest in sound to the name Christie chose, with its double meanings of 'leek' and 'wart', appears to have no obvious connection with the detective, the word 'poirier', meaning a 'pear-tree' offers a much more fruitful area for investigation. Its sound provided the first syllable of Poirot's name '*poir*', and for the second one need look no further than the French word 'perdr*eau*', meaning 'a young partridge'. The unusual juxtaposition of these two words can only be a subconscious association in the author's mind with the well-known carol, *The Twelve Days of Christmas*, whose repetitive chorus ends, 'And a partridge in a pear-tree.'

The truth of this conjecture would seem to be confirmed by Agatha Christie's choice of titles for the 1938 volume, *Hercule Poirot's Christmas* and the 1960 collection, *The Adventure of the Christmas Pudding and a Selection of Entrees*.

APPENDIX II – THE NAME 'HASTINGS'
The name of Poirot's occasional assistant is no less carefully chosen than that of Agatha Christie's main protagonist. His nomenclature has a very respectable literary history. Shakespeare hinted at the essence of the character in *Richard III*, Act Three Scene One, when the young Prince of Wales, with a knowledge beyond his years, cries:
    'Fie! what a slug is Hastings.'
Goldsmith, at the end of *She Stoops to Conquer* has Hastings say:
    'Come, madam, you are now driven to the very last scene of all your contrivances.'
– surely a parallel prefiguring (together with the Burns poem) of all those occasions when Christie's Hastings would be delegated to assemble the suspects for Poirot's latest denouement.

And Hastings' habit of pipe-smoking was clearly taken from Thomas Hood, who in a poem of 1839 wrote:

'Twas August – Hastings every day was filling.'

SIMON BRETT WRITES:

Though, as I mentioned, I was unable to make contact with Mr Mint, a letter accompanying his essay did make clear the unfortunate fact that its standard – or perhaps the startling originality of its thinking – did not meet with the examiners' approval. Osbert Mint was not awarded his doctorate. When last heard of – in the early Seventies – he had returned to the United States and was apparently working in a fast food restaurant.

Simon Brett's first crime novel was published the year before Agatha Christie died, though the two events are unrelated. He has seen *The Mousetrap* three times.

GOOD TIME HAD BY ALL

ROBERT BARNARD

'It was murder,' said the first housemaid firmly. 'Murder by suffocation.'

'Nonsense, Ethel,' said Cook. 'We've never had murder in this house.'

'Well, there's a first time for everything, as I'm sure you remember, Mrs Cornforth. . . There was veronal on the bedside table. She was probably so drugged she didn't struggle. As a rule it's difficult to suffocate people, even if they're sleeping.'

'What would you know?' demanded Thomas, the under-footman, jealous that it had been she who had found the body when she went into the bedroom with the morning tray of tea and biscuits.

'A great deal,' said Ethel with infuriating self-confidence. 'I wasn't with Dr Mackenzie for two years for nothing.'

'Oh, and I suppose he took you with him on his rounds, did he? Had you by his side at his post-mortems?'

Mr Eames the butler put up his hand in rebuke. This was becoming unseemly.

'Let's have no more of this squabbling. If it was murder we shall be informed in the Family's good time. I wouldn't be surprised if Ethel isn't entirely wrong about the cause of death and the poor lady did it herself.'

'What, after a night of passionate love?' asked the irrepressible Ethel.

'There's been nights of passionate love in this house that have left the lovers more depressed than ecstatic,' said Thomas, who found the neurotic sex-lives of some of his betters incomprehensible. 'Anyway, what call have you to say that Mrs Heatherington-Scott had had one?'

'I know her. She's been here before. Always insists on a room to herself with a lock on the door.'

'She'd no call to mention that,' said Mrs Cornforth. 'All the bedrooms in this house have locks.'

''Course they do. The Prince of Wales used to visit.'

'The old Prince of Wales,' said Eames pedantically. 'The last but two – King Teddy as he became. You're too young to remember, my girl.'

'But I've heard the stories! Anyway, there she was in her own room, and no call if she didn't want to to open the door to anyone, not even her husband.'

'Especially not her husband,' said Thomas.

'But the fact is, she did. And the question is, who to?'

'*If* she did,' said Cook heavily. Everything about Cook was heavy, except her hand with pastry. 'I've heard no hevidence so far that the poor lady did.'

'I did her room when she was here last year,' said Mary, the second housemaid, and Ethel's great ally. 'Going by form she'll have had someone in there with her.'

'There'd been two heads on those pillows,' agreed Ethel, 'and two bodies between those sheets, however hard they tried to disguise it.'

'You noticed a lot before you ran screaming down the corridor,' said Thomas spitefully.

'I noticed first and then I ran screaming. I thought it would be expected of me. Anyway, the forensic scientists will be able to confirm she had someone in with her. Brilliantine leaves traces.'

'Oh ho!' said Thomas. 'Lord Heptonstall, you mean!'

'He uses lots of it,' agreed Ethel. 'But all the men use some.'

'I don't know what's got into you, young lady,' tut-tutted Cook. 'You read too many of them detective stories.'

'Well, they're more educational than *Lucky Star* or *True Romance*, Mrs Cornforth.' Ethel thought for a minute. 'I hope the police notice the mud.'

'Mud?'

'A bit of hard mud, very light-coloured, by the bed.'

This had them all looking at each other.

'I didn't leave no mud when I cleaned the floor yesterday,' said Mary.

'She could have left it herself,' said Mrs Cornforth.

'When she never went outdoors yesterday?' asked Ethel. 'Or if she did it was no further than the grounds. Too busy making a dead set at young Mr Merrivale. Anyway, that wasn't Frensham earth I saw, not local.'

'Sir William took some of the gentlemen shooting yesterday,' Thomas pointed out. Thomas had now got over his pique and was thoroughly caught up. This was too good a thing to be distracted from by pique.

'So he did, Thomas,' said Ethell. 'Harpington way. Has anybody cleaned any boots today?'

'Light mud,' said Bob the odd-job boy, relishing his moment of glory. Usually he was much put down. 'Sort of clay-y like.'

They all looked at each other.

'Which side of the bed was it, the piece you found?' asked Mr Eames.

'The far side. Where the bedside table is. The side she slept on.'

'And where the window is,' said Thomas. 'And she's a lady who always sleeps – slept – with her window open.'

'Was the door locked when you went up this morning?' asked Mary.

'Of course it was. Otherwise whoever it was would probably have come in from the corridor. I used my house key, the same as I did yesterday. Hers was on the floor by the bedside table – she'd probably knocked it off when she had a glass of water, or when she took the veronal.'

'That veronal must be strong,' said Mary. 'Otherwise she'd have surely woken up, with someone coming in through her window.'

'Not her,' said Thomas. 'She was drinking and dancing till two or half past. Not just last night either, but the night before as well.'

'When I took the tray in yesterday morning,' said Ethel, 'she didn't register a thing.'

'Well, she certainly didn't today,' said Thomas. 'So what you reckon is, she had her boyfriend in, and after he left someone climbed in the window and smothered her in her sleep?'

'That's right. She'd have been too far gone to hear. She always was. I had orders not to take in tea until half past ten.'

'The gentleman who'd been in with her would naturally have gone back to his room well before people started stirring.'

'Particularly if he was a married gentleman.'

'Particularly,' agreed Thomas, 'if he was a married gentleman. The question is, what do we do now?'

'Draw up a list of suspects,' said Ethel promptly. 'Drat that bell.'

'Thomas will see to it,' said Mr Eames, who was beginning to enjoy himself. 'Is lunch under way, Mrs Cornforth?'

'Everything under control,' said Cook, 'in spite of hinterruptions and hupsets.' She looked at Ethel, who had secured a notebook and pencil. 'I suppose we're all on this list of suspects?'

Ethel shook her head regretfully.

'No. It would have been lovely, but it couldn't really be one of us, could it? She's only been here two weekends, and none of us had worked for her in the past. . . No, it couldn't be one of us.'

'She could have seduced Thomas,' suggested Mary.

'The idea!' said Mrs Cornforth. 'Mrs Heathington-Scott would never've gone outside her class, and neither would Thomas.'

'I'm not so sure about Thomas,' said Ethel, 'but she'd have

stuck to her own circle. An exclusive lady, Mrs Heatherington-Scott, not to say expensive as well. Anyway none of us went to Harpington shooting yesterday. Right. So that means the eight ladies and gentlemen sleeping here last night. Top of the list goes the husband, of course.'

Ethel, who later in life wrote scripts for *Mrs Dale's Diary* and *Upstairs, Downstairs*, licked her pencil and wrote in a bold, well-schooled hand: Captain James Heatherington-Scott.

'Why top of the list?' asked Bob.

'Because in a domestic murder the husband or wife is always the obvious suspect. You'll know why if you ever marry.'

'Why wait till they are away on a weekend?' asked Mrs Cornforth. 'Why not do it at 'ome?'

'And be even *more* the obvious suspect?' asked Ethel pityingly. 'Besides, he may have been driven over the edge by her carryings-on. Because carry on she did. Though if you ask me he's a nasty piece of work who wouldn't bat an eyelid whatever she might do. . . Then there's master and mistress.'

She wrote again: Sir William and Lady Warboys. When Cook once more expanded her bosom to protest, Mr Eames put up his hand.

'No, Mrs C. We must be scientifical about this. All must be equally under suspicion, though we all know the master or mistress would never think of doing such a thing.'

'Anyone any idea why the master and mistress ask the Heatherington-Scotts?' asked Ethel. 'They're a good twenty years younger, and they've only known them a year or two. Yet this is twice they've been here – first last Spring, and now for the New Year party.'

'I heard the master say that they were fun,' said Mr Eames. 'He likes young people with a lot of life in them. Not that he'd ever for a moment think of. . . taking advantage, so to speak, of a young woman of loose morals like Mrs Heatherington-Scott.'

There was a brief moment of silence before Ethel spoke again. Ethel knew a lot more about what the master would and would not think of doing to a young woman than Mr Eames did.

'Then there's Colonel and Mrs Swanton. I should think we're all agreed about them.'

'A nice gentleman,' said Mary. 'Always courteous, never too demanding, and generous with it. His lady's a bit more fussy, but a real lady nonetheless.'

'Right,' said Ethel. 'A thoroughly suspicious pair, if you went by detective stories. Then there's Lord and Lady Heptonstall.'

There was another moment's silence.

'I'm not one to speak ill of my betters, as you know,' said Mrs Cornforth, 'but her Ladyship's remarks within Thomas's hearing about my profiteroles Angels would not forgive!'

'Mean, cross, nasty-tongued bitch, and his Lordship is if anything worse,' agreed Mr Eames. 'Mind you, it's the first time they've been here, and if I'm any judge it'll be the last. Sir William and her Ladyship have been noticing things, I can tell you.'

'Then there's Mr Merrivale,' said Ethel. 'Mr Raymond Merrivale. I don't mind saying I think he's a lovely gentleman!'

'Oh he is!' said Mary. 'It's always "I wonder if you'd mind" with him – never "do this, do that" like it is with the Heptonstalls. He's smashing.'

'Smashing!' said Cook disparagingly. 'What kind of a word is that? I suppose all this henthusiasm has nothing to do with the fact that he's a very handsome young man, has it?'

'Everything,' said Ethel. 'The old sex urge, and don't run it down, Mrs Cornforth. Still, he's a married man, and his wife is in her seventh month, from what I hear: that's why she had to send her apologies at the last moment. . . Well, if you go by character it'll be the husband or one of the Heptonstalls who did it. But of course you can't just go by character.'

'No, you can't!' said Thomas, coming back through the baize door positively pink with self-importance. 'You've got to look at *evidence*, that's what you've got to do!'

'All right, out with it,' said Ethel. 'What's happening

upstairs?'

'Upstairs? Bill is ministering to master and mistress and the house-guests, sick as a toad that he's missing all the fun. It's outside that things are happening!'

'Outside? You mean round her window?'

'That's right. Five coppers from Addlesfield, and a French gentleman with moustaches you could uncork a bottle with who's staying with the Chief Constable. I heard one of the constables say he was a tip-top detective from London.'

'And what was he doing?'

'He was looking at the marks of a ladder just under her window. He asked me where a ladder like that could be found, and I took him round to the one that hangs on the side of the potting shed. It had earth on one end.'

'Be pretty funny if a gardener's ladder *didn't* have earth on it,' commented Cook.

'It corresponded!' said Thomas, who as talking in exclamation marks. 'They took it over to the rose-bed under her window and the marks corresponded. And there was more of that light earth there.'

'Why did he talk to you about that anyway?' demanded Ethel. 'I'd've thought he'd've talked to the gardeners.'

'He wanted to talk to me anyway, the French gentleman,' said Thomas, oozing conceit. 'He said he could see I was a young man with all his wits about him.'

Ethel's silent opinion was that Thomas's strong point lay very much lower down than his brain. She said: 'But he must have had some *reason* for wanting to talk to you.'

'Because I was on last night. That's why Bill is kicking himself. He pulled rank and went to bed at half past eleven, leaving me on for the late-night drinks. I was the one around just before they all went to bed.'

'And?'

'Well, like I told the foreign gentleman, there was dancing in the sitting room, and this Mrs Heatherington-Scott she was dancing with Mr Merrivale.'

'Oh – you told him that!' chorused Ethel and Mary.

''Course I did. You've got to be truthful, like in a court of law. If they are innocent they have nothing to fear, that's what they always say. I told him they danced very intimate-like, with her twigging his ear and whispering in it, and dancing closer and closer. I was surprised because she'd been throwing herself at him all day and not getting anywhere much.'

'And did you tell the foreign gentleman that her husband was going mad with jealousy?'

'No I didn't, because he wasn't. He was changing the gramophone records. Same as happened last year with her and Sir Harry Dexter.'

'Oh yes, I remember: she had him panting after her all right!'

Mr Eames was just getting up, convinced that juniors and upstarts were usurping the stage and it was time for him to be where the action was, when he was interrupted by the bell. Soon it was time for luncheon, and the whole of the downstairs staff was occupied in one way or another. Any conversation there was was snatched in odd moments of repose.

'You were wrong about that foreign gentleman,' said Mr Eames to Thomas in the kitchen between courses. 'He's Belgian.'

'Same thing.'

'It is not the same thing. Don't you remember "gallant little Belgium" during the war?'

'Mr Eames I'm only twenty-three. I was born the year it started.'

'Well, we'd never have called France "gallant", I can tell you. France and England never pulled together, for all they might find themselves on the same side.'

After lunch the Belgian gentleman talked to several of the below-stairs staff and they were severally repelled or enchanted. Bill, the first footman, who had nothing to tell him, said his foot itched to kick him up the b.t.m., while Mary said she felt she was being taken by one of those continental gigolos to the Strand Corner House, as a preliminary to being seduced.

'You shameless hussy!' said Cook, and thought accordingly worse of the foreign gentleman for arousing such fancies.

It was gone three before they could have another real talking-over of the crime. They pooled the information they had gleaned or guessed from their several interrogations, and then began in again.

'So far as I can see it's practically certain Mr Merrivale was in there with her early on in the night,' said Ethel. 'They're hardly making a secret of it, and after the exhibition they seem to have made, if Thomas is right, he couldn't deny it.'

Mr Merrivale, clearly, had lost favour.

'I think the foreign gentleman thinks there may be more than one of them in it,' said Thomas. 'He keeps going on about "grey cells".'

'I've never been inside the local police station,' said Ethel. 'You wouldn't expect them to paint it pretty pink, would you?' She thought, looking dubious. 'It doesn't sound likely. Why should there be a conspiracy? Merrivale could have done it on his own when he was in there with her, and the gentleman who came in from outside didn't need a partner either. Now, let's think a bit about this mud.' She turned towards Bob. 'How many pairs of boots were there this morning?'

Bob blushed at his unaccustomed prominence, but said promptly: 'Four, like I told the foreign gentleman.'

'The foreign gentleman won't have a notion how things are done below stairs. There may be something he's missed. Whose were they?'

'The master's, Colonel Swanton's (I know because he takes size 12), Captain Heatherington-Scott's (he had his name in his) and one pair more. I think they were that Lord Something's.'

'They were,' said Mary. 'I found them outside his door when I took master and mistress their early morning tea.'

'He may be a lord but he's no gentleman,' said Mr Eames loftily. 'We are not an hotel.'

'And the other boots would have been just inside the baize door as usual,' said Ethel thoughtfully. 'Given to one or other of us last night. Anyone could have retrieved his. . . Still, the fact that Lord Heptonstall had the use of his all night does rather direct the spotlight on him.'

'What do you sound like, girl?' said Mrs Cornforth. 'One of those books you read.'

'There was one thing I remembered when the foreign gentleman was asking questions,' said Mary eagerly. 'He was ever so gentle and nice, but sort of piercing – went right through you –'

'That's enough of that, my girl!'

'– well anyway, I remembered the last time she was here this Mrs Heatherington-Scott made a set at Sir Harry Destry, like Thomas said, and – well, we all know what happened that time, don't we? Anyway, I was dusting in the library on the morning they all left, and I remember Mrs H.-S. and Sir Harry walking into the library, he was looking very suspicious and upset, and both were talking very low. Well, I slipped out, of course, as mistress likes us to –'

'They expect servants to be invisible, but they expect the work to be done all the same,' put in Ethel.

'– anyway they never saw me, but before I went I heard her say, in a slinky sort of voice. "It would be a pity if your wife got to know. I believe she's delicate – the nervous type, isn't she?"'

The reaction was gratifying.

'Blackmail!' said Mr Eames.

'That's what it sounded like,' agreed Mary. 'A bit of blackmailing on a small scale.'

'Well!' said Cook. 'To think of someone in that station of life resorting to blackmail!'

'Not unknown,' said Mr Eames sagely. 'I could tell you a thing or two about the Countess of Warwick and letters from King Teddy. Had it directly from Sir Alan Lascelles's valet. If you can blackmail the R.F. . . . !'

'Anyway,' said Thomas, 'this really puts Mr Merrivale back in the spotlight, doesn't it? If she started to put pressure on. . .'

'Ah, but she wouldn't have, would she?' said Ethel. 'Not till just before they all left. She'd have let him get in as deep as possible and *then* started the pressure. . . Not that I've any time for *him* any longer – going on like that when his poor wife was near her time.'

'That's exactly the time many gentlemen *do* go astray,' said Bill. 'I believe when Teddy was acting the goat in this house the Princess of Wales was carrying Queen Maud of Norway as she now is.'

'I think you'll find,' said Mr Eames, 'that King Teddy acted the goat pretty well irrespective.'

'Did I hear something,' said Cook frowning, 'about Lady Destry having been ill?'

Mr Eames was thunderstruck.

'You're right! It had gone completely out of my mind. I heard last summer that she'd. . . This needs to be looked into. I shall telephone Sir Harry's butler.'

'You never would, Mr Eames,' said Mary admiringly. 'That's two counties away!'

'Desperate situations call for desperate measures,' said Mr Eames grandly. But as he departed for the pantry the bell rang for afternoon tea to be served. It was five o'clock before they could hear the results of his conversation.

'Terrible,' he told them – and to be fair it was entirely without relish that he spoke. 'Really shocking. The lady had always been a bit flighty in her mind – nervous, delicate, taking odd fancies. Last summer she had some kind of shock – nobody knows what. Sent her completely overboard. Bouleversed, as they say across the Channel. Confined to an a.s.y.l.u.m. Private, constant attendance, no expense spared. Shocking!'

'Diabolical!' said Mrs Cornforth. 'She deserved everything she got!'

'The question is, how often she – they, it must be – tried it,' said Mary. 'Had they been bleeding Colonel Swanton or Lord Heptonstall dry?'

'Or even master?' put in Ethel.

'As far as I can see only Mr Merrivale is in the clear,' went on Mary. 'Even if he had been out shooting, he wouldn't slip into a lady's bedroom in muddy hunting boots.'

'I wouldn't wear muddy hunting boots if I was going to climb in through a bedroom window and murder a lady,' said Ethel. The words took time to sink in – to herself as much as to the rest. 'It's not as though a gentleman would only bring one or two pairs of shoes with him to a house-party.'

They sat there thinking. Finally it was again Ethel who spoke.

'It was a blind,' she said. 'That mud was a red herring. It seemed to let Mr Merrivale out. In fact it could simply have been broken off Lord Heptonstall's boots at any time during the night. The ladder could have been put up against the wall any time of night –'

'Going out by the gun-room window,' said Thomas, 'which master announced to all of them was faulty, and that was why Rover slept there.'

'Very good with dogs, Mr Merrivale,' said Ethel. 'Yes, he went out, put the ladder against the wall briefly to leave traces, threw a bit of mud through the window, and the key, and scattered more mud around the rose bed. It was a red herring.'

'What do you think really happened?' asked Mary.

'I think she was dead before he left her room. I think they had their fun, she took the veronal to sleep soundly, then when she was far gone he smothered her.'

'But why? You said yourself she wouldn't have begun putting the pressure on yet.'

Ethel shook her head in puzzlement, but a gleam had been coming into Eames's eyes.

'I think,' he said, 'I've been forgetting something.' He got up in his stately way and went over to his pantry. He emerged with an old edition of *Burke's Landed Gentry*. It was very dog-eared, for he seldom took up any other book for his own amusement. He thumbed through it till he came to Merrivale.

'Merrivale, Sir John, Knight, father to our young Raymond. . . Married Georgiana, widow of Sir Francis Destry, Bart. . . Let's see: Destry, Sir Francis, deceased 1914, issue: Henry Edward. . . They were step-brothers, Sir Henry and our Mr Merrivale, with only a year or two's difference in their ages.'

'Brought up together, most likely,' said Ethel. 'It was revenge, revenge pure and simple. Young Mr Merrivale came here to get it. I do think he's noble! I expect he hoped to have as little as possible to do with her, but when she made a dead set at him, as she did at all young married men, that was no longer possible. He had to improvise. That was what he came up with. I don't mind saying I don't blame him a bit! I always did say Mr Merrivale was a lovely young man!'

They were pulled up by the bell. It was Mr Eames's, and in a moment he was back, and as much in a rush as a butler can be. Drinks and snacks were required in the library. Everyone was assembling there – family, house-guests, the Chief Constable, the Belgian gentleman. For a time there was chaos. Mr Eames and Bill and Thomas collected trays and glasses, decanters were dusted down, all variety of bottles were sought. When they went up to the study Ethel and Mary waited outside with the little trays of sundries, catching glimpses of the people in the room, all of them nervously talking in high voices. Bill came out swearing, on his way to look for *sirop de cassis*. Mary peeped in to get another look at those wonderful moustaches and said to herself that they were nothing like corkscrews, more like one of those curved oriental swords that would cut right through you.

Finally everyone was served. Bill and Thomas came out, followed by Mr Eames, who shut the door behind him, but somehow not quite to – a thing never known to happen before. He led Bill firmly to the baize door and down the stairs, never once looking back to see if he was being followed. In the hall Thomas looked at Mary and Mary looked at Ethel.

'Better stay and listen,' said Ethel. 'Make sure he gets it right.'

Robert Barnard was once Professor of English at the University of Tromso. Now retired from academic life, he has written a number of critically acclaimed detective stories as well as books about Charles Dickens and Agatha Christie.

CAUSE AND EFFECTS

CATHERINE AIRD

'Of course you must come with us, Henry, dear. I insist. Besides Margot will be so pleased.'

'I really don't see why any hostess should be pleased to see a total stranger arrive at her dinner party.' Henry Tyler had had an unexpected few days' leave and had descended on his married sister and her husband in the small market town of Berebury in Calleshire without a great deal of warning.

'You're not a total stranger. . .'

'To my certain knowledge, Wendy, I have never set eyes on anyone called Margot Iverson in my life before.'

'I know that,' said Wendy Witherington placidly, 'but you're my brother and that's the same as my knowing her on her knowing me.' Logic had never been Wendy's strong suit.

'I still don't see why she should be pleased to see me on Saturday evening,' said Henry Tyler mildly.

'Because you're a man, that's why.'

'And may I ask if she will be so delighted to see me because I happen to be a male member of the human race. . . ?' There was nothing in his face to show how much he enjoyed teasing his only sister. 'Or is it only that I don't understand why as a consequence of being a mere male?'

Henry worked at the Foreign Office in London, where ambiguity had been raised to an art form. Wendy's mind was a much more literal one.

'Because you're an extra man, dear,' she said.

'Ah.'

'And because of Arthur's Cousin Amy,' went on his sister. 'She always upsets the table.'

'Dipsomania?' enquired Henry Tyler with interest, 'or is she just a clairvoyant?'

'Don't be unkind,' said Wendy severely. 'Cousin Amy can't help being there. She hasn't anywhere else to go but. "The Hollies".'

'She doesn't always have to upset the table, though, when she is there, does she?' remarked Henry Tyler in a tone that at least one ambassador had been known to call 'eminently reasonable'.

'Arthur's Cousin Amy,' responded his sister firmly, 'works as a secretary at a girls' boarding school. She's as poor as a church mouse, that's why she has to come to Arthur and Margot's in the holidays.'

'And what happens,' asked Henry mischievously, 'when Cousin Amy isn't there and your friends have an extra man?'

'Oh, that's no problem,' said Wendy at once. 'Margot just asks Miss Chalder to stay on. She's Arthur's dispenser and receptionist. Young but quite presentable.'

'So Arthur's a doctor. . . ' divined Henry without too much difficulty.

'Oh, didn't I say? He's our general practitioner.' Wendy giggled. 'Actually, when she's not there Margot calls Miss Chalder their deceptionist.'

'Always saying the doctor's out when he's in?' Deception was another of the subjects that they knew rather a lot about at the Foreign Office. 'That sort of thing?'

'And saying,' said Wendy, 'that he's been held up at a confinement when he's forgotten all about somebody.'

'Is he a good doctor?' asked Henry. It wasn't entirely an idle question since Wendy and Tom Witherington had two young children upon whom their bachelor uncle doted.

'How does one ever know that, Henry?' Wendy had more intelligence than her pleasant calm looks might have led the casual observer to suspect. She wrinkled her brow. 'There was some trouble at the end of last year about a little gipsy child who died from a burst appendix. Arthur said he'd never had their second message, and the fuss all died down, but he's always come when we've sent for him.'

'Quite so,' said Henry Tyler. 'I shall look forward to Saturday evening then.'

'And I shall telephone Margot,' said his sister.

Later that evening Henry, who was a firm believer that time spent in reconnaissance was seldom wasted, raised the matter of the dinner party with his brother-in-law.

'Don't worry, old chap.' Tom Witherington was reassuring. 'They do you very well at "The Hollies". Very well indeed.'

'So Dr Iverson is a successful doctor,' murmured Henry Tyler (which he knew was not the same as being a good one.)

Tom Witherington frowned. 'Couldn't say, but he is sound on food and drink.'

'How is it that their entertaining is so – er – reliable then?'

'Oh, you mean how is it that they can afford the pukka style if he isn't successful?' His brother-in-law's brow cleared. 'That's easily explained. W.H.M.'

Henry Tyler thought for a moment, 'That's an acronym I haven't come across.'

Tom Witherington grinned. 'I don't suppose it matters in the Foreign Office as much as it does in some other spheres. W.H.M. stands for Wife Has Means. . . Margot has the money and Arthur has the ideas for using it. You'll see for yourself on Saturday.'

'I can hardly wait,' said Henry Tyler politely.

As dinner parties went, noted Henry on the night, it was neither large nor particularly intimate. Ten people sat down in the dining-room at 'The Hollies' after partaking of a well-chosen sherry – a good Macharnudo, Henry thought – in the drawing-room.

Margot Iverson had welcomed him most hospitably. 'How nice to have someone here from the Foreign Office. You can tell us what they think of Il Duce.' She was a plain woman with the apparent placidity of the overweight, but she didn't look as if she missed much. Like those of all good hostesses, her eyes were everywhere.

'I'm afraid,' said Henry Tyler with every appearance of regret, 'That's not my Department.'

Dr Iverson was equally welcoming, 'What a pity it's dark. Otherwise you could have seen the garden, although there's not much to look at at this time of the year.'

'Arthur's garden is a delight,' said Wendy at his elbow. 'In the summer his vegetable garden is as neat and attractive as the one at Villandry.'

'It's mostly my gardener I have to thank for that,' said the doctor modestly, 'but, yes, I do take an interest. 'Now let me introduce you to Major Anderson. He's the Chairman of our local Bench . . . '

The announcement about dinner being served, Henry observed with approval, had come at just the right length of time after the sherry had been drunk. It followed a brief absence from the room of the doctor.

'Just checking on the claret,' he boomed as he came back. 'Edith's very good but there are some things that need watching.'

'My cousin is something of a wine connoisseur, Mr Tyler,' said Miss Amy Hall as he escorted her in to dinner. The doctor's cousin was a thin anxious woman with her hair drawn in two neat earphones. 'Now, tell me what you think of Haile Selassie . . . '

The first course had been awaiting them on the dining-room table. Potted shrimps in attractive little ramekins, and prettily adorned with watercress, stood on plates at each place. It was clear that the Major's wife was the chief lady guest, as she was seated on Dr Iverson's right, the Major sitting on Margot Iverson's right.

A Mr and Mrs Locombe-Stableford made up the party. Henry

had already discovered that he was a solicitor and his wife a power in the Red Cross. Henry found himself next to the Major's wife.

'I hope you enjoy your visits to Calleshire,' she said. 'A very fine county.'

'Indeed.' Henry passed her some thin, crustless brown bread and butter and listened to a long story about fox-hunting. Across the table he could hear Mrs Locombe-Stableford talking to the doctor about someone's gall-stones. ('Seven as big as marbles, the surgeon said.')

Edith, the parlourmaid, cleared away the first course.

'Jolly good tiger-frighteners, what?' said the Major to Margot Iverson.

'He usually calls them horses' doovers,' sighed the Major's wife to Henry, 'which is worse.'

'Strange how we have taken to some French words and not others, isn't it?' remarked Henry diplomatically as the parlour-maid came into the room with a pile of dinner plates and the vegetable dishes.

'I hope you'll take to a good French claret,' chimed in Arthur Iverson jovially. 'One of the St Emilion hill wines. Château Balestard la Tonnelle, and just ready for drinking. . . ah, thank you, Edith. Put it down here. Carefully, now. . .'

Obediently the parlourmaid lowered a serving dish bearing a large fillet of beef on to the table in front of the doctor. He put his hands out to take up the carving knife and fork and Amy Hall murmured something to her neighbour about Arthur always having wanted to be a surgeon really.

'My dear,' he said to his wife, 'aren't you going to tell our guests about our new addition to the dining-room?'

All eyes turned towards Margot Iverson at the other end of the dining table. She almost pouted. 'I wasn't going to tell them, Arthur. I was going to show them later.'

'Very well, dear.' The doctor turned his attention back to the carving. He was indeed good at it. After having carefully removed the browned edge of the fillet he sliced the meat quickly and evenly. Edith took the plates to Margot Iverson's end of the table, where the vegetables were served, and then handed them in turn to the guests.

Henry passed the horseradish sauce and then the gravy to the Major's wife. 'And salt?' he enquired. The career of one of his Foreign Office contemporaries had been said to have foundered after he said 'Pepper and salt' to the wife of a diplomat with uncertainly coloured hair and a poor command of the English language.

'Now you really must tell us what you think of the Abyssinian question, Mr Tyler,' Brenda Waters said as soon as Edith had withdrawn.

'Dear lady, I am but an errand boy in the Foreign Service. . . ' At the other end of the table he could hear Margot Iverson exchanging stately platitudes with Mr Locombe-Stableford. Henry Tyler would not have described her as a happy woman, but afterward he could not say that she had seemed at all unwell. She certainly complained of nothing in his hearing.

Her moment came at the end of the first course when, without any apparent signal, the parlourmaid came back into the room.

'There,' challenged Arthur. 'How did Margot summon up reinforcements? Tell me that if you can.'

'Perhaps,' suggested Tom Witherington slyly, 'Edith was listening at the door. . . '

'Did you hear that, Edith?' said Arthur Iverson. 'Well, were you?'

'No, doctor.'

'Bush telegraph?' The Major had served in Africa.

'Oh, do tell us,' pleaded Wendy Witherington. 'We'll never guess.'

'A bell-push under the carpet by my foot,' said Margot Iverson calmly. 'Arthur got an electrician to come in and do it during the week.'

'Clever stuff,' exclaimed Tom as Edith brought in the puddings.

She placed a hot Normandy pudding for the doctor to serve and a crème brûlée for her mistress to offer to those who preferred it.

'A great nation, the French,' said Mrs Locombe-Stableford, eyeing the puddings.

'In some ways, yes,' said Henry, a Foreign Office man to his fingertips even on Saturday evenings. 'But not all.'

'You mustn't forget Cook's special wine sauce with the Normandy pudding,' said Margot Iverson. 'She's very proud of it.'

'Or the Barsac,' said Dr Iverson. 'I think the ladies will like it. . .'

It was late by the time the meal was done and later still when the company rose from the coffee cups in the drawing-room.

It was early, though, the next morning when Wendy Witherington came back from answering the telephone. 'That was Brenda Waters,' she said, looking shocked. 'You won't believe this but Margot Iverson died in the night . . .'

'No! Surely not. . .' exclaimed Tom.

'What on earth from?' asked Henry.

'Brenda doesn't know,' said Wendy, 'but apparently poor Margot started being sick about one o'clock in the morning and then had a most frightful pain in her tummy.'

'At least Arthur would have been there,' said her husband. 'Nothing like having a doctor in the house.'

'He got very worried and immediately sent for one of the consultants from the hospital.'

'I should think so. . .' murmured Henry.

'And the consultant wanted to know what she'd had to eat, of course. . .'

'Of course.' Tom Witherington looked very solemn.

'. . .And whether anyone else had been taken ill.'

'Naturally,' said Henry.

'They were just going to check that we were all right when Margot suddenly got quite excitable and delirious – so unlike her.'

Henry nodded. Margot Iverson had struck him as a very controlled woman.

'And then. . .' Wendy's voice began to quaver, 'her breathing got very slow. Brenda says she was in a coma by the time they got her into the hospital. And then she just died. . . oh, isn't it too awful?'

Both men nodded.

Wendy sniffed. 'I think I'll just ring Phyllis Locombe-Stableford. . .'

'No,' said Tom Witherington quietly. 'I don't think I would if I were you, Wendy.'

'Why ever not?' Wendy stared at her husband. 'She was there too last night.'

'That's why,' said Tom. 'And she may not want to talk about it. Or have been asked not to by her husband. . . ' he put his arm round his wife. 'I think you're forgetting something about old Locombe-Stapleford.'

She was close to tears now. 'What's that?'

'That he isn't only a solicitor.' Tom went on steadily, 'He's the Coroner as well.'

Beyond speech now, she nodded her comprehension. 'Brenda said they were doing a post mortem this morning. Oh, poor, poor Margot. . .'

Henry Tyler said, 'I have to be back in Whitehall tomorrow, Wen. I must be with my Minister at ten but I'll come back for the funeral. . . or if anyone else wants to talk to me. . .'

In the event the persons who wanted to talk to Henry Tyler went to the Foreign Office to see him – where they found his rank to be rather higher than that of errand-boy. In fact he had his own office and a considerably larger area of carpet than anyone in Berebury suspected.

The two policemen who were shown into his room did not

appear to be daunted by this. 'Detective Inspector Milsom,' said the senior of the pair, 'and my assistant, Detective Constable Bewman. We are making enquiries into the sudden death of Mrs Margot Iverson.

Henry Tylor bowed his head. 'Anything that I can tell you, Inspector, I will, but my acquaintanceship with Mrs Iverson in the event was brief.'

'It is the event,' said Milsom dryly, 'which interests us. You were, I understand, one of the guests on the fatal night. . . '

'Indeed,' said Henry, noting with the appreciation of an expert the inspector's choice of words.

'And partook of the complete meal?'

'Oh, yes, Inspector. And very good it was, too.'

'Save for Mrs Iverson, sir. It didn't do her any good at all. Quite the reverse you might say.'

'Are you telling me,' said Henry cautiously, 'that Mrs Iverson – er – consumed. . . .'

'Ingested was the word the Home Office pathologist used, sir.'

'Ingested that from which she died at that meal?'

'It would seem so, sir. And we want you to tell us everything you remember about it.'

Henry cast his mind back over the evening. 'I think we all ate the same. . . '

'That is one of the things that is making our enquiries difficult.' Detective Inspector Milsom had his notebook at the ready.

'And from the same dishes. . . no, I forgot. The first course was on the table when we went into the dining-room. Potted shrimps.' He looked sharply at the policeman. 'Shell-fish can be dangerous in their own right.'

'The potted shrimps were put on the table by the parlourmaid immediately before the guests entered the dining-room,' said Milsom.

Henry hesitated: but not for long. 'Our host did slip out to attend to the claret. . . '

'That was before the shrimp dish reached the dining-room,' said Milsom, revealing that he already knew a great deal about the evening. 'It was – er – safely in the kitchen at that stage.'

'And,' said Henry as lightly as he felt the conversation warranted. 'I suppose you are sure that Edith wasn't harbouring a grudge against her mistress.'

'As sure as we can be,' said Milsom.

Detective Constable Bewman stirred. 'Besides, if you remember, sir, the potted shrimps had a solidified butter glaze on top.'

'So it had,' said Henry appreciatively. The constabulary had certainly done its homework. 'And Mrs Iverson would certainly have noticed if that had been disturbed.'

'I think we can go a little further than that, sir.' Milsom gave a faint smile. 'Human nature being what it is, my guess is that any maid worth her salt would have put a slightly imperfect dish in front of anyone but her master or mistress for the cook's sake.'

'Quite so,' said Henry gravely. He had forgotten the old joke about a policeman being the best kitchen range-finder in the world. 'Well, apart from the potted shrimps I think I can assure you, Inspector, that one way and another all the other dishes were shared.'

'This is what all the other guests say, sir, and that is what is puzzling us.'

'What about after we all left?' said Henry.

'The experts assure us that symptoms occur between one and four hours after this particular substance has been ingested.' The detective inspector went on, in tones totally devoid of emphasis, 'Unfortunately Dr Iverson went out after the dinner-party to pay a late visit to a man with pneumonia about whom he was worried an so cannot tell us anything about the time immediately after the guests had left. By the time he got home his wife was already beginning to be unwell.'

'I see.' Henry frowned. 'Well, after the potted shrimps we had the beef – and very good it was, too.'

'I understand that Cook has an excellent relationship with the butcher. She got him to send round the largest and best fillet he had,' said Milsom.

'The vegetables, as I recollect, Inspector, were Brussels sprouts and glazed carrots.' The man on the Belgium desk at the Foreign Office was being driven to despair by what was coming out of Brussels at the moment but Henry saw no reason to say so.

'We think we can give the vegetables a clean bill of health, sir.'

'Finished up in the kitchen, were they?' divined Henry. 'I say, Inspector, what about the horseradish sauce? It brought a tear to my eye.'

'Home-made, Mr Tyler, by Cook, according to Mrs Beeton's recipe with cream, white wine vinegar, a little castor sugar and some mustard – and horseradish, of course.'

'I have heard,' said Henry slowly, 'that on occasion – by accident, usually – aconite has been known to have been mistaken for horseradish.'

'Picked by Cook herself in the kitchen garden,' said Inspector Milsom with evident approval. 'She says that when she asks the gardener for produce she feels she doesn't always get the best.'

'Human nature doesn't always change, does it?' said Henry absently. They knew quite as much about human nature at the Foreign Office as they did down at any police station. 'Besides, coming back to your problem, Inspector, nearly everybody had some of the horseradish sauce.'

'Exactly, sir. Our problem is that while Mrs Iverson appears to have ingested that from which she died at the dinner party there is no dish from which some or all the guests did not share.'

'Difficult,' agreed Henry, 'and made more so, I imagine, by the fact that both the Coroner and the Chairman of the Magistrates' Bench were there.'

Detective Inspector Milsom said with deep feeling that this had not helped in the investigation so far. 'They both insist that there was no way in which their hostess could have been poisoned before their very eyes – and both the parlourmaid and the cook swear that she didn't take anything afterwards. What with the doctor going straight out and the deceased going down to the kitchen to thank both staff for a very good meal there wasn't time – even if she took it herself, which is unlikely from all I hear.'

'That means Edith and Cook liked her,' said Henry at once. 'And I understand there were no money troubles. . . .'

'None,' said the inspector stoutly. 'She was very well-off, was Mrs Iverson.'

'And yet. . . .' began Henry.

'Yes?' The policeman leaned forward.

'It does seem almost staged, doesn't it?'

'Just what the chief constable said. . . .' the detective inspector lowered his head.

'I'm sorry, sir, I shouldn't have said that.'

Henry Tyler waved a hand airily. 'My dear fellow, we spend our time here working on things that shouldn't have been said, but unless they are,' he added thoughtfully, 'nobody gets anywhere. That case of pneumonia?'

'Genuine,' said the inspector. 'The doctor had visited the man earlier in the day and said he would be back later that night when he thought the pneumonia would have reached its crisis.'

'Mrs Iverson hadn't been beastly to Miss Amy hall, I take it?'

'Kindness itself, I understand, sir.' He coughed. 'That doesn't mean that Miss Hall enjoys being a poor relation. Very few people do, sir. However, both staff agree Miss Hall fitted in as well as anyone could in the circumstances. Cook is the most observant woman, and parlourmaids have to be of a noticing cast of mind, otherwise they wouldn't be any good for the job, would they, sir?'

Henry confessed it was something that hadn't crossed his mind before.

'Like detective constables,' said the inspector generously. 'Constable Bewman here pointed out that each guest had their plate handed to them by Edith but I can't see how that would give the murderer any scope.'

Henry frowned. 'She would have done it in a preordained way, of course,' mused Henry. 'The lady on the host's right first, and then the one on his left. My sister was served after them, I think, and then Miss Amy and Mrs Iverson.'

'That would have meant,' said the inspector alertly,' that anyone who knew where you were all sitting would have been able to work out who would get which plate in the pile.'

'Oh, yes, Inspector.' Henry Tyler smiled faintly. 'It's an interesting little puzzle when you think about it like that. The quickness of the hand deceiving the eye and all that. Except that we don't know whose hand.'

'Yet. . . ' responded Milsom.

Detective Constable Bewman scratched his head. 'But even if you knew beforehand who was going to get – say – the fifth plate, how could you put poison on it and not on the other plates?'

'Difficult,' agreed Henry Tyler, 'isn't it?'

'But not impossible,' growled Milsom.

'According to the pathologist, the timing is wrong for her being poisoned except at the meal. He's prepared to swear to that.'

Henry Tyler screwed up his face in an effort of recollection. 'There were some glazed onions and Duchesse potatoes round the fillet. . . our host put those on the individual plates before he handed them to Edith.'

'We thought of that, sir,' said the inspector, a touch of melancholy in his voice. 'Both were brought in from the garden – home grown – and never left the kitchen until Cook gave them to Edith for the table. Apparently the doctor's very particular about his potatoes. Never lets seed be used that's more than two years out of Scotland.'

'Quite right,' said Henry stoutly. 'I think the same should go for the Scots race, too.'

'Not everyone had the same pudding,' said the inspector with a certain tenacity. 'Some had one and some had the other.'

'And some, Inspector, I fear, had both.'

'And those that had the Normandy pudding,' said Detective Constable Bewman, 'had the wine sauce that went with it.'

'It was a splendid sauce,' said Henry appreciatively.

'Consisting, I understand,' said Milsom heavily, 'of a small glass of brandy, ditto of Madeira, a gill of water, an ounce of unsalted butter and a little caster sugar.'

'You should try it some time, Inspector,' said Henry.

'It was handed round,' said Milsom, ignoring this frivolity, 'by Edith in a sauce boat on a tray.'

'No room for monkey business there,' agreed Henry. 'Or with the fruit and nuts.'

'Two bowls of each were placed within easy reach of all the guests,' said Milsom. 'In theory, I suppose, the nearest piece of fruit could have been doctored, but I don't see myself how the murderer could have been sure the victim would have picked it.'

'No.' Henry noted how the detective inspector's speech had now widened to include words like 'poison' and 'murderer'. 'I can't tell you if Mrs Iverson had any port.' He grinned. 'I did and it was splendid.'

'Vintage,' said Milsom. '1912 and nothing wrong with it at all.'

'Just as well to check though,' agreed Henry gravely.

'The doctor had decanted it himself,' the policeman informed him, reddening slightly, 'before the guests arrived.'

'You can't be too careful with a really crusty port,' said Henry.

'Someone,' said Inspector Milsom meaningfully, 'seems to have been altogether too careful to my way of thinking.'

Henry Tyler nodded. 'Careful and very clever, Inspector. It takes a great deal of prestidigitatory skill to poison someone before your very eyes so to speak.'

'That's not a word that I know, sir, but I think I take your meaning.'

'We are talking of the art of the conjuror. . .'

'Ah,' said Milsom.

'Where did the patter come in then?' enquired Detective Constable Bewman. 'You would have all been talking normally like, wouldn't you, sir?'

'Yes. . . that is, I suppose so.' Henry cast his mind back to the small talk of a small town. 'Conversation was very general. The nearest thing to a conjuring trick was the new bell-push that had been fitted under the carpet for Mrs Iverson.'

'That was the doctor's idea, sir. Cook tells me he'd seen it somewhere and wanted one for his wife. The parlourmaid likes it because it saves her. . .'

'Just a minute,' said Henry, a thought beginning to burgeon in his mind. 'You, Constable, said something about a conjuror's patter.'

'You don't get that many silent ones, sir,' responded Bewman stolidly. 'Not on stage, anyway.'

'It did occur to me that the doctor did choose an odd moment to draw attention to the bell's being there. It would have been much more subtle just to have allowed his wife to demonstrate it when the time came and then to turn it into a talking point.'

'Out of character you might say?' suggested the inspector. 'And what, might I ask, sir, was he doing at the time he was talking about the bell?'

'Oh, he wasn't doing the talking at that point, Inspector. It was Mrs Iverson who was telling us about it after he mentioned it.'

'So,' reasoned the inspector, 'all the guests were looking at her?'

'I suppose we were.'

'So,' said Milsom patiently, 'what was the doctor doing while she was talking?'

Henry Tyler cast his mind back to the fatal evening. 'He was carving the fillet of beef. He'd just begun. He took off the first slice, you know the rather well-done, brown bit at the end, and laid it on one side of the serving dish and then he cut the next slice off for the first lady and so on.'

'We can't work out how he could have killed his wife while he was sitting at the opposite end of the table,' said Constable Bewman naïvely.

'You have rather got it in for the doctor, haven't you?' said Henry easily.

'Most male murderers are widowers,' growled Milsom. 'What we don't like, Mr Tyler, is that Mrs Iverson was poisoned in full view of the Coroner and the Chairman of the Bench.'

'"Aye, there's the rub," as William Shakespeare so wisely said,' murmured Henry.

'And Miss Chalder is a very good-looking girl.'

'Ah, so that's the way the wind blows, is it?' said Henry, his mind beginning to stray. 'Mind you,' he added fairly, 'doctors are able to get their hands on poison more easily than most of us.'

'Oh, didn't I say, Mr Tyler? It wasn't a medical poison that was used to kill Mrs Tyler.'

'No?' If Henry thought that there was a contradiction in terms about the words 'medical poison' he did not let it show in his face.

'More of a horticultural poison,' said the inspector, 'although not intended as such.' He consulted his notebook. 'The substance was called ethylene chlorohydrin if that means anything to you, sir.'

'I'm afraid not,' said Henry regretfully.

'Used to speed the germination of seeds and potatoes,' said the inspector, 'and as a cleaning solvent.'

'And it's odourless,' chimed in Constable Bewman helpfully.

'So there was no need to have anything highly scented or smelling strongly on the table,' said Henry at once.

'I hope you never take it into your head to commit a murder, sir,' said the Inspector. 'You do seem to have an eye for essentials.'

'And how much of this – er – horticultural poison does it take to kill a human being?' asked Henry, ignoring this last.

'Not a lot,' said the inspector quietly. 'Something under a fifth of a teaspoonful – say four or five drops – added to which it is highly soluble.'

'It seems to me,' said Henry Tyler, in the last analysis a Ministry man, 'that this stuff, whatever it is, is something that ought to be put a stop to.'

'Very possible, sir,' said the inspector smoothly. 'And after the fruit and nuts?'

'We all moved back into the drawing-room for coffee,' said Henry, 'and I performed my party trick with the cream and the back of a spoon.' He looked up. 'It's not a conjuring trick, Inspector.'

'I'm glad to hear it, sir.'

'It's a question of how to get the cream to float on top of the coffee.'

'Very difficult, I'm sure, sir.'

'Not when you know how.'

'I think that is going to be the case with the ethylene chlorohydrin, sir.'

'Er – quite, Inspector. Well, with the coffee it's all a matter of putting the sugar in first and stirring well. That increases the surface tension on the top of the coffee – or is it the specific gravity? – so that when you dribble the cream slowly down over the back of the spoon it stays on the top.'

'And Bob's your uncle, so to speak?' said the inspector, paying unconscious tribute to an old nepotism.

'It worked,' said Henry. 'Whether it distracted everyone else long enough to slip five drops of something into Mrs Iverson's coffee, I wouldn't know, Inspector.'

'But we would, Mr Tyler. You see, Mrs Iverson never drank coffee. And we have it on the authority of those sitting near her that she did not drink it that evening.' He coughed. 'If I may say so your sister was particularly emphatic on the point.'

'Good old Wendy,' said Henry, then frowned. 'I say, Inspector, that does rather leave every avenue explored, doesn't it?'

Detective Inspector Milsom assented to this sentiment with a quiet nod. 'Every avenue that we can think of.'

'What we want, then, Inspector,' he said bracingly, 'is a new avenue or fresh look at an old one.'

'Either would do very nicely, sir.' With an ironic smile Milsom said, 'Which do you recommend?'

'Oh, a new look at an old problem,' said Henry Tyler at once. 'We don't have new problems in the Foreign Office.'

'The only matter which you have brought to our attention, sir, which seems to have escaped everyone else's notice was the – er – untimely mention of the footbell.'

'Which doesn't get us very much furth. . . wait a minute, Inspector, wait a minute.'

'Yes, sir?'

'Suppose it does?' Henry ran his hands through his hair in a gesture of excitement that his sister would have recognized well. 'Suppose it was meant to turn all eyes towards our hostess?'

'And to take them off your host?' said Milsom astringently.

'Exactly!'

'Well?'

'Well, if it was intended as a distraction, then that must have been the moment when he poisoned his wife. That follows, doesn't it?'

'It's a thought worth considering, sir.'

'Watch out, Inspector, if you can talk like that in response to one of my brainwaves we'll have you working here.'

'No, thank you, sir. We've got enough troubles of our own in Calleshire.'

'I think you're going to have one less in a minute.' He brought his fist down on his desk with a bang. 'Inspector, until this moment I have always felt that the benefit of a classical education was over-rated.'

'Indeed, sir?'

'But not now! Parysatis, wife of Darius, killed Statira, wife of Artaxerxes, in much the same way as Mrs Iverson was murdered.'

Detective Inspector Milsom leaned forward, his notebook prominent. 'Tell me. . .'

'Now I know what else it was Dr Iverson did when he went through to see to the claret before dinner.' Henry rubbed his hands. 'First he probably smeared a little horseradish sauce or even some colourless Vaseline on the righthand side of the carving knife. Then he added a fatal dose of your ethylene stuff to it and put it back on the carving rest. . .'

'With the other blade facing upward.' Detective Constable Bewman could hardly contain his excitement. Then his face fell. 'But why didn't the first guest get the poisoned beef?'

Detective Inspector Milsom said quietly, 'Because the doctor laid the first slice of the fillet – the piece that you don't give to guests – to one side of the carving dish . . . Mr Tyler said so.'

'But put it on his wife's plate later without anyone noticing,' said Henry. 'Only the left hand side of the carving knife touched the next piece of meat, while the right hand side had been neatly wiped on the outside piece, so everyone else's meat was unaffected.' He sat back in his chair. 'Parysatis did it with a chicken and I should have thought of it before.'

Catherine Aird is Chairman of the Crime Writers' Association during the Agatha Christie Centenary. She has lived all her life in the East Kent village where her father was a doctor. She acted as his dispenser, an experience which has proved invaluable in her 'Inspector Sloane' novels, set in the deceptively comfortable English village first made famous by Agatha Christie.